The Lost Summer

Also by Tom Milton

The Lost Summer

Tom Milton

NEPPERHAN PRESS, LLC
YONKERS, NY

Published by Nepperhan Press, LLC
P.O. Box 1448, Yonkers, NY 10702
nepperhan@optonline.net
nepperhan.com

PUBLISHER'S NOTE
This is a work of fiction. Names, characters, places, and incidents
are the product of the author's imagination or are used fictitiously,
and any resemblance to actual persons, living or dead, events, or
locales is entirely coincidental.

Printed in the United States of America

Library of Congress Control Number: 2020943972

ISBN 978-1-7320634-7-1

Cover art was licensed from Publitek, Inc.

For Marie

More tortuous than anything is the human heart,
beyond remedy; who can understand it?
Jeremiah 17:9

Yonkers, 2005

ONE

OVER THE YEARS since that lost summer Brigid often thought about Laura, and she imagined what could have happened to her, but she didn't find out what actually happened until she met with a police detective, thirty-seven years later.

He had left a message with her mother, who was home at the time. Her mother never paid attention to the caller ID but automatically picked up the phone whenever it rang, out of habit from the years she had spent attending the phone in a clinic where she worked, and on a piece of note paper she had neatly printed the name of the caller, Vijay Patel, and his phone number. She had also noted that he was a police detective.

Brigid returned his call as soon as she got home from work, but he didn't answer, so she left a message, hoping they wouldn't end up playing a long game of phone tag. She had no idea why a police detective would call her, and she was curious, though not concerned. As far as she knew she hadn't done anything that deserved a police investigation.

The call was a topic at that night's dinner, which they ate as usual in the dining room. Her mother had cooked a casserole of chicken with garlic and white wine with carrots, new potatoes, and only enough tomato to make the sauce faintly pink, a long way from the hearty red sauces that Brigid remembered from her childhood. Her mother, whose parents were immigrants from Calabria, had ventured several years ago into Northern Italian cooking, with recipes from a popular cookbook by a woman from Emilia-Romagna. And now instead of red wine they drank white wine with their dinner.

Brigid's adopted daughter, Nhu, had showered after work and changed into the comfortable clothes she wore around the house. She had come home an hour ago after completing her shift in the emergency room at St. John's Hospital, her need for sustenance having priority over her need for rest. Though she was only five three and weighed no more than a hundred ten pounds, on these evenings after a shift she ate like a famished linebacker.

"What do you think the detective wanted?" her mother asked while passing the casserole to Brigid. Her mother, who was now eighty-three, was as sharp as ever.

"I have no idea," Bridget said, spooning some food from the casserole onto her plate.

"Detective?" Nhu said, patiently awaiting her turn with the casserole. "What detective?"

"A detective who called your mother today."

Nhu paused long enough to pile her plate with chicken, carrots, and potatoes. Setting down the casserole, she asked: "Is it someone you know?"

"I don't know any detectives."

"I know a detective," Nhu said after chewing and swallowing a mouthful of food. "They brought him in last week with a gunshot wound."

"I hope it wasn't serious," Bridget said.

"It could have been worse. The bullet hit him in the shoulder, but it was less than five inches from his heart."

"He was lucky," Brigid said.

"Yeah. Carlotta, could you please pass the water?" When she was a kid, Nhu had called her grandmother Nonna, but around the age of sixteen she decided it was cool to call her Carlotta, and seeing that her grandmother thought it was cool, she had called her Carlotta ever since, though Brigid couldn't bring herself to call her mother anything but mom.

"He didn't say where he was from," her mother said, referring to the detective.

"He's probably from Yonkers," Brigid said. "Where else?"

"It could be anywhere."

"What's his name?" Nhu asked, chewing.

"Vijay Patel."

"That's Indian."

"Yeah. Patel is a common Indian name. It's like Smith or Jones."

"We have a Patel in the ER."

"Well, maybe they're related," her mother suggested jokingly.

"He's a physician. A good one." Nhu was a physician assistant, which meant that she could do almost anything that a physician could do. "So maybe you did something, mom, that we don't know about."

Brigid laughed and said: "I've done a lot of things that you don't know about."

"You mean even Carlotta doesn't know about them?"

"Not even my mother knows about them." But as she said this Brigid was conscious of how hard it was to put something over on her mother.

"You never committed a crime, did you?"

"Yeah, I did. I got traffic tickets."

"That's not a crime. I mean a real crime like you can be put into jail for."

After a pause Brigid revealed: "I was put into jail once."

"You were?" Nhu said, impressed. "What for?"

"For demonstrating against the war."

"You mean the war in Vietnam?"

"Yeah, that was the war of my generation."

"My generation too," Nhu said, having somehow made it to America as an orphan of that war, eleven months old.

"You're right. I'm sorry."

"There's nothing to be sorry about. I'm blessed to have you as a mother."

Brigid reached out and covered her hand. "I'm blessed to have you as a daughter."

"And I'm blessed to have you as a daughter and a grand-daughter," her mother said, reaching across the table and covering both their hands.

"We're like a volleyball team," Nhu said, "before a match."

They all laughed.

It brought back the time when Nhu played volleyball at St. Catherine College. She lacked the useful height for the sport but she played as a digger, a tough digger who would rather crash on the floor herself than let the ball touch it.

"Speaking of Vietnam," Nhu said, helping herself to seconds from the casserole. "I had a patient last night who was a veteran. He was your age, mom."

"What was he there for?"

"A kidney stone. It was stuck in his ureter, and he was in horrendous pain."

"I never had a kidney stone, thank God."

"I never did either," her mother said. "But your father had one. When I took him to the emergency room a nurse said it was the only thing a man could have that was anywhere near as painful as having a baby."

"Was it really painful having me?"

"I don't remember. Pain is an easy thing to forget."

"You mean physical pain," Brigid said, knowing from her experience as a psychiatric nurse that it could be almost impossible to forget mental pain.

"Oh, yeah" her mother said. "The pain from losing your father will never go away."

Brigid shared her mother's pain. She had been close to her father. She had inherited his Irish features: the fair skin, the reddish hair, and the green eyes. It was less than a year since her father had died from a heart attack, and she was still in mourning for him.

"I'm glad I had twenty-two years with him," Nhu said, taking a pause from ingesting food.

They were silent for a while, and then Brigid said: "Tell us more about your veteran."

"He was a nice guy. He said he was sent there when he was only nineteen. Imagine being sent to kill people at that age."

"It was evil," Brigid said simply.

"He said he was sorry for what he did there but he was glad that Vietnam is recovering."

"He must still have nightmares about it."

"He didn't mention having nightmares. We didn't talk much until I gave him a painkiller, and then he was so thankful he took my hand and held it for a while."

"That was nice."

"He was a nice guy."

They are in silence for a while, and then her mother said: "You never told me you went to jail."

"I didn't want you to worry about me. But I did go to jail, and I spent a night there."

"How did you conceal that from us?"

"A priest got us out. He took responsibility for us, so there was no need for you and dad to get involved."

"A priest? What priest?"

"Well, he wasn't a priest yet at the time. He was only a seminarian."

Her mother frowned in disapproval. "When did that happen?"

"It happened the summer when Laura and I were doing our internship in the city."

"You mean the summer of 1968?"

"Yeah. The lost summer," Brigid added wistfully.

"Why do you say that?" Nhu asked with her fork stopped above her plate. "Did you lose something that summer?"

Brigid nodded. "Yeah. I did."

"I hope it wasn't your innocence," her mother said.

"It wasn't, at least the way you mean. It was something in my heart and soul." She paused, then smiled. "But I've been greatly compensated. From both of you, I've gained so much more than I lost."

"Should we do the volleyball thing again?" Nhu asked.

Brigid laughed happily. "No, we don't have to. We know what we mean to each other."

That night she lay in bed, thinking. Her memory had been jogged by the conversation at the dinner table. In particular she remembered what it was like spending a night in jail with Laura and other demonstrators—the fear of impending punishment, the concern for her parents, the lack of sleep, the stink of armpits and excrement. Having Laura with her at least gave her some company, but it didn't give her much relief because she knew they were both in trouble. It was a long depressing night, but her spirits were lifted the next morning by the appearance of Kieran who had come to bail them out. They were carrying no identification, and like the others they had refused to provide any information about themselves. To get them released, Kieran had to reveal their names, but only on the condition that their parents wouldn't be contacted because he was taking responsibility for them. It must have helped that he was wearing clerical clothes, and though he was only a seminarian the police must have assumed that he was a priest. At that time, as Catholics, they respected priests.

For all his natural charisma Kieran was only twenty-five then, not much older than her daughter now. Of course, she herself was only twenty, and she looked up to Kieran as if he was from an older generation. She hadn't seen him in many years, but she had followed his career from the time when he resumed his Jesuit formation to when he published his latest book. He was now a highly regarded thinker in the fields of theology and ethics, a professor at Fordham University, and a popular speaker at events attended by Catholics who believed that their church should play a greater role in achieving social justice.

The questions from her daughter and comments from her mother made Brigid think about what she had lost. In a way, it *was* her innocence, or at least illusions associated with a state of innocence. Along with her fellow demonstrators she believed that with the message of love and peace she could change the world by convincing the government to end the war. Though she still believed she could change the world, now it was by helping people recover from their wounds of war. The main illusion she had lost was that she could change the world on a larger scale. But she still believed that Kieran, through his teaching, writing, and speaking, could change the world on a larger scale, and that he could convince the government to pursue policies of peace and justice. He was still the beacon that showed the way.

The next morning she got up as usual at six o'clock. It was early January, still not light, which made it harder to get up. After spending a half hour in the bathroom she went downstairs and found her mother in the kitchen. Her mother was always the first one up.

She hugged her mother, conscious of her mother's lean body, which her younger brother had inherited. She herself had to control her weight, which she did by limiting food intake and going to Pilates twice a week. But she was grateful for her good health and the fact that at fifty-seven, unlike so many people her age, she didn't need to take any medications. She only took vitamins, which she bought in three-month supplies.

Her mother had already made coffee, prepared oranges, and sliced the bread that she bought from a bakery in her old neighborhood, Nodine Hill. When her mother was growing up there the two main languages were Italian and Polish, and now the main language was Spanish, but an Italian bakery had survived, operated by the grand-daughter of the man who had started it. Along with bread, her mother always bought some treats, of which Brigid's favorite were the pignoli cookies. They were to die for.

They had breakfast together at the table in the kitchen. They didn't talk much because her mother read the local newspaper, which was delivered every day, and Brigid checked her email on her phone, especially to see if there were new appointments or cancellations.

Her mother had retired eight years ago when she was seventy-five. She would have kept working but the doctor who ran the clinic retired at the tender age of sixty-five, and her mother didn't respect the people who took over the practice. Her mother had gone to the Cochran School of Nursing right after high school and gotten certified as an RN. She worked for a while at St. John's, the same hospital where Nhu worked now, and then she took a job at a clinic across the street from the hospital, where she worked as a nurse and eventually as the office manager because she was good with numbers, details, and records. She easily mastered the art of processing claims, and her reputation led other clinics in the building to ask her to help them, which she always did. In fact, for years she taught a course in processing claims that was sponsored by the community college.

7

Now she spent her work time at the neighborhood church, St. Brigid, after which she had named her daughter. The church was in walking distance from her house, and she went there for the early morning mass several times a week. She was active in the altar society, and she served on the parish council. She had a good relationship with the priest, Father Paul, who was the same age as Brigid and had been at the parish for his second assignment almost twenty years, beyond the normal period of rotation. He came to dinner at their house at least once a month.

Brigid was about to leave for work when her phone rang, and since she rarely got a robocall on that phone she immediately answered it.

"Hello. This is Vijay Patel," a man's voice said with no trace of an Indian accent. "I would like to speak with Brigid McBride."

"This is Brigid," she said. "How can I help you?"

"I'm a detective with the police department in Peekskill, and I would like to meet with you at your convenience."

"Yeah, sure. What's this about?"

"It's too complicated to explain over the phone," he said. "But I can assure you that you're not under investigation. We only want to see if you can help us with an old case."

"Okay." She had never been to Peekskill, though she knew it was the site of a race riot in 1949 when a violent mob attacked a concert promoting civil rights and featuring Paul Robeson, Pete Seeger, and Woody Guthrie. "But I can't meet with you during the week. I could meet with you this Saturday."

"That would be fine. Would the morning work for you?"

"Yeah, sure. You could come to my house."

"What time?" he asked.

"Oh, I don't know. Around ten?" At that time her mother would be at a church meeting and Nhu would be at a yoga class, so there wouldn't be anyone else around.

"Fine. What's your address?"

She gave him her address, ended the call, and went upstairs to get ready for work.

About twenty minutes later she said goodbye to her mother,

left the house, and started walking toward Broadway. When she reached Broadway she headed north, going down the hill. As she passed St. Brigid she saw Father Paul standing outside the front door, having his morning cigarette. She stopped to exchange a few words with him, noticing that after more than thirty years of living in America he still had a lilting brogue from his native Ireland. It made his voice even more soothing, and though she had never sought his help she knew a lot of people whom he had counseled, and they all adored him.

From there it took her only about fifteen minutes to get to the building where she worked. It was the same building where her mother had worked before retiring. Along with three other buildings, all in a row, it provided offices for doctors who were affiliated with the hospital. They covered many specialties, and if you needed a doctor with any specialty you were likely to find one in those buildings.

Her building was the next to the last. It was the tallest, and it probably had the most floor space. Her office was on the fourth floor. In the elevator a child with his mother asked why there wasn't a second floor, and his mother patiently told him that there probably was a second floor but it was for mechanical equipment, like for heating and air conditioning, and that seemed to satisfy him until his next question.

Brigid got out of the elevator and followed the corridor to her office. She had inherited the practice from Wesley Osborne, her mentor and a pioneer in treating people who suffered from post-traumatic stress disorder. He had done his initial work on veterans but he later expanded his practice to victims of rape and other types of trauma. He believed that a lot of mental disorders were caused by trauma, and that they could be most effectively treated with cognitive behavioral therapy. He taught Brigid everything he knew, and he supported her getting a doctorate in psychology so that she would have the qualifications to take over the practice someday. A year ago he died from pancreatic cancer, leaving her with this office in Yonkers and an office in the Bronx. By then they had taken another partner into the practice, a psychiatrist about ten years younger than Brigid. His name was Alberto, and he had grown up in a Puerto Rican neighborhood of the Bronx, so he was bilingual, which was necessary for serving patients in Yonkers and in the Bronx.

Brigid had joined this practice after completing her master's degree in mental health. Before that she had worked as a nurse in the emergency room at St. John's Hospital, in an operating room at Phelps Hospital, and on a surgery floor of White Plains Hospital. She had been attracted to the practice because Wesley specialized in treating mental disorders of veterans. Back then they were treating veterans of the war in Vietnam, but now they were also treating veterans of the wars in Afghanistan and Iraq. Though they had patients with post-traumatic stress disorder from other experiences, Brigid's primary mission was to help veterans, and with the current wars there were always more veterans who needed help.

Entering the office, she was greeted by Clara, the office manager. Clara was in her late forties, and she had been with the practice since Brigid joined it more than twenty-five years ago. She was the oldest daughter of immigrants from the Dominican Republic, and she grew up in the same neighborhood where Brigid's mother had grown up. She now lived in a house on Morsemere Avenue, a few blocks from where Brigid lived.

"*Buenos días,*" Clara greeted her.

"*Buenos días. Como estás?*"

"*Muy bien, y usted?*"

"*Bien. Hoy tenemos un hermoso día.*"

"*Gracias a Dios.*"

"Are there any changes in my appointments?"

"Yes, a few. Mr. Sanchez cancelled. Today is his son's birthday, so I rescheduled him for next Tuesday. You had an opening then."

"Okay. So I have nothing at nine-thirty?"

"You have a new patient. Dr. Daly called from the college. A student there had a breakdown this morning, and since you had a cancellation, I told him you were free."

"Okay. Did he send us information on the student?"

"I sent it to you. He's a veteran."

"Of Afghanistan or Iraq?"

"*Afganistán. Señor ten piedad.*"

Brigid went into her office and sat down behind her desk. The college had a lot of veterans as students now, young men and women returning from war. As veterans they had the benefit of paid tuition, but they also had the cost of their war experience. Based on the students that Brigid had seen, the cost outweighed the benefit.

Looking at her computer, Brigid saw the information that Clara had sent her. The student's name was Javier Ortiz, he was twenty-three years old, and he lived in South Yonkers. Dr. Daly, the college psychologist, had described symptoms that were typical of patients with post-traumatic stress disorder.

Brigid sat in silence, gathering her mind in preparation for seeing this student. She had treated a lot of patients for PTSD, going back to the men who had served in Vietnam. Back then, they were drafted, and they were mostly poor and nonwhite because boys from families with middle or high incomes could defer the draft by going to college and staying there indefinitely. If they had connections or a lot of money, they could get themselves classified as 4F for minor or nonexistent conditions. Now we had a volunteer army, but most of the young people who joined the military were from the same socioeconomic level as those who had been drafted for Vietnam, so in that sense nothing had changed. The politicians who sent them to war were mainly affluent white males who had no idea what it was like to be poor and had never served in the military. She remembered Kieran's definition of a politician as someone who sends other people's children to war.

She had left the door of her office open, so her thoughts were interrupted by Clara appearing and telling her that her patient had arrived.

Brigid got up and went out to the reception area, where she saw a young man slumped in a chair with his right hand wrapped in a fresh bandage. His head was bowed, though not enough to prevent her from seeing the look of despair in his brown eyes.

"Javier?" she said. "I'm Brigid. I work with Dr. Daly."

He raised his head and humbly met her eyes, saying: "I'm sorry."

"I know. Come into my office. We'll talk about it."

He followed her slowly, and she closed the door behind him. Gesturing toward one of the chairs, she said: "Please sit down."

When he did, she took the chair opposite him. In early days she had made notes while talking to a new patient, but now she no longer had to. She started by asking: "What's your program at the college?"

"Nursing," he said after clearing his throat.

"Really? I got my nursing degree at St. Catherine. How do you like the program?"

"I like it a lot. And I'm doing okay."

"What year are you in?"

"The second year."

"The first year is the hardest. At least it was for me. I hated the anatomy and physiology."

"I didn't mind it, though it wasn't easy."

She paused and then said: "So you live in Yonkers."

"Yeah. In a bad neighborhood."

"You live with your family?"

"There's only my mother and my sister, who's nineteen."

"Does she go to college?"

"No, she works in a restaurant. My mother wants her to go to college, but my sister wants to make some money."

"Where does your mother work?"

"In a law office, downtown. They needed someone who speaks Spanish, and her English isn't bad. I mean, considering that she was in her twenties when she came here."

"Where did she come from?"

"Santo Domingo."

"Did she come here by herself?"

"No. She came with my father. He stayed with her long enough to have two children, and then he took off."

"Is he in touch with you?"

12

Javier slowly shook his head. "We haven't seen him in many years. My mother thinks he got involved in some kind of criminal activity."

"Like drugs?"

"I don't know. Whatever it is, it keeps him away from us."

"So you grew up in Yonkers," Brigid continued. "Where did you go to high school?"

"I went to Saunders. My mother wanted to get me out of the neighborhood."

"Because of the gangs?"

"Yeah. I almost joined one."

"But you didn't join one. You went to Saunders. Did you like it there?"

"Oh, yeah. I wanted to be a mechanic then."

"Did you graduate from Saunders?"

"Yeah, and I got a job. The job wasn't bad, but I could see it wasn't going to get me out of the neighborhood so I joined the army."

"You joined the army to get out of the neighborhood?"

"Yeah. The job wouldn't have done that for me."

She understood, having heard it from veterans many times. "So where did you do your basic training?"

"Fort Jackson."

"What was that like?"

"I didn't mind the training, but I did mind the people in town."

"Why did you mind them?"

He shrugged. "They were racist. They made us feel inferior, you know?"

"I don't know, but I can imagine."

"It was better upstate at Fort Drum, where they sent me after basic training. I was in the 10th Mountain Division."

She knew what they were—they were the first to be deployed to Afghanistan in late 2001, only months after the attack on 9-11. "Did you go to Afghanistan?"

"Oh, yeah. We were there for about eight months. We came back for a while, and then we were redeployed there."

"So how long were you in Afghanistan?"

"About two years in all, with a break in the middle."

Gently, she asked: "Do you remember a lot about what happened there?"

"Well, I try not to remember, but it comes back."

"How does it come back?"

"In nightmares. And in flashbacks."

"Tell me about what happened this morning."

He took a long, deep breath. "I was in the bathroom before my eight-thirty class. I was washing my hands, and I was looking into the mirror above the sink when I saw someone behind me. I wanted to turn and smash whoever it was, but I stopped myself and instead I punched the mirror."

"Did you think the person behind you was real?"

"Well, at first I did, but then I wondered if it was only my imagination, so I punched the mirror."

"*Was* there anyone behind you?"

"No. After punching the mirror, I turned around and saw there was no one."

"You know, what you did in that bathroom is a hopeful sign."

"Punching a mirror?"

"Realizing that the person behind you was only your imagination. That's progress. And if it's okay with you, I'd like to see you twice a week and help you continue making progress. *Te parece bien?*"

"*Habla español?*" he said, looking surprised.

At least he didn't look astounded like the way a kid in the hospital had looked at her as if she was a cat talking human language. "*Por supuesto. Vivo en Yonkers.*"

"You have a good accent. Where did you learn Spanish?"

"From friends and patients over the years. So we have to work around your classes. What days are good for you?"

He gave her some possibilities, and they worked it out with Clara.

After he had left she returned to her office, feeling that the day had gotten off to an unusually good start.

On Saturday morning, precisely at ten, the doorbell rang. She was in the kitchen checking the grocery list her mother had left on the table, and she went directly to the front door. When she opened it she saw a young man with glossy black hair and keen black eyes. In his tweed jacket, button-down shirt, and rep tie he could have been a model for Brooks Brothers, except that he wasn't tall enough.

"I'm Vijay Patel," he said, flashing a badge. "It's not initials, Vijay is my first name."

"I'm Brigid McBride. Please come in."

He waited for her to step aside, and then he followed her into the house.

"Would you like some coffee?"

"If you already have it made," he said, "but I don't want you to go to any trouble."

"We always make more than enough in the morning, so I just have to heat it up. Come into the kitchen."

He followed her into the kitchen, saying: "This is a nice house. Have you lived her long?"

"I've lived here since I was born," she said, going to the counter to get the filter coffee pot. "Except for the years when I lived in Tarrytown."

"Do you live here with your family?"

"I live here with my mother and my daughter. All three of us are healthcare professionals."

"Are you a doctor?"

"I'm a doctor of psychology," she said, pouring the coffee from the pot into a stainless steel pan that also served as the lower half of a double boiler.

"So you treat patients with mental disorders. What kind of disorders?"

"All kinds of disorders, though I specialize in post-traumatic stress disorder."

"That must be a tough job."

"I'm sure it's no tougher than being a detective," she said, turning on the flame under the pot.

"I guess our jobs are similar—if you consider crime a symptom of mental disorder."

Brigid smiled, acknowledging that this detective was a clever young man.

When it was ready she poured the coffee into the mugs that Nhu had given her years ago. One of them said LOVE and the other PEACE. He took his coffee black and she lightened hers with half and half.

Then, with mugs in hand, they went into the living room and sat down in the armchairs that faced each other in front of the fireplace, where during the winter her parents had spent their evenings after dinner, her father with a glass of Jameson, neat, and her mother with a snifter of sambuca, talking with each other, enjoying each other's company.

After taking a sip of coffee he said: "According to records of the NYPD, you were arrested for participating in a demonstration in front of the Whitehall induction center in July of 1968. Is that correct?"

"Yes, it's correct." She didn't understand why he would bring up something that had happened so long ago. Wasn't there a statute of limitations?

"Well, one of the people arrested with you was a young woman named Laura Hughes. Did you know her?"

"Yes, I knew her well."

"What was your relationship?"

"We were students in the nursing program at St. Catherine College."

"Were you close friends?"

"We were very close."

He took a sip of coffee. "How did you get involved in the demonstration?"

"We were members of an organization whose purpose was to end the war in Vietnam."

"What was the name of this organization?"

"The Catholic Peace Fellowship."

"Was it sponsored by the church?"

"No. It was founded by Catholics who didn't agree with the

church's position on the war. At least the position of Cardinal Spellman."

"What was his position?"

"He supported the war. He convinced the government that Vietnam was a Catholic country that had to be saved from communists."

"It was mostly a Buddhist country, wasn't it?"

"Yeah, it was. But politicians never let facts get in the way."

He smiled faintly. "So you were members of the Catholic Peace Fellowship. Who were the other members?"

"They were mostly lay people, but they were also priests and nuns who believed that the church's mission on earth was to help the poor."

"What did that have to do with the war?"

"The boys who were drafted to fight the war were usually poor. They didn't have the money to buy their way out."

He nodded as if he understood. "Could you give me names of members of this organization who knew Miss Hughes?"

"Well, it's been a long time. What are you trying to find out?"

"I'm trying to find out what happened to her."

"What do you mean?" she asked, perplexed. It was thirty-seven years ago that Laura had mysteriously disappeared, and now this detective was trying to find out what happened to her.

"I'm sorry. I should have told you upfront. We found her body a week ago."

"Her body? Oh, my God." Since she still hadn't lost all hope that Laura was alive, being told they had found her body was a shock. "Where did you find it?"

"On an estate outside of Peekskill. The estate belonged to a landowning family that went back to the eighteenth century. It had hundreds of acres of land and a manor house that wasn't occupied for many years. Last fall the heiress sold the estate to a developer, and when they were clearing the land they found the body."

"Where was it?" she managed to ask.

"It was in the family mausoleum. It was easy to identify. There was a tag on a suitcase that gave her name and an address in Poughkeepsie."

"What kind of suitcase was it?"

"A hard shell suitcase."

"What was in the suitcase?"

"A lot of clothes."

That was Laura. She always took a lot of clothes when she traveled.

Resuming, the detective said: "We contacted the Poughkeepsie police, and they had a case of a missing girl named Laura Hughes. They never found a trace of her, so they closed the case. And now, after thirty-seven years, they've reopened it. Since the body was found in Peekskill, I'm working with them."

"I assume they told her parents."

"They told her mother. Her father's deceased."

Brigid felt bad for her mother, who had lived all those years without knowing what had happened to Laura, and now she had learned that her daughter was dead.

"I talked with her mother, and she told me that her daughter had a friend who lived in Yonkers. She didn't remember your name, but we found you after searching to see if Miss Hughes had a police record. She did have a record, and that led us to you."

"Well, I don't know if I can help you. When she was reported missing, I told a Poughkeepsie police detective everything I knew. And then when her father hired a private detective, I told him everything I knew."

"I understand. But it's possible that they missed something."

"Yeah, I guess. So go ahead."

The detective leaned forward in his chair. "Now, when was the last time you saw her?"

"It was when she was going to Canada to see her boyfriend, who had gone there to avoid the draft."

"How was she going to Canada?"

"She was taking the train."

"Where were you living then?"

"In the East Village. It was the summer after our second year of nursing school, and we were doing an internship."

"An internship?" he said, slightly raising his eyebrows.

"That's what we told our parents we were doing. We were really trying to end the war."

"How were you trying to end the war?"

"We were demonstrating against it. Peacefully," she added so he would understand that they practiced the principle of nonviolence.

"Where in the East Village were you living?"

"On the fifth floor of a tenement on East 4th Street between Avenue A and Avenue B. Back then it was a poor neighborhood, but it's been gentrified."

The detective made some notes, and then he said: "Since you were living in the city and she was taking the train to Canada, she must have gone to Penn Station."

"That's where she was going. She wouldn't let me go there with her to see her off, so we said goodbye in front of our building."

"Did she have a suitcase?"

"She always traveled with a suitcase."

"Well, as I said, there were a lot of clothes in the suitcase they found with her remains. There were not only summer clothes but also winter clothes."

Brigid was surprised. "Are you sure there were winter clothes?"

"I'm sure. There were sweaters, wool slacks, gloves, and a winter jacket."

"But she didn't have any winter clothes at our apartment. We were there for only two months of the summer. So where would she have gotten winter clothes?"

"The train to Montreal stops in Poughkeepsie, so she must have stopped there and gotten them from home."

She remembered that Laura had chosen that time to go to Canada because her parents were at their cabin in the Adirondacks with her little brothers, so she could have gone home and gotten winter clothes without their knowing. "But why did she have winter clothes? She was only going to Canada for the rest of the summer. She was planning to return for the fall semester. At least that's what she told me."

"She might have wanted the option of staying in Canada."

"Yeah, she might have. She really loved that guy."

The detective was silent for a while as if in respect for the girl's feeling, and then he said: "After getting winter clothes from home she must have intended to get on the train and continue the trip to Montreal. But she evidently didn't. Do you think she could have changed her mind about going to Canada?"

"She could have, but I don't think she would have. As I said, she really loved that guy."

"Did you ever meet him?"

"No, I never did. He went to Canada before I met Laura. They were high school sweethearts."

"That's what her mother told me. Her father was against the relationship, which probably had the effect of strengthening it." He paused again. "And after you said goodbye in front of your building, you never saw her or heard from her again?"

"I never did. But you have to understand, I assumed she didn't contact me because she didn't want to reveal where she was. I mean, it could have led the police to her boyfriend, who was wanted by the law."

"I understand. From what her mother told me, her parents assumed the same thing, which is why it took them so long to hire a detective to find her." He took a last sip of coffee and set down the mug. "After so many years, it's impossible to say how she was killed, but—"

"She was killed?"

"Evidently. The vertebrae in her neck were damaged, so either she was killed by whiplash in a car accident or by someone who assaulted her and broke her neck."

"Oh, my God," Brigid said with pain in her heart.

"So this could be a murder investigation."

After a long silence she asked: "Where do you think she could have been killed?"

"We think it could have happened between her home and the Poughkeepsie train station."

"How could it have happened?"

"Well, her mother said she could have walked to the train station, which was less than a mile from her home, and she could have run into someone on her way to the station."

"You mean someone who assaulted her?"

"Right. So we're checking people with criminal records who might have been around at the time."

"But how did her body end up in Peekskill?"

"Whoever killed her must have taken her there."

She searched her memory, looking for something that would fit into the new paradigm that the detective had given her, but she couldn't find anything. At last she said: "I wish I could tell you more, but I can't think of anything."

"It's okay. I appreciate the time you've given me." He got up from the chair without using his arms to help him. "If you do think of anything, please contact me."

"I will," she said.

After seeing him out she returned to the chair where she had been sitting and leaned back and closed her eyes. Over the years she had imagined all kinds of things that could have happened to Laura, including her being killed, but she had still hoped that Laura was alive. And now that this hope was obliterated, the only thing she had left from that lost summer was her love for Kieran, which was rooted so deeply in her heart that it had survived the assaults of time.

TWO

WHEN SHE WAS in fifth grade at St. Brigid School the teacher asked the students to write about the person who was their role model. The teacher explained what the concept meant, and she gave them a week to submit their papers.

Brigid had to think about this assignment. She loved and admired both her parents, and she didn't like having to choose between them. For a while she considered avoiding the issue and writing about the Blessed Mother, which would also make the assignment easy. But then she decided to face the issue, and she took a walk along Broadway to consider whether to write about her mother or her father. When her walk took her past the hospital it was like a sign. Her mother worked there as a nurse, and if she understood the meaning of role model it was someone you wanted to be like. And it became clear that she wanted to be like her mother, whose profession she could easily imagine pursuing. Her father worked for a beer distributor, and though she understood what he did, having accompanied him during his workday as a school assignment last year, she couldn't imagine doing what he did. For one thing, she didn't have his outgoing personality which enabled him to connect with people regardless of their age, gender, race, or ethnic background. From watching him in action she could tell that his customers liked him, ranging from an old Dominican man who owned a bodega in south Yonkers to a young Korean woman who operated a fruit and vegetable store in Bronxville. They liked him, and they liked his product because they made extra money selling it.

That was the difference between her parents: her mother was serious, and her father was fun, and for her it was a blessing to have them both. It was evidently also good for their marriage because instead of producing conflict their difference made them talk about things and helped them arrive at compromises. Even as a child Brigid understood when they kidded each other about their difference, her father joking about her mother's need for order and reason, and her mother joking about her father's need for humor and feeling.

So she ended up writing about her mother, making in her paper her first declaration of what she wanted to do with her life. And when in her senior year of high school at Sacred Heart she applied for the nursing program at St. Catherine College, she was strongly supported by both parents. Since her father started working directly after high school, and her mother got her degree in nursing from a two-year school, Brigid would be the first in her family to enroll in a four-year college. Of course her parents and her grandparents were very proud of her.

Brigid was familiar with St. Catherine because it was only a twenty-minute walk from her house, north of the hospital on a hundred acres that overlooked the Hudson River. The property had belonged to the Morrissey family, who had bought it during the last half of the nineteenth century from the heirs of an estate that went back to the colonial period. A fourth generation Morrissey, whose children had no interest in maintaining the property, had donated it to the Sisters of the Redemption for a college, which had started as a two-year school for training nuns and evolved into a four-year college for women. The college was still Catholic, and the sisters were still involved in its faculty and administration, though now it had more lay employees than nuns. Its nursing school had an excellent reputation, easily placing its graduates in hospitals that spanned the region from the Bronx to northern Westchester. So Brigid felt lucky to have been admitted to the program.

There were about sixty students in Brigid's cohort, most of whom commuted from their homes but some of whom lived in a dormitory. In that respect, the program was representative of the college's student population, eighty percent of whom commuted, taking a train from the city, riding a bus from nearby areas of the county, or driving a car from remote areas. During her first year of the program Brigid dispersed along with most of the other students immediately after her last class to go to her job at the checkout counter of the supermarket on Palisade Avenue, so she didn't get to know any of her classmates very well.

That all changed in the fall of her second year when she and Laura were assigned to be lab partners in microbiology. She had noticed Laura in some of her classes the previous year, but they hadn't exchanged more than a few words with each other. Laura was a natural beauty, with radiant blond hair and pure blue eyes, and she had an aura that deterred other students from approaching her. The impressions that they had of her, which ranged from an image of her as a glamorous movie star to an image of her as a remote virgin, proved to have nothing to do with reality when Brigid got to know her.

While working with Laura their first day in the lab Bridget realized that her partner was a shy girl who had limited confidence in her own abilities as a student. Though they both found the course difficult, Laura was overwhelmed by it, and she was grateful for having a partner who could help her with it. When the lab period ended, Laura asked Brigid if she could go to the pub with her. Since the drinking age was eighteen at that time the college had a pub on the lower floor of Wagner Hall, next to the cafeteria. Expecting tougher courses in the second year of the nursing program, Brigid had cut back on the days she worked at the supermarket, so she happened to be free that afternoon, and she accepted Laura's invitation.

The pub had a bar with three sides, the bottles of liquor on the back wall, and the bartender in the middle. He was a graduate student in a business program, and he was talking with two girls who were sitting at the front side of the bar. He greeted Brigid, who had gone there occasionally, and he paused his conversation long enough to serve her and Laura. They ordered beers, which they carried over to an empty booth.

"I haven't been here before," Laura admitted, sitting across from her with her hands clasped around her bottle.

"I've only been here a few times," Brigid said. "I'm not a regular, even though my father sells beer to them."

"Your father sells beer?"

"Yeah. To bars and grocery stores. He doesn't sell it to supermarkets. The big guys have those accounts."

"My father's a plumber. He has his own business, but it's just him and an assistant."

"Does your mother have a job?"

"Oh, yeah. She's a secretary at IBM."

"That sounds like a good job," Brigid said.

"It is," Laura said. "It provides our healthcare benefits."

"My mother's a nurse. She works at the hospital where we do our clinicals."

"Is that why you want to be a nurse?"

"Yeah. She's my role model." Brigid paused to take a sip of beer. "So why do you want to be a nurse?"

"I want to help people," Laura said simply. "And being a nurse seems like a good way to help people. Except—"

Brigid waited, but the girl didn't continue. "Except what?"

"Well, I don't know if I have the ability."

"I'm sure you do. And if you want to help people, you have the right motivation."

"But I don't know if I can handle some of the courses. I mean, this microbiology course is really difficult for me. I'm not very good at memorizing things."

"It's a lot of things. But it helps if you understand what they do, and how they work, instead of just being names on a list."

"I'll try that," Laura said hopefully. "Were you good at school?"

"I was good enough to get into this program, but I wasn't a star student. I had a lot of competition."

"Where did you go to high school?"

"Sacred Heart in Yonkers."

"I've met some other girls from there. Was it only girls?"

"No, we had boys. It's one of the few coeducational Catholic high schools."

"I went to a public high school. There were times when I

wished I was in a school with only girls. And that was an attraction of St. Catherine."

"I heard they're thinking about going coed here."

"I hope they don't until we graduate."

"Yeah, boys can be a distraction."

Laura nodded as if she knew from personal experience what Brigid meant. She took a sip of beer, and then she said: "You're not in a dormitory. Where do you live?"

"I live on Greenvale Avenue, near St. Brigid. It's walking distance from the college."

"So you don't have to take a bus here?"

"Only if it's raining, or snowing."

"I wish I lived closer. Sometimes I miss my family."

"Where do they live?"

"Poughkeepsie."

"How often do you see them?"

"About twice a month. My parents drive down here on Sunday, and we go out for lunch at a place on the river."

"Do you have any brothers or sisters?"

"I have two brothers, who are younger. I don't miss them, but I do miss my parents."

"I have a younger brother. He's going to Manhattan College next year."

"Do you have a good relationship with him?"

"It's all right. At least it's better than when we were younger."

"My brothers are ten and twelve years younger, so I don't have much of a relationship with them." Laura paused. "There're so many years between us because my father was called back to active duty not long after I was born."

"Was there a war then?"

"Yeah, in Korea. He was in the marine reserves, and they called him up. It took him a while to recover from it," Laura added, staring at her bottle.

"Was he wounded?"

"Yeah. He was wounded badly in his right leg. They had to do several operations before he could walk again. But he only has a slight limp now."

"My father was in Europe during World War II. He doesn't talk about it much."

"My father doesn't talk much about his experience either."

"How does he feel about the war in Vietnam?"

"He supports it, being a veteran. It's the only thing we argue about."

"Are you against it?"

"I'm completely against it," Laura said with unexpected fervor. "What we're doing there is morally wrong."

"Well, I'm against it too," Brigid said, based on her feelings. "I wish there was something we could do about it, but what could we do?"

"We could join a group that opposes the war."

"What group?"

"A group here at the college," Laura said. "It's called the Catholic Peace Fellowship."

"Is it sponsored by the college?"

"Not officially, but the college chaplain is involved in it. And so are some nuns. But most of the members are students."

"How do you know about it?"

"The girl who lives across the hall from me is a member. She's on the basketball team, and the captain of the basketball team is the leader of it."

Being a commuter student, Brigid didn't follow the college's sports. The only sport she followed was baseball because her father was from the Bronx, so he was naturally a Yankees fan. "If you're against the war, then why haven't you joined this group?"

"I'm not good at joining things. I never have been," Laura said with lowered eyes. "But if you joined with me, I wouldn't have a problem."

"Well, let's find out more about it," Brigid said, responding to the girl's need for company.

"We could talk with the girl across the hall from me."

The girl's name was Jenny, and when they met her in the pub two weeks later she brought with her another girl, whose name was

Teri. They were both taller than the average girl, but neither of them was six feet. They were in training for the basketball season, so instead of beers they ordered sodas, which they brought to a booth with Brigid and Laura. Since they were done with basketball practice for the day they had all the time in the world, and when they finally left the pub it was dark outside.

Laura and Jenny headed for their dormitory while Brigid and Teri walked to the bus stop. On the way Brigid learned that Teri had a twin brother whose name was Tim, and he was her personal reason for opposing the war. Their father was a war hero, and even though Tim was deferred from the draft because he was a student at Fordham, he felt a need to go to war in order to prove his manhood to their father.

Brigid left the girl at the bus stop, and from there she headed home. As she walked along Broadway she thought about what she had learned about the Catholic Peace Fellowship, which Jenny and Teri referred to as the CPF. They said it was founded by Jim Forest and Tom Cornell, who had been involved in the Catholic Worker movement, and it was supported by prominent Catholic activists, including Daniel Berrigan, Dorothy Day, and Thomas Merton. The group at St. Catherine College derived their values from the papal pronouncements *Pacem in Terris* and *Gaudium et Spes*, and they based their position against the war on the just war doctrine. Though she had been raised as a Catholic, these names and ideas were unfamiliar to Brigid, who had never given much thought to the role of her church in the modern world, so the conversation in the pub had opened up a whole new dimension for her. Teri had given her and Laura copies of the papal pronouncements and the just war doctrine, and Brigid stayed up late that night reading them. It was around two when her mother, on a trip to the bathroom, advised her to turn off her light and go to sleep.

In the college library the next morning, after reviewing her notes for a class, she reviewed the reading material from the Catholic Peace Fellowship, directing her attention especially to the passages that she had identified last night. In the encyclical *Pacem in Terris* she had highlighted the passage: "Governmental authority, therefore, is a postulate of the moral order and derives from God. Consequently, laws and decrees passed in contravention of the moral order, and hence of the divine will, can have no binding force in conscience, since 'it is right to obey God rather than men'." In that context the encyclical quoted St. Thomas Aquinas, who said: "A law which is at variance with reason is to that extent unjust and has no longer the rationale of law. It is rather an act of violence." So the laws that authorized the war were acts of violence.

After skimming through two more sections she came to the pastoral exhortations, which began by saying: "We exhort Our sons to take an active part in public life, and to work together for the benefit of the whole human race, as well as for their own political communities. It is vitally necessary for them to endeavor, in the light of Christian faith, and with love as their guide, to ensure that every institution, whether economic, social, cultural, or political, be such as not to obstruct but rather to facilitate man's self-betterment, both in the natural and in the supernatural order." Later, the pope talked about a longing that he felt most keenly— that peace be assured on earth. He ended by recalling how Christ had brought us peace and by ardently praying for it. That was the foundation of their mission.

She then reviewed *Gaudium et Spes*, which covered many of the same issues. In the section called "The Avoidance of War" she had highlighted the statement: "Any act of war aimed indiscriminately at the destruction of entire cities or extensive areas along with their population is a crime against God and man himself." She understood how this statement applied to the use of atom bombs at Hiroshima and Nagasaki, and she could see how it applied to the bombing of cities and the exfoliation of forests in Vietnam. So that was the basis for their claim that the war in Vietnam was a crime against humanity.

Finally, she reviewed the booklet on the just war doctrine, which set the four conditions for legitimate defense by military force. First, there must have been an act of aggression against your nation or against the community of nations that inflicted lasting, grave, and certain damage. Second, all other means of resolving the conflict must have been shown to be impractical and ineffective. Third, there must be serious prospects of success. And fourth, the use of arms must not produce evils that are worse than the evil to be eliminated.

Assessing the war in Vietnam by those conditions, she found that there had not been an act of aggression against her nation or against the community of nations that inflicted lasting, grave, and certain damage. All other means of resolving the conflict had not been shown to be impractical and ineffective. Whatever the generals claimed, there were no serious prospects of success. And based on the sufferings of the Vietnamese people, the use of arms had definitely produced evils that were worse than the evil to be eliminated, namely, the presumed "evil" of communism.

So the war in Vietnam was not just.

At the pub after their next lab Brigid and Laura agreed to join the CPF, and that was when Laura told her about her boyfriend, Owen. He was two years older, and after graduating from high school he went directly to work as a mechanic in a local garage. He had played with cars as far back as she could remember, and when they didn't function he loved diagnosing the problem and fixing it. He was doing well at his job when he received a draft notice. Since he was a Quaker he was a genuine conscientious objector, and he assumed that they wouldn't take him. But the government ignored his beliefs, and they ordered him to report for active duty. At that point he did what many young men like him were doing—he fled to Canada. That had happened during Laura's first year in nursing school, and it helped to explain why she was aloof. Right now, Owen was living in Nova Scotia, working at a garage in a rural area, repairing trucks and tractors as well as cars. He didn't exchange letters with Laura for fear that it would leave a trail for the FBI to find him. Instead, every Sunday evening he called her from a pay phone, and she took his call at a pay phone in her dormitory. The phone was in a tiny room with a door that she could shut, so she had privacy. At times she had to cut their conversation short because another girl wanted to use the phone, but at least they had a way of communicating with each other.

So Laura had a personal reason for joining the CPF, and when they were introduced to the group at their next meeting she embraced their mission. There were about fifty people at the meeting, including the college chaplain, Father Justin, and two nuns, Sister Audrey and Sister Maura. Brigid had taken an English course with Sister Audrey, who had kept the students engaged with outrageous one-liners. The leader of the group was Megan, a tall girl with dark hair pulled back in a ponytail and commanding dark eyes. After dealing with the minutes of their last meeting she asked a girl named Angela to give them a report on her trip to Washington last Saturday.

Standing at the front of the room, Angela recounted how she and eleven other members of the group had taken a train to Washington for a demonstration to be held at the Lincoln Memorial. It was the first large national demonstration against the war, and it was attended by more than a hundred thousand people. The crowd included CPF groups from other colleges as well as a wide variety of other groups. The speakers included Dr. Benjamin Spock, poet Robert Lowell, and writer Norman Mailer. They were all governed by the principle of nonviolence, and their crowd was orderly and peaceful.

Meanwhile, another crowd of protesters had gathered at the Pentagon around a core of people from the Youth International Party, led by Jerry Rubin and Abbie Hoffman. These protesters provoked the soldiers and U.S. marshals who were guarding the Pentagon, and there were violent interactions between them. About seven hundred protesters were arrested.

"What were they trying to do?" a girl in the front row asked.

"They were trying to shut down the Pentagon," Angela responded.

"That would be cool. It would end the war."

"It wouldn't end the war," Father Justin said. "It would only start another war."

"Violence only leads to more violence," Sister Audrey said.

"But the politicians aren't listening to us," another girl said. "They keep sending more and more boys to die in Vietnam."

"We have almost half a million troops there now," another girl said.

"So we're not stopping them."

"The only way to stop them," Father Justin said, "is to get a majority of people in this country to oppose the war. And we can do that with our apostolic mission."

"The Yippies got the news coverage," the girl who had raised the issue said. "It was all about them. It wasn't about our peaceful demonstration."

"I think we should *do* something," a girl said heatedly, "and not just talk."

"What would you do?" Father Justin asked.

"If I were a boy, I'd burn my draft card."

"You're not a boy," Megan pointed out. "So you don't have a draft card."

"Well, I *should* have a draft card. If women had equal rights with men, I'd have one."

"You mean equal rights to die in Vietnam?"

"Yeah. It's not fair that boys get drafted and girls don't."

"It would be fair," Teri said, "if neither boys or girls got drafted. It would be fair if neither of them were sent to war."

"I agree," a girl who hadn't yet spoken said. "If the politicians want to have a war, they should fight it themselves."

"Yeah, that would be a way to get rid of them."

"Okay, okay," Father Justin said. "You're veering off the course of nonviolence."

"I know the Yippies got press coverage," Megan said, "but so did the peaceful demonstrators. We had more than a hundred thousand people there. Think about it."

"Next time we could have a million people," Teri said.

"We could," Sister Audrey said. "So let's plan the next time."

As she walked home Brigid reflected on the meeting. Clearly, there were girls in the group who felt that they should move beyond just talking and start doing things like the Yippies were doing. But their leaders had made a good case against this change in tactics, and from their exchange as they left the meeting Brigid could tell that Laura agreed with their leaders, repeating what Sister Audrey had said, that violence only leads to more violence. Brigid had listened to the girls who wanted to take dramatic action, and she empathized with their position, so while she leaned toward Laura's position, she had to admit that those girls had a point. For a moment she imagined standing up to the marshals at the Pentagon and being arrested. She didn't know where that idea had come from, and it surprised her.

At dinner that night with her parents and her brother she ate in silence, still thinking about the meeting, still not knowing which side of the issue she was on.

"Brigid, you're very quiet tonight," her mother said.

"I'm sorry," she said, trying to snap out of it.

"Did something happen at the college?"

"No, nothing happened. I went to a meeting," she added, "and I was thinking about it."

"What was the meeting?"

"A meeting about the war."

"Oh. Who was at the meeting?"

"Students, mostly. But also the college chaplain and two nuns."

"Then it couldn't have been a bad meeting."

"It wasn't a bad meeting. But there was a debate about what we should do to end the war."

"We should pull out," her father said, "and let those people fight among themselves. We have no business being there."

Brigid was relieved, though not surprised, to hear her father take this position. Like Laura's father, he was a veteran. He was drafted at the age of twenty, right after meeting her mother, who was working at the family's grocery store to help pay for nursing school. Her father, who still lived in the Bronx, came to the store to deliver beer, he met her mother, they fell in love, and after he was drafted her mother waited for him throughout the war. Among his objections to that war, it separated him for more than three years from the woman he loved.

"I agree," her mother said. "All the money we're spending on this war we could be spending on health care."

"What was the issue of the debate?" her brother Brady asked. He could be a little nerdy, but he usually asked good questions.

"The issue was whether we should continue our tactics of nonviolence, or change our tactics and do things like the Yippies did last Saturday at the Pentagon."

"Who are the Yippies?" her father asked.

"They're people who believe in taking action to end the war."

"You mean like those riots in Washington last week," her mother said.

"They did that to get attention," her father said.

"Well, that's the point. They got attention. But we had people in Washington who were demonstrating peacefully, and they didn't get any attention."

"Those Yippies, or whatever you call them, got the wrong kind of attention," her mother said. "It didn't get people on their side."

"But it sent a message."

"What was the message?" her father said.

"That the war is a crime against humanity," she quoted.

"I agree that it's wrong, but where did you get the idea that it's a crime against humanity?"

"From a papal pronouncement."

"You're reading papal pronouncements?" her mother asked, impressed.

"Yeah. The values of our group are based on them."

"What's this group?"

"The Catholic Peace Fellowship."

"I never heard of them."

"I did," her brother said. "They're a group of Catholic lefties."

She knew that her brother was teasing her, so she didn't object, especially since the politics of their family were somewhat to the left of center. At least they voted for Democrats.

"You said the college chaplain was at the meeting. Does the college sponsor this group?"

"No. But it allows us to meet on campus."

"You also mentioned some nuns."

"Yeah. They're faculty," Brigid said. "I had one of them for my second English course, and the other one I'll probably have for a religion course."

"Are they like the nuns we had at St. Brigid?" her brother asked as if he hadn't been impressed by them.

"No, they're college professors."

"Well, I hope I don't have nuns as college professors."

"Brady," their mother told him. "Don't be disrespectful."

"I'm sorry," he said. But making a comeback he asked Brigid: "So where do *you* stand on the issue that they debated at your meeting?"

"I think I'm on the side of nonviolence," she said carefully. "But I don't know. When I heard the arguments for taking action, I understood them. I mean, those girls may have brothers or boyfriends who will go to war unless we end it."

"If they drafted me," her brother said, "I'd go to Canada."

"They won't draft you," their mother said. "You'll be in college."

"For four years. But what if the war's still going on when I graduate?"

"It won't be," Brigid said, having her own personal reason now for ending it.

From then on she watched the evening news on television, with or without her parents. A particular event that caught her attention occurred less than a week after the CPF meeting. Along with three others Philip Berrigan, a Catholic priest who was a younger brother of Daniel Berrigan, protested against the war by seizing and damaging draft records. Known as the Baltimore Four, they occupied the draft board in the Baltimore Customs House and performed a sacrificial protest using their own blood and blood from poultry, which they poured over draft records. They were arrested and charged with felonies.

Believing that this was the kind of action the CPF should consider, Brigid went to the college library the next day to find out more about Philip Berrigan. From microfilm of newspapers she learned that like her father he was drafted at the age of twenty and did combat duty in Europe during World War II. He went to the College of the Holy Cross after the war, graduated with a degree in English, and joined a religious society that served African-Americans, who were still dealing with the legacy of slavery, especially in the South. He was ordained a priest five years later and became active in the Civil Rights movement of the early Sixties. He was imprisoned for his activities, but that didn't stop him. According to one article, he was involved in the founding of the CPF along with Jim Forrest and Tom Cornell. With his recent action in Baltimore he seemed to have violated the principle of nonviolence, though the violence of that action was against things, not against people, so you could argue in a narrow sense that it conformed with the principle of nonviolence.

Brigid processed this information, which she shared with Laura the next time they went to the college pub. Laura listened, and after some resistance she agreed that acts of violence against things didn't necessarily violate the principle of nonviolence. But she maintained that if such acts even inadvertently hurt people, then they were morally unacceptable. And Brigid agreed that this was where they should draw the line.

THREE

THERE WERE SEVERAL major events that fall before the end of the semester. On the last day of November Eugene McCarthy, a U.S. Senator from Minnesota, announced that he would run against Lyndon Johnson in the primaries for the nomination as his party's candidate in the presidential election. He had served in Congress for almost twenty years, so he had a lot of experience in government, which included being a member of the Senate Foreign Relations Committee. Over the past few years McCarthy had become known for his opposition to the war, and he planned to campaign as an antiwar candidate.

Along with her colleagues in the CPF, Brigid welcomed this development, and she went back to the library to find out more about McCarthy. She learned that he was born in a small town in Minnesota northwest of the Twin Cities, and that he went to St. John's Preparatory School and St. John's University, which were founded by the Benedictine monks of St. John's Abbey in Collegeville, Minnesota. He earned a master's degree from the University of Minnesota, and he taught in public schools for a while before taking a position as a professor of economics at St. John's University. After three years in that position he entered the novitiate at St. John's Abbey, but after nine months he left the monastery and enlisted in the Army and served as a code breaker for military intelligence during World War II. After the war he became an instructor in sociology and economics at the College of St. Thomas in St. Paul, Minnesota. He was elected to the U.S. Congress in 1948 with support from labor unions and farmers, and ten years later he was elected to the U.S. Senate. His positions on most issues were left of center, which placed him out of his party's mainstream. His decision to run against Johnson was considered quixotic at best, and he wasn't given a chance of winning. A crucial test would come in New Hampshire, where the first Democratic primary was scheduled for March 12.

Meanwhile, the war in Vietnam went on. Less than two weeks after McCarthy's declaration of candidacy the general in charge of the war effort, William Westmoreland, told the press that he was absolutely certain that we were winning. But only about a week later the Secretary of Defense, Robert McNamara, announced his resignation, which suggested that he was having second thoughts about the war. At the same time a battle was raging in the Mekong Delta, with U.S. and South Vietnamese forces engaging the Viet Cong forces. As usual it was impossible to tell who was winning the battle.

By then the semester was almost over. Brigid had to study for exams, and she helped Laura prepare for the final in microbiology. On the day before the students in the dormitory went home for Christmas recess, the CPF had a meeting to discuss recent events in the war and McCarthy's announcement. They agreed that they would find a way to help him in the New Hampshire primary, and Megan promised to have a plan when they returned in January. Brigid and Laura left the meeting resolved to participate in the CPF action in New Hampshire.

Brigid spent the recess catching up on sleep and helping her mother with the holiday events. On Christmas Eve they went to the apartment of her mother's parents on Nodine Hill, where her grandmother had prepared a traditional Feast of Seven Fishes, and on Christmas after they attended mass at St. Brigid her father's parents came to their house for a dinner of roast leg of lamb, mashed potatoes, carrots, and peas with apple crumb-cake for dessert, which Brigid had made the day before. Her father and his parents drank beer with their food, while she and her mother drank red wine. Her brother had a Coke.

When her grades for the fall semester arrived by mail she was happy to see that she got an A in microbiology. She also got A's in her other courses, but those she had expected. A few days later in a phone call she learned that Laura had gotten a B+ in microbiology, and Laura was very happy with that, having worried about passing the course. And they were assigned to be lab partners for the second part of this course in the spring semester. It was as if someone knew they made good partners.

In the CPF meeting after they returned from recess Megan gave them an outline of the plan for helping McCarthy in New Hampshire, which she and Teri and two other girls had developed over Christmas recess. The group had sixty-four members, who would be divided up into four teams of sixteen. A team would go to New Hampshire for each of the six weekends leading up to the election. Megan's team and Teri's team would go for two weekends. They would travel to New Hampshire on a bus driven by Angela's boyfriend, who was a licensed bus driver. They would leave on Friday morning and return on Monday afternoon. They would stay in motels, with four girls to a room. They would pay for the bus, the motels, and food with money they would raise for the project.

"That's basically it," Megan said, looking at Teri. "Have I forgotten anything?"

Teri shook her head, saying: "You covered the key points."

"So let's have your questions."

A lot of hands went up, and Megan called on people by name. "Carolyn?"

"You said we're sleeping four to a room. How can we do that?"

"The rooms will have two queen size beds, but if you don't want to share a bed you can always bring a sleeping bag."

"Well, I don't know if I want to share a bed with Carolyn," a girl joked.

"Next question. Sandy?"

"What kind of bus?"

"It's a reconditioned school bus that Angela's boyfriend uses for his business. It's in good condition. It's not like the busses we rode to elementary school."

"I hope not. They were the pits."

"What if there's a problem with the bus?"

"My boyfriend's also a mechanic," Angela said.

"I'd like to have a boyfriend like that. Where did you find him?"

"I didn't find him. He found me."

"We won't ask where."

"Next question?"

"Most of us don't have Friday classes," a girl said, "but I think we all have Monday classes. So if we come back on Monday afternoon, we'll miss those classes."

"Just tell your professor you have an important mission."

"They'll understand," another girl said. "They're all against the war."

"And half of you," Megan pointed out, "will only miss one Monday class because you're only going for one weekend."

"Who decides which team we're on?"

"We thought we'd ask for volunteers for Teri's team and my team. The rest of you can decide which team you want to be on."

"Who are the other two leaders?"

"Angela and Marianne. Next question?"

"You said we'll raise money for this project. How much will we need?"

"We have a budget. We'll divide the total by sixty-four, and that will be the suggested contribution. If you can't afford it, that's okay. If you can afford more, that's also okay. But somehow we'll raise the money."

"We'll help," Sister Audrey said.

"And I'll help too," Father Justin said.

"Thank you, sisters, and thank you, father. That would reduce the suggested contribution. Next question?"

"What are we going to do in New Hampshire?"

Megan smiled. "I thought you'd never ask. We're going to the major cities, where we'll go door to door and ask people to vote for McCarthy in the primary. That's why we need to be there on weekends, when people will be at home."

"Will we have campaign materials?"

"Oh, yeah. We'll also have our own materials. Our message is that the war in Vietnam is morally wrong, and that McCarthy is committed to ending it."

"Has he said how he'll end it?"

"From what I gather, he'll end it by having the two sides

negotiate. But he wouldn't tell them what to do. It's their country."

"From what I heard," a girl said, "he should be a good peacemaker. He almost became a Benedictine monk."

"Really? That's cool. But I'm glad he didn't become a monk."

"Yeah, that would have been a real waste."

"Are there any more questions?" Megan asked.

"I have one," a girl said. "When do we start going to New Hampshire?"

"The first weekend in February, and we'll go there until the weekend before the election."

There was a silence, and then Sister Audrey said: "Can I say something?"

"Since when do you need permission to talk?" Sister Maura asked her.

"Yes, please," Megan said, smiling.

"I think your plan is excellent. You're taking action, and you're doing something positive. You're doing the most effective thing to change our country's policy. And that's to change our government, peacefully."

"You're also supporting a good Catholic," Sister Maura said.

"Do we get extra points for that?" Megan joked.

"Of course you do. You're too young to have campaigned for John Fitzgerald Kennedy, but we campaigned for him. And we helped him get elected."

"So you girls can do something that'll change the world."

"Thank you, sisters," Megan said.

"I second what they said," Father Justin said. "You've found exactly the right thing to do in this situation."

"Thank you, father. Will you give us your blessing?"

They bowed their heads while the priest gave them a formal blessing, concluding with the sign of the cross.

For the rest of the month of January the standing of McCarthy in the national polls was far below that of Lyndon Johnson, and it wasn't rising, despite the events in Vietnam that were turning public opinion against the war. The major event was the Tet

Offensive, launched at the end of January by the combined forces of the Viet Cong and the North Vietnamese army. The largest offensive of the war so far, it was a well-coordinated campaign of surprise attacks against military and civilian targets in more than a hundred towns and cities throughout South Vietnam, including the provincial capitals and Saigon. A major target in Saigon was the U.S. Embassy, which the attackers penetrated by blowing a hole in the wall that surrounded it. Though they were eventually overwhelmed, their ability to come so close to taking over our embassy revealed the vulnerability of our position and undermined the credibility of our government's claim that we were winning.

A few days after the launching of Tet a photograph appeared in newspapers and on television that showed the chief of the South Vietnamese police executing a captured Viet Cong officer. The photograph showed the outstretched arm of the executioner holding a pistol and firing directly at the head of the victim, who was standing in a plaid shirt with his hands evidently tied behind him. What made the action even more shocking was that the victim looked like a kid.

Brigid saw this photograph the day before she left for New Hampshire with Teri's team, which she and Laura had volunteered for. It appeared on the front page of the newspaper that was delivered to their house every day, and it was a subject of their conversation at the dinner table that evening.

"If that policeman is the kind of people we're fighting for," her father said, "then we should get the hell out of there."

"I agree," her mother said. "He killed that young man in cold blood."

"But they're in a war," her brother reminded them.

"Even in a war," her father said, "it's not legal to kill prisoners."

"And it's not moral," Brigid said.

After a silence her mother asked: "Are you all packed?"

"Yeah. I'm not taking much."

"You need to take enough for three days."

"I'm taking enough."

"Are you taking my sleeping bag?" her brother asked her.

"No, I won't need it. I'm going to share a bed with another girl."

"Which girl?" her mother asked her.

"Laura. The girl from Poughkeepsie."

"Oh, yeah. I hope we can meet her someday."

"You will. We could have her here for dinner on a Sunday when her parents don't come down to see her."

"That would be nice."

"So you're going there in a bus," her father said. "Who's going to drive it?"

"A girl's boyfriend. He's a licensed bus driver."

"That doesn't mean he's a good driver."

"I'm sure he'll be careful." She understood their concern because it would be the first time she went on a trip without them. "Don't worry."

The next morning, after her parents had left for work and her brother for school, Brigid left the house with an overnight bag that contained two outfits, underwear, a nightgown, a pair of boots, and toiletries. The plan was to meet at the college in the parking lot where the bus would be waiting for them. It would take them about five hours to go from Yonkers to Manchester, the largest city in New Hampshire. Their campaign would focus on that city and on Concord, Derry, and Nashua, the next three largest cities.

The bus was scheduled to depart at ten with the plan of riding for two hours, stopping at lunchtime for an hour, and continuing for another two hours. Everyone had been asked to arrive at the college by nine-thirty, and Brigid got there about ten minutes early. She had no trouble spotting the bus, which was painted a bright blue with yellow letters on the side that said "Catholic Peace Fellowship."

Teri was already there, standing by the bus with a clipboard. She greeted Brigid and checked off her name and asked her to put her bag into the storage compartment, which she promptly did. Since she would be sitting on the bus for two hours she didn't want to get on board yet, so she strolled over to a spot where she could gaze out at the river. There was no wind, so the surface of the water was smooth, and it reflected the sheer rock walls of the Palisades on the other side. The view always made her wonder what might lie beyond those walls.

The last girls to arrive were the ones who lived in the dormitory, with the least distance to travel. Laura was among them, and she was carrying a hard shell suitcase that could have held enough clothes for a week. They had agreed to sit together on the bus, and as soon as Laura had stored her suitcase they climbed on board and took the seats immediately behind the driver, whose name was Jack. He had slicked-back dark hair, and he wore aviator sunglasses.

Before taking a seat across the aisle from them, Teri did a last count to make sure that her sixteen team members were all present, and then she told the driver they were ready to go. He shifted into forward gear, and as the bus got under way the girls cheered.

They headed up Route 9 and then got onto the highway that crossed the county and led to the Connecticut Turnpike. Brigid had travelled these roads before with her family, so there was nothing new to see, and she turned toward Laura, who told her what she had packed, anxiously wanting to make sure that she had brought the right things. Brigid assured her that she had, and then they settled into a quiet conversation that wandered from one topic to another. If asked what they had talked about she couldn't have remembered, but they didn't stop talking until the bus stopped for lunch on the other side of Hartford.

They were at a roadside restaurant that Jack knew from taking groups to Massachusetts. He recommended the pizza, so that was what most of the girls ordered before heading to the bathroom, which was their top priority. Brigid and Laura shared a pizza with sausages, resisting the temptation to wash it down with beer because that would probably necessitate another stop before they reached their destination.

During the last half of the trip they dozed off for a while, and they were aroused by the bus slowing down at the outskirts of Manchester.

The motel was part of a regional chain that Megan had made a deal with, committing to five rooms for six weekends. Instead of having to sneak two extra guests into a room she had gotten the owner of the chain to agree to having four girls per room on the grounds that they were like a family, and with the assurance that except for the driver, who would have his own room, there would be no boys. It had helped that the owner was Irish.

After checking in, Brigid and Laura and two other girls found their room and unpacked and lay down on the beds to rest. By then it was only around four, so they had time for a siesta before dinner, which they planned to have at the restaurant across the road. The beds were fine, the bathroom was clean, and the only limitation was closet space, though none of them had brought as many clothes as Laura. In deference to their needs Laura kept all but one of her outfits in her suitcase.

The restaurant was informal with a bar on one side and booths on the other. They ate with four girls to a booth while the driver sat at the bar, evidently relieved to be in the company of the bartender and the guys who were seated at the bar. Most of the girls had burgers, which were excellent, and most of them drank beer with their food. They were in bed by ten because they had to get up early in the morning, and they were exhausted from the trip. Laura was a restless sleeper, and once during the night she awoke from what must have been a bad dream, but Brigid didn't mind because she had no trouble getting back to sleep.

In the morning they had to take turns in the bathroom, which slowed things down, and they were late meeting at the bus after breakfast for the trip to the campaign center. When they got there the day's activities were still being organized. A lot of other college students were gathered there, waiting for instructions, milling around and socializing. After a discussion among several girls who were seated behind an official table, their group was assigned to a working-class neighborhood with specific streets and addresses for them to cover.

They rode there on the bus, which the driver left in the parking lot of a neighborhood school, and then they dispersed in pairs, with campaign material and helpful maps from the campaign center. Brigid and Laura were paired together, and when they found their assigned street they took opposite sides, with each of them going from house to house.

Since it was cold and there were patches of snow on the ground, Brigid wore her boots, with tights under her skirt and a scarf wrapped around her neck. She carried her campaign material in a tote bag that she had been given at the campaign center. The bag had "VOTE McCarthy" emblazoned on it, so there was no doubt about her purpose. With a prepared script in her head she rang the doorbell of her first house and waited for someone to answer.

Finally, the door was opened by a woman who looked at her warily and said: "I'm sorry, but if you're selling something, I'm not interested."

"I'm not selling anything," Brigid said. "I only want to tell you about Eugene McCarthy, who's running for President of the United States."

"I never heard of him. Who is he?"

"He's a Senator from Minnesota. I can give you his background," Brigid said, reaching into her tote bag, "but the most important thing about him is, he wants to end the war in Vietnam. He wants to stop sending our boys over there to be killed."

"I'm all in favor of that," the woman said. "I have two teenage sons, who will be drafted and sent to Vietnam if the war goes on."

"Then vote for McCarthy in the primary." She handed material to the woman. "Vote for peace and justice."

The woman took the material, saying: "I will. Thank you."

As she checked the address and entered information into the boxes on the sheet that they had given her for collecting data, Brigid couldn't believe how easy that had been.

But they weren't all that easy. The next one was a man who looked at her scornfully and said he was a Republican before closing the door on her. And the next one was an old woman who didn't know what a primary was.

Still, after two blocks of houses she had positive reactions from most people. The best was after almost two hours when her fingers were numb from the cold. It was a modest house, and the door was opened by a woman around her mother's age. Before she could say anything the woman said: "You poor dear. You look so cold. Come in and warm up."

"Thank you," she said. "But I have to keep going."

"You want to tell me something, don't you?"

"Yes. I want to tell you about Eugene McCarthy, who's running for President of the United States."

"Then please come in and tell me about him," the woman said, opening the door further and stepping aside to let her pass.

"Well, only for a minute," Brigid said, relenting.

"I'll make you a cup of hot chocolate. Would you like that?"

"Yes, but you really don't have to."

"I know I don't have to, but I want to." The woman led her into the living room where a man around her father's age was sitting in an easy chair, reading a newspaper. "Jim, this young woman is campaigning for Eugene McCarthy."

"You are?" the man said, lowering his newspaper. "I heard good things about him."

"Are you a college student?" the woman asked her.

"Yeah. I go to St. Catherine in Yonkers."

"You've come a long way," the man said. "What's your name?"

"Brigid McBride."

"Ah, that's a good Irish name."

"I'm only half Irish. My mother's Italian."

"So was mine. Please sit down and tell us about Eugene McCarthy."

"You two can talk," the woman said, "while I make the chocolate. Do you like it sweet?"

"No, only a little sugar please. But I don't want you to go to any trouble."

"It's not any trouble."

As the woman left the room Brigid unbuttoned her coat and sat down on a sofa opposite the man. Her fingers, as they warmed up, were tingling.

"What are you studying at St. Catherine?" the man asked her.

"I'm working toward a bachelor's degree in nursing."

"That's more than an RN, isn't it?"

"Yes. It's a four-year degree. An RN is a two-year degree. But there's nothing wrong with a two-year degree," she added. "My mother has one."

"She does? So does my sister. It's a wonderful profession."

"Do you have children?"

"We have two," he said. "Our older daughter must be around your age. She's twenty."

"I just turned twenty."

"She goes to Salve Regina in Newport. It's a Catholic college that was founded by the Sisters of Mercy."

"I've heard of Salve Regina. It's a very good college."

"Our daughter likes it. She's studying English. She wants to be a teacher."

"St. Catherine is a Catholic college too. It was founded by the Sisters of the Redemption."

"Do you live in a dormitory?"

"No, I commute. I live within walking distance."

"I wish our daughter went to a college within walking distance. We don't see her as often as we'd like to, and living in a dormitory costs a lot of money."

Emboldened by the conversation, she asked: "What do you do for a living?"

"I work in a factory. I'm the union steward."

"That must be a lot of responsibility."

"It is. But I like it. I was a first sergeant in the army."

"Were you in World War II?"

"Yeah. I missed Korea, thank God. And I sure as hell wouldn't want to be in this war. It has no purpose that I can see, except to line the pockets of the owners of the defense industry. You know," he told her, "old Ike was right to warn us about the military-industrial complex."

"So you're against the war in Vietnam?"

"Completely," he said. "I always wanted to have a son, but now

I'm glad I have two daughters. At least they won't be drafted."

"How old is your other daughter?

"She's sixteen. She's a sophomore in high school. She works at a supermarket on Saturdays, or she'd be at home now."

"I work at a supermarket," she said as the woman returned bringing a mug.

"Here's your chocolate," the woman said. "Be careful, it's hot."

"Thank you," she said, taking the mug.

"Brigid goes to a Catholic college in Yonkers," the man said. "She's working toward a bachelor's degree in nursing."

"That's wonderful," the woman said. "What are you doing so far from home?"

"I'm with a group of girls who are helping with the campaign of Eugene McCarthy. We're members of the Catholic Peace Fellowship."

"I don't know that organization. What's its mission?"

"Peace and justice. And right now our main priority is ending the war in Vietnam."

"God bless you," the woman said. "How is the campaign going?"

"The people are nice. I mean, a man who was a Republican closed the door on me. But he didn't slam it."

The man and the woman both laughed.

"Okay," the man said. "I know that McCarthy wants to end the war. But what will he do for working people?"

"I have background material," she said, reaching for her tote bag. "His career has been based on support from labor. His platform includes raising the minimum wage, improving benefits, and strengthening unions."

"Then he sounds like the right candidate," the man said, taking the material.

Concerned that Laura might be wondering what happened to her, she drank the chocolate as quickly as possible, thanked the couple, and went on her way.

Around noon they met at the bus, which took them for a lunch break at the campaign center. The lunch consisted of sandwiches prepared by volunteers, but the girls were so hungry they would have eaten anything. It gave them a chance to rest, and it was the right time for a break because people at home would be having lunch and wouldn't appreciate being interrupted by the doorbell. They resumed their campaign around two and continued until around five. By then they were hoarse and weary from being on their feet all day.

Back at the motel Brigid and Laura lay on their bed and shared their experiences. Of course Laura had been anxious about talking with strangers, but after a few houses she got used to it. Her only bad experience was a guy in his twenties who made a pass at her.

The next morning they went to the early mass at the nearest Catholic church, and then they returned to their neighborhood, where they still had a lot of streets to cover. Until around noon there were fewer people at home than on Saturday, presumably because they were in church, but during the afternoon almost everyone was at home, so they had a very productive day. In the evening, at the restaurant across the street, Teri gave them data on their activity, and they were amazed at how many people they had talked with.

On Monday, during the trip home, the girls talked less and dozed more than they had during the trip to New Hampshire, and when they arrived at the campus they dragged themselves off the bus and headed home or to the dormitory. Since it was the middle of the afternoon, Brigid found no one at home, so she was able to climb upstairs and crawl into bed, where she slept until the early evening.

Of course at dinner her parents wanted to hear all about her trip, and she gave them enough details to satisfy them. In particular, she told them about the nice couple who had invited her into their home to warm up.

Three weeks later she and Laura made a second trip with Teri's team. By then McCarthy was still only about 15 percent in the national polls, and no one expected him to do much better than that in New Hampshire. In the meantime the war was still escalating. The Tet Offensive was halted, but the Viet Cong and the North Vietnamese army were causing havoc. We had more and more troops there, and the casualties were mounting.

With special permission the members of the CPF stayed up most of the night in the student lounge on March 12, the day of the New Hampshire primary, watching the results on television. At first it wasn't clear what had happened, but eventually it began to look as if McCarthy had pulled off an upset. By the next day the final results showed that he had come close to beating Johnson, an amazing feat for a little known Senator against an incumbent President. Believing they had contributed to it, the girls felt good about what they had done, and they were praised by the chaplain and the nuns at their next meeting.

On March 16, only four days later, Robert Kennedy announced that he would run for President. That created a dilemma for their group because while they liked both McCarthy and Kennedy, some were loyal to McCarthy and others leaned toward Kennedy. It didn't help that their mentors were divided, with Father Justin sticking with McCarthy and the sisters favoring Kennedy, if for no other reason than they had supported his older brother.

Two weeks later Lyndon Johnson announced that he would not seek reelection, which left the race open to McCarthy and Kennedy. It was assumed that as incumbent vice president Hubert Humphrey would enter the race, but he was associated with the war, so he would have a disadvantage among the growing number of people who opposed the war.

The next primary was in Wisconsin on April 2. It was too late for Johnson's name to be taken off the ballot, and it was too early for Kennedy to have organized a campaign, so McCarthy won easily, though he wouldn't be tested against Kennedy until the latter got organized.

On April 4 Martin Luther King was assassinated in Memphis, Tennessee, and riots erupted in many cities, raising awareness of the civil rights issue, which recently had been overshadowed by the war in Vietnam. This issue, along with the war, was on the agenda for the next meeting of the CPF, for which Father Justin had invited a guest speaker.

Brigid learned from Teri that the speaker's name was Kieran O'Donnell, and that he had spent the past two years in the novitiate program at the Jesuit seminary in Hyde Park. The seminary was now in the process of moving to Syracuse, so he had been there for the past several weeks. Since he already had a bachelor's degree in theology from Fordham University he was on a fast track to becoming an ordained Jesuit priest, which normally took about ten years. They said he knew Daniel Berrigan who at the time was teaching at Le Moyne College, near the new location of the seminary. Having completed the first phase of his studies, Kieran was about to begin a period of ministry that would extend through the summer until he took his first vows of poverty, chastity, and obedience.

Of course his main attraction was that he knew Daniel Berrigan, who was increasingly active in the antiwar movement. In January, ignoring danger and threats from our government, he had gone to Hanoi and helped to negotiate an exchange of prisoners. Based on his experience there, he graphically described the pain and suffering caused by our bombing of that city. For people who supported the war Daniel Berrigan was a traitor, but for people who opposed the war he was a hero. For the girls in the CPF he had the charisma of a rock star.

When she entered the room where they had their meetings Brigid noticed a tall, lean man in clerical attire talking with Father Justin. His back was to her, so she didn't see his face until he finally turned around. And the sight of his face, with its wavy dark hair, its fine features, and its dazzling blue eyes, literally took her breath away. She had never seen such an attractive man.

In a daze she sat down in the seventh row, afraid of getting too close to this man. She looked around and was glad to see Laura approaching her.

"Is that the speaker?" Laura asked, sitting down next to her.

"Yeah," she said hoarsely.

"He's really cute. And he's going to be a priest?"

"Yeah."

"What a waste."

Brigid said nothing. She just sat there, calming herself. For the first time she understood what girls meant when they said they had a crush on someone.

Megan went through the formalities of beginning the meeting, and then she introduced Kieran, saying: "We have a special guest today. As you probably know, Kieran O'Donnell is a novice from the Jesuit seminary at Hyde Park. For the past several weeks he's been in Syracuse, where Daniel Berrigan is teaching at Le Moyne College. Kieran is about to begin—an experiment. Is that what you call it?"

Kieran nodded. "But it's not like an experiment you'd do in a chem lab. It's a ministry."

"They have their own language, the Jesuits," Father Justin said.

"Whatever they call it, he's here to talk to us about our ministry, and to tell us about his plans for this summer. Please welcome Kieran O'Donnell."

The girls applauded, and Kieran moved over to the podium.

"Thank you, Megan," he said in a sonorous voice. "Thank you, father. Thank you, sisters. And thank you, members of the Catholic Peace Fellowship. I've heard from Father Justin about your activities, and I want to congratulate you for helping to defeat Lyndon Johnson in the New Hampshire primary. I know that technically Johnson won that primary, but it was so close that he realized that it was time for him to step aside and make way for candidates who will change our policy on the war. And now we have two good men competing for the nomination. But let's not forget that Hubert Humphrey has the support of the party's establishment, and he's going to announce his candidacy any day now. If he wins the nomination, we won't have a real change in government. We'll have more of the same thing."

"You don't think Humphrey wants to end the war?" Father Justin asked.

"I think he wants to, but he's not in a position to do what he wants. And he's so connected with the war, he might not get the votes of people who oppose it."

"Then he could lose against Nixon?"

"He could. And then the war would go on forever."

"So we have to support McCarthy and Kennedy."

"Yes, we do. But we also have to do more."

"Like what?"

Kieran paused. "I think you all know what Philip Berrigan did in Baltimore."

"You mean pouring blood on draft records," a girl said.

"That's right. It was an action that sent a message."

"What was the message?" Father Justin asked.

"That people were willing to sacrifice their blood to end the war. They were doing what Jesus did when he sacrificed his blood for us."

"I wonder if that's an apt analogy."

"I think it is. That's what they intended."

"But what good did it do?"

"It gave us some martyrs for the cause. We all know that since the early days of Christianity, our cause has been advanced by martyrs."

"The cause of the Vietnamese was also advanced by martyrs," Megan said.

"That's a good point. Those Buddhist monks who became martyrs by setting themselves on fire had a lot of influence on public opinion in this country."

"I can't imagine setting myself on fire," a girl said.

"I can't either," another girl said.

"An American boy your age, no, younger than you, set himself on fire only last fall. He did it to protest the war."

"Where did that happen?" Teri asked.

"In Syracuse. He was a high school student. Without any warning he went into the cathedral and then came out and doused himself with gasoline and set himself on fire."

"Mother of God. I didn't know about that."

"It didn't make the front page of the newspapers. But it happened right outside the cathedral."

"Did he die?"

"Not right away. He was taken to the hospital with burns all over his body. Father Berrigan went to visit him there."

"I hope you're not going to recommend that we follow his example," Father Justin said.

"If you mean the example of that boy, no. But I *am* going to recommend that we follow the example of the Berrigan brothers."

"You mean become martyrs by going to prison?"

Kieran nodded. "We should be willing to go to prison for the cause of peace."

"As a way of demonstrating our commitment, I agree. But I don't agree with the idea of going to prison for acts of violence."

"I'm not advocating acts of violence against people. You know that, father. I'm advocating acts of violence against the machinery that sends our boys to war."

"But pouring blood on draft records didn't stop them."

"It slowed them down. It put a spoke into the wheels of their machinery."

"Did Philip Berrigan go to prison?" a girl asked.

"No, not yet," Kieran said. "They were going to sentence him, but I heard that the process was interrupted by the assassination of Dr. King."

"Then he'll be stuck in prison," another girl said. "He won't be able to do anything there."

"He'll be able to speak out against the war, and being a martyr he'll have authority."

After a silence Sister Audrey said: "I like the idea of putting spokes into the wheels of their machinery, but you have to be careful that you don't hurt anyone."

"That's the challenge," Sister Maura said. "When you attack things you can accidentally hurt people. And you can't justify hurting people by saying it was an accident."

"Yeah," Megan said. "Like our government justifies hurting civilians in Vietnam by calling it collateral damage."

"We all agree on that point," Kieran said. "We won't allow collateral damage."

When the meeting ended, Brigid and Laura went to the pub. They ordered beers and sat in a booth and talked about Kieran.

They agreed that he had made some good arguments, and they liked the way he had stirred things up. In their conversation Brigid didn't reveal how the sight of his face had affected her. Since he was about to leave and do his ministry she didn't expect to see him again, so she decided to keep it to herself.

Laura was talking about her boyfriend when Kieran appeared in the pub. He went to the bar and ordered a beer, which he sipped for a while facing away from them. And then he turned around and saw them.

Approaching them, he said: "You girls were at the meeting, weren't you?"

"Yeah, we were," Laura told him.

"I thought I recognized you. Do you mind if I join you?"

Feeling as if she had curled up into a ball, Brigid was speechless.

"No, not at all," Laura said.

He sat down across from Laura, next to Brigid, who had to shift over.

"How do you think the meeting went?"

"I think it went well. It made us think about what we're doing."

"I hope it did. As I said, I think we have to do more."

"Where are you going on your ministry?"

"I'm going to the city."

"Where in the city?"

"A poor neighborhood."

"But what does that have to do with the war?"

"It has everything to do with the war. Who do you think they're drafting into the army?"

"Poor people."

"Right," he said. "And most of them are people of color."

"So there's a racist element in the war."

"There's a racist element in everything we do. Our country was born in the mortal sin of slavery, and we're still a long way from redeeming ourselves."

"So what exactly are you going to do?"

"I'm going to put a spoke into the wheels of their machinery."

"Like Philip Berrigan did."

"Yeah. I don't know how, but I'll find a way. I have almost the whole summer."

"Will you act alone or have people to help you?"

"I'm going to need people to help me. The truth is," he quietly admitted, "I came here hoping to recruit people."

Still speechless, Brigid curled up even more.

"How many people?"

"Two would be enough."

"Can they be girls?"

"Why not? You girls have done such a good job in your ministry."

"Well, I don't know who could join you in the city," Laura said, shaking her head. "Most of our members live in Westchester."

"Whoever joins me," Kieran said, "could live in the apartment I'll have for the summer."

"You mean live with you?"

"The apartment has two bedrooms. And remember, I'm a Jesuit seminarian."

"So girls wouldn't have to worry about you?"

"No, they wouldn't."

Brigid had kept her eyes on Laura most of the time, but now she turned and looked at Kieran, and the thought of sharing an apartment with him made her feel lightheaded.

"Could you excuse me?" Laura said. "I have to go to the bathroom."

"I'll go with you," Brigid said.

Kieran got up and let her out of the booth, and she followed Laura out of the pub and down the hall. In the safety of the bathroom Laura asked her: "What do you think of the idea of us joining him this summer?"

"I think it's crazy."

"I know it is. But I feel like doing something crazy."

Laura wasn't acting like the shy girl that Brigid was used to, and it made her wonder if Laura had a crush on Kieran too. "Is it Kieran?"

"Oh, no. I'm not interested in him. I have a boyfriend. I just think it's an opportunity for us to influence more people. And I don't want to spend the summer with my parents."

"Speaking of parents, what would we tell them?"

"I don't know. We'd have to think of something. But I haven't decided to do it. I only wanted to know what you thought of the idea."

"I still think it's crazy."

"Yeah, it is. But let's tell Kieran we'll think about it."

"How do you know he'll want us?"

"He will. I can tell."

So they agreed to tell him they would think about it, and he told them he would wait for their decision. He acted like he wanted them to join him.

FOUR

THEY HAD FINISHED their last exam and the students in the dormitory were packing to leave for the summer vacation when the story of Catonsville broke in the news. A group of Catholic activists had gone to the draft board in Catonsville, Maryland, and gathered draft files, taken them in wire baskets to the parking lot, dumped them out, poured homemade napalm on them, and set them on fire. Among the nine members of the group were Philip and Daniel Berigan as well as a former priest and nun who had gotten married. While the records were burning they recited the Lord's Prayer and explained why they were protesting the war in Vietnam. Of course they were arrested and put into jail, but they would be released pending their trial.

Catonsville was on the agenda of the last CPF meeting of the academic year, which was held two days later. The group had no plans for the summer, but some of the members had their own plans, which they described briefly. Brigid and Laura didn't mention what they were thinking about doing because they hadn't made a decision, and they didn't join in the discussion about Catonsville, which focused again on the issue of whether any kind of violence, even against things, was justified in the name of peace. About half of the members approved of the action at Catonsville while the chaplain and the nuns had reservations, reiterating the argument that violence only leads to more violence.

Brigid and Laura were in the pub after the meeting when Kieran appeared and joined them. He apologized for missing the meeting, explaining that his trip from Syracuse had taken longer than expected. After greeting them he went right into the subject of Catonsville, and he was obviously impressed by it. His eyes were glowing as he said: "I don't know who thought of using napalm, but what a great idea. Think of the symbolism of burning draft records with the weapon we're using to burn Vietnamese women and children."

"I guess it put a spoke into the wheels of their machinery," Brigid said. She was still flustered by the presence of Kieran, but she was more composed now.

"A major spoke," Kieran agreed.

"But can't they reconstruct those records?" Laura said.

"I'm sure they can, but bureaucracies take forever to do things."

"So it'll slow them down."

"Yeah. It'll slow them down."

After a silence Brigid asked: "Is that the kind of thing you want to do this summer?"

"Yeah, it is. If possible, I want to go beyond what they did at Catonsville."

"But they're going to prison for what they did," Laura said.

"Of course they are. That's the idea."

"So how does going to prison help the cause?"

"Their being willing to make that sacrifice for their beliefs gives them moral authority."

"Well, I don't know about you," Laura said, "but I don't want to go to prison."

"I don't either," Brigid said.

"You won't have any risk of going to prison," Kieran said. "I promise you."

"But if you want to go beyond what they did at Catonsville, you'll go to prison, and if we help you, we'll go too."

"No, you won't. You won't be involved in what I do."

"Then what would we do in the city this summer?"

"You'll demonstrate against the war. And the worst that can happen is you might get arrested and put into jail for a night."

"My parents wouldn't like that," Laura said.

"Mine wouldn't either," Brigid said.

"They wouldn't have to know about it," Kieran said. "But anyway, it probably won't happen. The demonstrations will always be peaceful."

Brigid took a sip of beer and asked: "If we won't be involved in what you're going to do, then what do you need us for?"

"That's a good question," Kieran said, smiling. "I need you for moral support while I work out what I'm going to do."

"Will you tell us what you're going to do?" Laura asked.

"When I know what it is, I'll tell you the basic idea. But I won't give you the details, so you won't be accessories."

After a silence Laura said: "Before we make any decision, we'd like to see the apartment you told us about."

"That's easy," Kieran said. "I'm going there tomorrow. I could meet you there, or we could meet on the train. I'll be coming from Peekskill."

"I'm done with exams," Laura said. "So I'm free."

"I'm free too," Brigid said. "I'd rather meet you on the train. Just tell us what train you'll be taking, and we'll get on at the Yonkers station."

Kieran had a train schedule with all the stops from Peekskill to Grand Central, so they were able to determine when his train would stop at Yonkers, and they arranged to meet then in the second car.

That evening she told her parents she was going into the city with a friend the next day to do some shopping. Of course her mother wanted to know who the friend was, and Brigid told her it was Laura, the girl she had shared a bed with during their campaign in New Hampshire. Her mother reminded her that she would like to meet Laura, and Brigid assured her mother that she would meet her, sooner or later.

The next morning after her parents had left for work she called a taxi and asked for a ride to the Yonkers train station, with a stop at the college to pick up someone. The taxi left them at the station about fifteen minutes before Kieran's train was due. At the entrance to the station a beggar asked them for money, and they each gave him a dollar, for which he blessed them. They climbed the stairs to the platform for trains going south, and they stood and waited in the warm sun. As they waited they had time to start working on the story they would tell their parents if they decided to spend the summer in the city. When the train arrived they had gotten as far as deciding that Kieran would already be a priest, and that he would be doing social work in a poor neighborhood where there was a need for nursing skills.

They found him in the second car of the train in a seat that could accommodate four people. He let the girls sit at the window, through which they could look out at the river. Its surface was wrinkled by a mild breeze, and across the water the Palisades were lit up by the morning sun.

On the way to the city they didn't talk about the war, they talked about their backgrounds. Kieran told them he had lived in Peekskill until he was twelve when his family moved to Jefferson Valley to have a bigger house for all their children. Kieran was the oldest, and he had thought about being a priest since his confirmation. His parents weren't crazy about the idea, but they had four sons, so they could spare one of them. After getting his bachelor's degree in theology at Fordham University he had begun his novitiate at St. Andrew-on-Hudson, which was in Hyde Park though in the church it was often referred to as Poughkeepsie. He had liked the novitiate well enough, but by the second year he was eager to move on to the next stage of Jesuit formation, a three-year period of graduate studies in philosophy and religion. He was glad that he would return to Fordham for this stage instead of doing it at Shrub Oak, which had a reputation among seminarians as a ball breaker and had mercifully been closed. For his ministry this summer he had proposed serving people in a poor neighborhood, coordinating his activities with social workers and healthcare workers, which fit nicely with the story that the girls were creating for their parents. His proposed ministry didn't include antiwar activities, which made them feel better about not including such activities in their story.

When they arrived at Grand Central the girls let Kieran lead the way. Though Brigid lived about twenty minutes by train from Manhattan she didn't go there very often. In that respect she was like most of the people who lived in her neighborhood. Few of them commuted to the city for work, and even fewer went to the city for entertainment. Her father almost never went there. He didn't have to because the company he worked for was based in Yonkers. So when people visited from out of town and expected him to know his way around the city, they were mistaken. He could only tell them how to get to Yankee Stadium.

The girls followed Kieran through the concourse and down to the subway, where he bought tokens for them. Then they followed him down to the platform and waited for the local. It was late in the morning, so the platform wasn't crowded. A long-haired guy with a guitar and a harmonica attached to his neck was singing: "A Hard Rain's A-Gonna Fall."

They found seats on the subway and rode down to Astor Place, where they got off. The girls followed Kieran out of the subway and onto a street. He got his bearings and then led them across a street and down an avenue. The buildings were old and mostly had three or four stories with fire escapes. The people on the sidewalk were mostly young and wearing jeans with a variety of tee shirts. Their hair was mostly long and flowing.

When they turned off the avenue Brigid noticed a sign that said 4th Street, which they entered after crossing Avenue A. In the middle of the block they stopped at a building with a brown brick face that had five stories with a fire escape in front. Kieran opened the door with a key and led them up the stairs, not stopping until they had reached the fifth floor.

Though the girls were out of breath Kieran wasn't fazed. He unlocked a door and let them into an apartment. They were in a room with windows overlooking the street. It was furnished with a sofa, two chairs, and a floor lamp. It was evidently the living room. A door led directly to another room, which had a single bed, and then there was a long narrow room that led to a room with a queen size bed. Finally, there was the kitchen, a large room with a wooden table and six chairs in the middle. On a spacious wall was a poster of Peter, Paul, and Mary. Against the wall opposite the poster was a stove, a refrigerator, and a deep sink. To the right of the sink was another entrance to the apartment. To the left was a door that opened into a bathroom, which had a footed tub and a toilet with a pull chain. The tub had a shower curtain on a ring suspended from the ceiling, and the toilet was on a raised platform like a throne. The kitchen had windows overlooking a courtyard in back of the building. Across the courtyard you could see the backs of other buildings.

Kieran explained that the apartment was a railroad flat, typical of the tenements that were built in the neighborhood during the previous century. Its tenant was a folk singer who was touring Europe with his group. Kieran was sub-letting the apartment for fifty dollars a month, but he didn't expect the girls to contribute. He proposed that if they joined him they could have the larger bedroom with the queen size bed and he would take the bedroom in front. He pointed out that their bedroom would be close to the bathroom.

After looking around, Laura asked about closet space, and Kieran said there were no built-in closets because people didn't have so many clothes back then, but there was space in the long narrow room that separated the bedrooms. The tenant had installed a pole there, which extended for the length of the room, and below was a chest of drawers.

Leaving Kieran in the kitchen, the girls went into the living room and stood at the windows, looking down at the street.

"What do you think?" Brigid asked.

"I think it's okay," Laura said. "At least we'll get exercise coming up those stairs."

"We won't have much privacy."

"Oh, he won't bother us."

"So you want to do it?"

"Yeah. Why not? I mean, how else would we spend the summer?"

Brigid would have been working, saving money, which raised the question of how she would pay for this adventure. The apartment was free, but she would need to pay for food and other necessities. "My only question is, can I afford it?"

"I have some savings. I can manage."

"I guess I can too."

So they agreed to give it a try after reassuring each other that if things didn't work out, they could always leave and go home.

On the train to Yonkers they worked out the rest of the story they would tell their parents. They weren't going to lie, they were only going to embellish the truth, and they had the right motive for what they were doing—to prevent their parents from worrying.

Brigid decided to broach the subject at the dinner table that evening. She felt that if she took her parents aside after dinner without her brother it would make the conversation more serious, and that he could provide a note of levity. She waited until they had started eating, and then she momentously announced: "I have an internship this summer."

"Really?" her mother said. "What is it ?"

Prepared, she said: "It's helping a social worker in the city, in a poor neighborhood."

"What neighborhood?" her father asked her.

"The East Village," she said.

"You mean the Lower East Side?"

"No, it's north of there." She wished she knew the geography of the area better so that she could be more precise.

"That's a cool area," her brother interjected. "It has a lot of artists and musicians."

"How would you know?" her father asked.

"I have a friend whose older brother lives there. He's a rock musician."

Brigid wasn't sure if this information helped or hurt her case. At least someone from their neighborhood lived there.

"I hope he's not on drugs."

"All musicians aren't on drugs."

"A lot of them are."

"You say it's a poor neighborhood," her mother resumed. "Is it safe?"

"Oh, yeah." She quoted Kieran, saying: "It has a low crime rate.

It's basically a neighborhood of immigrants."

"Where did they come from?"

"Italy, Ireland, and Eastern Europe, the same as Yonkers."

"There are poor neighborhoods in Yonkers," her father said. "So why do you have to work in the city?"

"Because that's where my internship is."

"Well, who's the social worker you'll be helping?"

"Father O'Donnell. He's a Catholic priest."

That silenced them for a while, until her mother finally said: "He's a priest but he's also a social worker?"

"That's not unusual. A lot of priests have ministries to help the poor." She paused, and then fired her last bullet. "He's a Jesuit."

That silenced them again, until her mother asked: "How did you meet him?"

"He came to the college to recruit students to help him this summer. He especially wanted nursing students."

"How many students did he recruit?"

"Two of us. The other is Laura, the girl I went to the city with today."

"That girl keeps coming up," her mother said wryly.

After a pause her father asked: "Is this a paid internship?"

"No. But I won't have many expenses. The place where we're staying is paid for."

"Good. Now, where exactly is it?"

"It's on East 4th Street, between Avenue A and B. We'll have an apartment on the fifth floor."

"Just you and Laura?"

"Yeah," she lied. She didn't want her parents to worry about them sharing the apartment with a man, even though they thought he was a priest.

"How long would you be there?" her mother asked.

"For six weeks." She had agreed with Laura to shorten the period to help sell the idea to their parents. If all went well, they would actually be there for eight weeks.

"Well, I know you're twenty, and you can do whatever you want, but your father and I would like to see the apartment before you go ahead with this. Okay?"

"Okay." She didn't mind having her parents assess the situation because maybe they would uncover something that she had missed.

"If Laura came with us," her mother added, "we could finally meet her."

"I'll ask her," Brigid said, trusting that her parents would be reassured by the good impression that Laura always made on people.

Later that evening she called Laura and made arrangements for them to pick her up at the Yonkers station the next day.

In the passenger seat of her father's car, half turned around, her mother politely grilled Laura while they drove to the city. In her own way her mother found out things that Brigid didn't know, including where Laura's parents had grown up, where they had met, and where they went to church in Poughkeepsie. Laura took the questioning in good grace, admitting afterward that her mother would have done the same thing to Brigid.

Her father found a parking place on 4th Street near the building. Her parents stood in front of the building and gazed at it, her father saying it looked like the building where he had grown up in Highbridge, and her mother saying it looked like the building where she had grown up on Nodine Hill. When they entered the apartment after the long climb upstairs her parents seemed at home there. Her father said it was almost exactly like his family's apartment, and her mother said that the only difference was that her family's apartment had a narrow hallway connecting the rooms, which had doors on them so there was more privacy.

As they went through the rooms her mother asked the girls which bedroom each of them would have, and unprepared for this question, they both said the larger bedroom, but they quickly explained that they hadn't yet made a decision.

In the kitchen her mother checked the stove to make sure it worked, and her father peered into the refrigerator, which was completely empty. He joked about the toilet on its throne, and after examining the lock on the door that entered into the kitchen he recommended that they replace it with a deadbolt lock.

They spent less than an hour in the apartment, and when they left, her parents seemed satisfied with it. To determine how safe the neighborhood was, they strolled around for a while, and her father remarked that there were a lot of weirdos on the streets. The girls explained that they were artists, writers, and musicians. Her father said he hoped they weren't on drugs, and Brigid's effort to ameliorate his concern was undermined by a whiff of marijuana smoke from a scruffy guy who ambled by them.

On the way back to Yonkers her mother told the girls that since they were both responsible she had no strong reasons for opposing what they wanted to do, but that she would like to talk with Laura's mother before she approved it. So that evening their mothers had a long phone conversation, and when it was over, the girls were given the green light.

Three days later, with a suitcase that contained a set of sheets for a queen size bed as well as her clothes and toiletries, Brigid joined Laura on the train from Poughkeepsie at the Yonkers station, and riding along the Hudson River toward the city in the sunlit morning she felt a freedom she had never experienced before.

When they arrived at Grand Central they followed the crowd and found their way to the subway, lugging their suitcases. They remembered to get on a local train and to get off at Astor Place, and once they got oriented, they walked over to Avenue A and then south. As instructed by Kieran they stopped at a coffee shop at the corner of 5th Street to get the keys for the apartment. The place was called Rigoletto, and it had about a dozen small tables plus a communal table where a group of guys was debating some issue. The ceiling was stamped metal, the floor was alternating back and white tile, and the hanging lights looked antique. A man with a full head of silver hair but a young face was standing behind the bar, talking with a guy who was seated at the bar with a cup of espresso. Guessing that the man was Carmine, the proprietor, Brigid introduced herself and asked him if he had an envelope for her. He said he did, and after rummaging through a drawer he found it and gave it to her. On their way out she noticed the bulletin board to the right of the door, where information was posted about events, concerts, art shows, and meetings.

They had no trouble getting into the building but having suitcases made climbing the stairs even harder, and when they entered the living room they plopped down on the sofa to rest. The first thing they did after getting up from the sofa was to unpack the sheets from Brigid's suitcase and make the bed in the room next to the kitchen. They laughed at the slip of the tongue they had made when Brigid's mother asked them which bedroom each of them would have, and they laughed even more at the thought of how her parents would react if they knew that a man would be sleeping in the other bedroom. Sharing this secret, along with the overall secret about their real mission in the city, made Brigid feel even closer to Laura.

They had just finished hanging up their clothes on the pole in the narrow room and putting their underwear in the chest below, with each of them taking a personal drawer, when they heard steps in the living room.

"It's me," Kieran said, evidently so they wouldn't think it was an intruder.

"We're here," Brigid said, controlling what she felt at the mere sound of his voice.

He joined them in the narrow room, saying: "So you met Carmine."

"Yeah. He gave us the keys."

"His coffee shop is the communications center for the neighborhood. Carmine always knows what's happening. You know, he's an opera singer. He sings at the Amato Opera, which is only a few blocks from here on the Bowery. His favorite role is Rigoletto."

Brigid listened to him, struck by how elegant he looked in his perfectly tailored clerical attire. It occurred to her that a photo of him would make an effective poster for recruiting Jesuits.

"We need to buy some things," Laura said.

"We should make a list," Brigid said. "Is there a supermarket around here?"

"It's not far," Kieran said. "Have you had lunch?"

"No. We came here directly."

"There're a lot of good places around here. If you like Italian, there's a grocery store that has takeout food, and there's a good pizza place. There's also a Chinese takeout place."

"What about breakfast?" Brigid asked.

"We can make coffee and have bagels. There's a Jewish deli that has great bagels."

"How do you know so much about this neighborhood?" Laura asked.

"I spent a few weeks in this apartment last summer. The folk singer is a guy I knew from high school, and we stayed in touch."

"What kind of folk songs does he sing?"

"Traditional songs, but also protest songs. You saw the poster in the kitchen. His group is modeled after Peter, Paul, and Mary."

They made a list of things for the supermarket. Before they left, the girls had to pee, and it made Brigid laugh to be sitting on that throne.

After eating lunch at a nearby Greek diner they went to the supermarket and bought the things they needed, including soap, paper towels, and toilet paper. On the way back to the apartment they passed Most Holy Redeemer, a church whose history Kieran knew. It had been built more than a hundred years ago by immigrants from southern Germany who were Catholics, and for a long time it was the heart of a community known as Little Germany. In fact, the German Catholic community referred to Most Holy Redeemer as their cathedral.

Though they were carrying bags of groceries Kieran urged them to go into the church. Inside, there were tall columns that led to a high vaulted ceiling. There were marbled walls and stained-glass windows that filtered the light from outside into many colors. It was truly awesome.

"It must have cost a lot," Brigid said.

"It did," Kieran said. "The stained-glass windows were imported from Germany. But it was a large community, with more than ten thousand parishioners, so they financed the project with a lot of small contributions."

"Is this a Gothic church?" Laura asked.

"It's German Baroque," Kieran said. "But the high ceilings make it feel Gothic."

As they continued walking back to the apartment he explained that the church was where he would attend daily mass. When he told them it was at six in the morning they declined his invitation to join him, though they agreed to go to Sunday mass.

Since they weren't ready to cook yet, and since none of them had much experience cooking, they had pizza for dinner that evening, which they took out from the place that Kieran had recommended. While they were waiting for their pie Kieran went to a nearby liquor store and bought a bottle of Chianti, which they drank with the pizza back in the apartment, sitting at the table in the kitchen.

They sat there and talked after finishing the pizza, long enough to finish the wine, and the girls went to bed in a mellow mood. As Brigid lay there with Laura by her side it was like they were sisters, and she felt blessed.

They were still in bed the next morning when Kieran returned from mass. He had bought a bag of bagels at the place he had told them about, and they had them for breakfast with coffee that Brigid made with the percolator that came with the apartment. While sitting at the table in the kitchen they began to develop a plan of activities. The girls would participate in demonstrations that were held almost daily at various locations, and Kieran would plan a dramatic action that would emulate the actions by the Berrigan brothers. For that he would have to meet with people who used violence as a tactic in order to learn things from them, but as he had promised, he wasn't going to involve the girls in his action.

They were still in the process of getting organized when they heard about the shooting of Robert Kennedy. They were seated at a table in Rigoletto when a guy came in with the latest edition of the *Daily News* and flashed the headline. In response to their questions the guy with the newspaper told them it happened in a hotel kitchen right after Kennedy's celebration of victory in the California primary. The guy who shot him was a Palestinian who had been waiting for him to come through the kitchen. Kennedy was taken to a hospital, where he underwent surgery for almost four hours, and his condition was still extremely critical.

"What's wrong with this country?" Laura asked.

"Our whole system is based on violence," Kieran said. "That's what's wrong. The shooter just followed the American way."

"He's a Palestinian," Brigid said. "You think he did it because of our support for Israel?"

"That could have been a motive, but it wasn't the reason why he did it."

"Then why did he do it?"

"To remove Kennedy as a candidate for president."

"Are you saying it was domestic politics?"

"I think it was. He had a motive, but he wouldn't have had an opportunity unless someone had told him where he could have a shot at Kennedy."

"Who would have told him?"

"People who don't want Kennedy to run for president."

"You mean there was a conspiracy?" Laura said.

"There must have been, just as there was in the assassination of his brother. One person can't do these things alone."

"So who are these people who don't want Kennedy to run for president?" Brigid asked.

"People who don't want to change the government," Kieran said. "People who don't want to end the war."

"People who are profiting from it?"

"Right. There are always people who profit from war, and they always have enough money to influence the government."

"If they have so much money, how can we stop them?"

"By waging war against them."

"If you mean using violence," Laura said, "then I don't agree."

"I know you don't," Kieran said patiently. "But if you apply the principles of the just war doctrine to what they're doing, you can justify using violence against them."

"I hope you don't mean killing them," Brigid said.

"I don't mean killing them. I mean stopping them from sending our boys to die in Vietnam."

"Well, we're going to stop them by demonstrating against the war."

"You'll be doing good. You'll be turning public opinion against the war, so that if we have a fair election we can change the government. But if they kill the candidates who would change the government, we're not going to have a fair election."

"So who will be the candidate now?" Brigid asked. "Does McCarthy have a chance?"

Kieran shook his head. "Not against Humphrey. With Kennedy out of the way he'll easily get the nomination."

"You're not suggesting that Humphrey was involved in the conspiracy, are you?"

"Oh, no. He's a good man. But he's controlled by the people who want the war to continue."

"Then they won't end the war," Laura said unhappily.

"They'll end it eventually, but only after they've gotten their last dollar out of it."

The girls both fell into a silence.

"Let's face it," Kieran said. "We're not going to change the government through an election. We need to have a revolution."

Brigid was inspired by this statement, though she had no idea of what a revolution might be. Whatever it was, if Kieran was going to lead it then she would follow him. At that point she would have liked to get involved in his action.

The next day they learned that Kennedy had died. As they joined a crowd in Washington Square to mourn his death they held hands and sang songs that were led by two guys with guitars. The songs were all about peace, and that was what everyone in the crowd wanted, but to Brigid it felt like a storm was coming, with lightning and thunder.

FIVE

DESPITE THE APPARENT odds against them Brigid and Laura decided to continue pursuing the strategy of the Catholic Peace Fellowship: to convert people to opposition against the war by appealing to their faith and their reason. But the tactics they had used during the academic year, which centered around speaking to groups of students at other colleges, weren't feasible in the city. Here the tactics centered around public demonstrations, in which the two girls had little experience. So they would have to find out where people were demonstrating and to join them.

From the bulletin board at Rigoletto they learned that there were regular demonstrations at Dag Hammarskjold Plaza, at 47th Street between Second and First Avenues, so on the Monday following the assassination of Robert Kennedy they walked to Astor place and took the subway to Grand Central and then walked to the plaza, where they found about forty people gathered. They were old and young, including a woman with a baby carriage. Some of them held signs that conveyed messages of opposition to the war.

As they approached the demonstrators Brigid noticed that the people her age were mostly wearing jeans and tee shirts and sneakers, unlike the skirts and blouses and flats that she and Laura were wearing. A girl wearing jeans and a green tee shirt with white letters that said PEACE ON EARTH stepped toward them and welcomed them and handed them fliers. They learned from the girl that she and her friend, who was standing next to her, were members of a group that promoted peace and justice. They were students at Mount St. Vincent College in the Bronx, where they were preparing to be teachers.

Taking the fliers, Brigid and Laura joined the group and stayed there for the rest of the morning. A lot of people walked through the plaza, so it was a good location for disseminating the message of peace and justice. There were interactions among members of the group, who exchanged information with each other about what was happening, and there were interactions with people walking through the plaza, who were usually polite but occasionally rude when approached with a flier.

For lunch they bought hot pretzels from a food cart on Second Avenue, and they stayed in the plaza for about two more hours. On their way back to the apartment they decided that they had to buy some appropriate clothes, make signs, and get fliers. They agreed that the perfect fliers were the ones they handed out on their visits to other colleges as members of the CPF. On one page, in simple terms, the fliers showed how the war in Vietnam failed to meet any criterion of the just war doctrine and was therefore morally wrong.

They found a clothing store on University Place that had a variety of affordable items including jeans and tee shirts. Since neither of them had ever worn jeans they had to try on several before they found the right sizes. Laura was taller and curvier, so it took her longer to find a pair of jeans that fit her. Then, after shuffling through a pile of clothes, they found tee shirts that were bright blue with words in white letters. Laura selected a shirt that said LOVE while Brigid selected a shirt that said PEACE, and they decided that since the tee shirts conveyed their essential message they wouldn't need signs.

On the same block they found a shoe store, where they bought sneakers, the most basic and the least expensive. Laura's feet were bigger and wider than Brigid's, so it took the guy who waited on them longer to find the right size. He packed the shoes in their boxes, tying cords around the boxes and attaching wooden handles to make them easier to carry.

Back at the apartment they changed into their new clothes, and looking at each other, they laughed at the thought of what their parents would say, or what the nuns would say. Though unlike high school the college didn't require uniforms, it did have a strict dress code under which shorts, mini-skirts, tank tops, tee shirts, and jeans were forbidden. It made them think of the song by Bob Dylan, "The Times They Are a-Changin'."

The next step was to get the fliers. Since it was summer the students who were CPF members wouldn't be at the college, so the person to call was Sister Maura. Using the phone that belonged to the folk singer, who kept it on a table in the living room, Brigid dialed the main number of the college and asked the receptionist to connect her with Sister Maura. It took a while but she finally got Sister Maura and told her she needed CPF fliers. Of course Sister Maura wanted to know why she needed them, but when Brigid told her she blessed their enterprise and agreed to give them a large supply.

The next day, properly dressed, they took a train to the Yonkers station and a bus to the college. They found Sister Maura in her office with several boxes on her desk. Invited to sit down, they told Sister Maura that they were living in the East Village and participating in demonstrations against the war. They told her more than they had told their parents, though they left out the detail that they were sharing an apartment with Kieran O'Donnell. From her reaction, they got the feeling that Sister Maura would have liked to join them.

With forethought Sister Maura had obtained four sturdy paper bags with handles, which could hold all the boxes of fliers, so with two bags each to balance the weight the girls were able to carry them and return to the city.

The girl from Mount St. Vincent was at the plaza the next day. She complemented them on their tee shirts and read their flier. The girl, who said she liked their flier, called to her companion to join her with Brigid and Laura, and they stood together for the rest of the morning. These two girls had more experience than Brigid and Laura in demonstrations, and they explained their strategy of being in locations where they would encounter a lot of tourists. Dag Hammarskjold Plaza was a popular location because it was one of the few public places in the city where large groups of people were allowed to gather without a permit, so it was like a home base. Some key locations where you could demonstrate in small numbers were the Isaiah Wall near the UN, the Empire State Building, Rockefeller Center, and Times Square. If there were no more than two of you, the police weren't likely to bother you as long as you didn't disrupt the flow of pedestrian traffic.

A few days later, following this advice, Brigid and Laura went to the Isaiah Wall, where they read the words of Isaiah inscribed in granite: "They shall beat their swords into plowshares, and their spears into pruning hooks; nation shall not lift up sword against nation, neither shall they learn war any more." They agreed that it was a perfect location for conveying their message. And they spent the day there, encountering more tourists than at the plaza, but also having to be more careful in the presence of police. At one point a young cop approached them, making them wonder if they might be doing something wrong, but after the way he chatted with Laura it was clear that he had only wanted to check her out.

In the presence of Isaiah's words the tourists were respectful of the girls' message, and instead of dropping them into the nearest trash container they kept the fliers, folding them and putting them into handbags or pockets for further reading.

That evening, with takeout Chinese food for dinner, they told Kieran about their day. They told him they felt they were making a difference, and he supported them, saying that their approach was the right thing for them. About his own day he only said that he had met with people who could help him carry out his action.

Lying in bed that night, after Laura had gone to sleep, Brigid wondered if Kieran would ever tell them what he planned to do. Though he had promised not to give them the details so that they couldn't be implicated, by now her curiosity was stronger than her fear of being implicated. But it was more than curiosity, it was her need to know what he planned to do so that she could understand him. Why did he have to do something more dramatic than the Berrigans? Why did he have to top their action at Catonsville? Was it a competitive male thing?

As she lay awake in bed she realized that in wanting to understand him she had moved from seeing him completely as a hero to seeing him partly as a human being, to caring about him. That was what love was, wasn't it? Caring about another person. And since she cared about him she didn't want him to be a martyr and go to prison. In fact, she didn't want him to be a priest, which led to a lot of speculation.

For two weeks the girls went and stood at the locations that the girls from Mount St. Vincent had recommended, and they felt good about what they were doing. At the same time they were enjoying the experience of being on their own, away from their parents, and they were exploring the neighborhood.

One afternoon, on their way home from a demonstration, they were walking down Second Avenue and they stopped in front of a building that looked like an old theater. A vertical sign said "Fillmore East," and letters on the marquee spelled out the groups that would be playing that weekend. The girls didn't recognize two of the groups, but they knew The Grateful Dead, which Brigid had heard on the radio and Laura had heard on record players in the dormitory. On impulse they decided that it would be fun to hear them live, so they went into the box office and bought two tickets for that Friday. Their seats were in the balcony, where it cost less than five dollars. They hadn't considered whether they should buy a third ticket for Kieran, and as they continued walking they wondered if they should have. But their feeling that they should have included him was outweighed by their desire to do something on their own. And in any case, after hearing about it, Kieran said he wasn't interested.

The concert was a blast. The theater was packed with people, and the girls felt lucky to have gotten tickets. Their seats in the balcony were perfect. They were far enough away from the stage so that the volume of the music didn't hurt their ears, and they were sitting in a cloud of marijuana smoke so thick that you didn't have to bring your own. About halfway through the concert the guys who were next to them shared a loosely rolled cigarette with them. Since neither Brigid nor Laura smoked, they hesitated, but then they went ahead and tried it. They had a little trouble inhaling smoke, but they adapted, and when the guys who had handed them the cigarette insisted that they keep it and finish it, they didn't protest. They were still high when they got back to the apartment. Luckily, Kieran hadn't waited up for them, as their parents would have, so they got away with it.

Lying in bed that night, they talked even more than usual, and it was then that Laura shared her innermost secret with Brigid. The night before her boyfriend left for Canada they had made love. They had done it in his bedroom while his parents and his sisters were sleeping. She would have liked to spend the night with him, but she had to leave early in the morning before his parents got up. At least she was able to meet him at the train station later that morning to say goodbye. Of course his parents didn't know he was going to Canada, and they certainly didn't know he had a girl in his room the night before.

When it came time for him to board the train she didn't want to be separated from him, and at the last moment she told him she was going with him. If he hadn't stopped her, telling her she should wait and join him after he was settled with a job and a place to live, she would have gone with him. And most of the time she wished she had.

"So you miss him."

"I do. But at least I can talk with him on the phone."

"Have you talked with him since we came here?"

"Yeah. I use the phone booth on the corner. The problem is it smells like pee. "

"Ugh, that's gross. Why don't you use the phone here?"

"They could trace the call. And I'm sure that the guy who lives here wouldn't appreciate having to pay for long distance calls to Canada."

"Do you still plan to join him?"

"Oh, yeah. After I get my degree in nursing, I'm going to Canada. It's been almost eighteen months since Owen went there, but our relationship has survived. In some ways it's gotten stronger. And I only have two years to go."

"God bless you," Bridget said, feeling that the bond between them had been cemented by Laura sharing her secret with her. And she gave Laura a heartfelt hug.

When they had stopped in front of the Fillmore they noticed a restaurant to the right of it called Ratner's. They asked Kieran about it, and he said it was an old Jewish restaurant, and it was excellent. He offered to take them there for brunch after mass the next Sunday.

They sat at a table in the window and while they perused the menus Kieran explained that Ratner's was a kosher dairy restaurant, and there was no meat on the menu because of the dietary rule of not mixing milk and meat. He said the restaurant was established right after the turn of the century to serve the Jewish immigrants who settled in the neighborhood. At that time it was a center of Yiddish culture, with several live Yiddish theaters, which now were theaters for Off Off Broadway plays.

Looking at an item on the menu, Brigid asked: "What are blintzes?"

"They're Jewish crepes."

"What are crepes?"

"You never had crepes? They're thin pancakes that are rolled around a filling."

"They sound good. I've only had the kind of pancakes that are stacked on a plate. They must be Italian because my mother makes them."

"They're not Italian," Kieran said. "They're American."

"I thought they were Irish," Laura said. "My mother makes them."

"Maybe they are. My mother makes them too."

The girls ordered the cheese blintzes, and Kieran ordered potato pancakes and split-pea soup. After taking their order the waiter brought them a plate of onion rolls, which were a meal in themselves.

While they were munching on the rolls Kieran asked: "So how do you feel about what you've been doing for the past two weeks?"

"I feel good," Brigid said. "We've made our case against the war to a lot of people."

"I agree," Laura said. "I think we've made a lot of people see why the war is wrong, and that may affect how they vote in the next election."

"You mean if they have a choice," Kieran said.

"Well, the way things look, they'll have a choice between Humphrey and Nixon, and maybe when he realizes that public opinion is against the war, Humphrey will want to end it."

"Maybe he will. At least with Humphrey there's hope of that happening. If Nixon wins, there's no hope at all."

"Nixon talks like he wants to end the war," Brigid said.

"He's a politician. He'll say whatever it takes to get elected."

They talked until their food arrived, and then they concentrated on eating. Brigid loved the blintzes, and she wondered if she could learn to make them.

When they resumed talking Kieran said: "I think you're doing good work. You're pursuing the strategy of turning public opinion against the war. My only question is which tactics would be more effective. And I think it would be more effective to demonstrate in front of an induction center."

"How would that be more effective?" Brigid asked.

"It would show people the evil being done to those boys."

"It wouldn't stop the evil."

"No. I'm not suggesting that you put a spoke in the wheels of their machinery. I'm only suggesting that you help people realize that our government is sending those boys to be killed so that capitalists can profit from the war."

"Those boys are mostly black or brown," Laura said. "Do you think people care about them?"

"I think they do. I still have faith in people. I still believe that they were created in God's image, and they're temples of the Holy Spirit. I just don't have faith in politicians."

"Politicians are people," Brigid pointed out.

"They're corrupt people," Kieran said. "I can have faith in people generally and still not trust specific people."

"At times it's hard to see things clearly. I mean, there are so many conflicts: whites against blacks, and rich against poor, and capitalists against communists."

"I'm with the blacks, the poor, and the communists," Laura declared.

"I think we all are," Kieran said.

"If Jesus was alive today," Brigid asked, "do you think he'd be a communist?"

"His followers shared whatever they had. They must have gotten that idea from somewhere."

"If we lived like that, we'd have peace, wouldn't we?"

"I think we would," Kieran said. "The cause of war is injustice, so if we want peace we should work for justice. And if you show people what our government is doing to those boys at an induction center, they'll see the injustice."

"Where is an induction center?" Laura asked.

"The main one is on Whitehall Street in Lower Manhattan."

"So let's go there," Brigid said, knowing that this was what Kieran wanted. She accepted his reasoning for why this tactic would be more effective.

The next morning, with packets of fliers, they walked to the subway stop at Bleecker Street and rode down to Bowling Green, where they got off in a different world. They were in the financial district, and most of the people walking around were dressed more formally than the people in their neighborhood. The men wore suits and ties, and the women wore dresses. Instead of wandering around aimlessly they walked as if they knew where they were going and how long it would take to get there.

As they headed over to Whitehall Street in the bright summer morning Brigid smelled salt from the sea, which at times when the tide was coming upriver she could smell in Yonkers, and it filled her with an inexplicable yearning.

The induction center was in an old multistory building. The way to its entrance was protected by rows of street barriers, and on the other side of one barrier was a group of about twenty people, obviously gathered to demonstrate against the war. It was similar to the group that gathered in Dag Hammarskjold Plaza, except that the people were mostly young and they carried signs that were more aggressive. One sign, held by an angry-looking guy, said: END THE FASCIST WAR.

Brigid and Laura joined the group, though they stayed at its edges and held their tongues as the people jeered at two army officers who arrived on a bus with a collection of boys for the purpose of having medical examinations, according to a guy behind the girls. The boys looked so young, and as Kiernan had said, they were mostly black and brown.

"Racist pigs!" a guy yelled.

"Fucking fascists!" a girl shrieked.

Brigid and Laura stood there for the next three hours, and during that time hundreds of boys were ushered into the induction center. The same guy behind them said that already a million boys had been inducted at that center.

As the girls were about to leave for lunch a journalist stopped and asked them if he could take a picture of them, and they assented, making sure he captured the messages on their tee shirts, though afterward Brigid wondered if he was mainly interested in their breasts. Well, if that was what it took to get publicity, she didn't mind.

For the next two weeks they went to Whitehall every day except Sunday. They had begun to feel at home in the group and to join in the catcalls. They got to know some of the regular members of the group, including a light brown girl with wire-rimmed glasses who had lost her older brother to the war and a stout black woman who had lost her son.

It could have been their imagination, but as time went on it felt like pressure in the group was building. The calls were getting louder, and the words were getting harsher. Finally, the group broke through the barrier and into the passage that led to the entrance of the induction center. Since Brigid and Laura were standing in the middle of the group, they were pulled along with it, and they ended up holding hands in a chain to block the passage.

A woman in the group started singing "We Shall Overcome," and they all joined her.

"Get back, get back," a cop urged them.

But they stood their ground, singing.

After a while more cops arrived, and a cop with a megaphone ordered them to get back behind the barrier. When they didn't budge, the cops moved toward them and started pulling selected individuals out of the group. The first person selected was Laura, who said to the cop who was holding her wrists: "May the Lord shine his light on you."

The cop said: "Come on, miss. Behave yourself."

When Brigid moved forward to help her friend another cop grabbed her. She and Laura were herded into a paddy wagon with two guys. The doors were slammed, and the vehicle moved, jerking the prisoners.

It took them only about ten minutes to arrive at the jail, where they were led out of the wagon and into a building that smelled like cleaning fluid. They were checked in by a cop behind a counter, and then they were put into cells, the girls in one cell and the guys in another. Their cell had two bunks, against the opposite walls, and a toilet in a back corner with no privacy, so the guards could see them at all times.

At the counter they were asked for a contact person, and they both gave Kieran, with the phone number of the apartment. They hoped he would come and get them released before the night, which they didn't want to spend in jail. They waited for him, lying on their bunks, and around five a guard delivered sandwiches. They were cheese sandwiches in cellophane wrap, and they tasted like they were from a vending machine.

By the time the lights were dimmed on their floor they were resigned to spending the night in jail. It was a long night, and their sleep was interrupted periodically by the cries of a woman down the hall. She sounded as if she was being tortured, but she was probably having nightmares or psychotic episodes. It wasn't the only thing that kept Brigid awake. She was also kept awake by the thought of how her parents would feel if they knew she was in jail.

The next morning she stood in front of the toilet to block the view while Laura peed, and then her friend did likewise for her. A few minutes later a guard came and led them out of the cell and to the area where they had checked in. They were glad to see Kieran there waiting for them. After checking out they left the building with him, not talking until they were beyond the hearing range of the police.

"I'm sorry you had to spend the night there," Kieran said, "but they didn't call me until early this morning."

Brigid understood. "So they wanted to teach us a lesson."

"Yeah. Did you learn the lesson?"

"I only learned that I never want to spend a night in jail again."

"Then you'll appreciate the sacrifices of our martyrs."

"I guess I will."

"How did they treat you?"

"They treated us well. I think it helped that we were girls."

"It usually helps," Kieran said, smiling. He unfolded a newspaper that he was carrying. "It also helps with photographers."

There was a picture of them with a caption that said: "Students arrested for demonstrating at the Army induction center."

"Oh, my God," Brigid said. "Is that *The Daily News*?"

"No, it's *The Post*."

She sighed in relief. "My father reads *The Daily News*, and if he saw that picture, he'd have a shit fit."

"Thank God my father doesn't read newspapers," Laura said. "He'd send in the marines."

"Well, you should be proud of yourselves," Kieran told them. "You achieved the goal. You raised awareness of the issue."

Now that they had been released, Brigid was able to feel proud of what they had done, though she didn't want to repeat the experience. While it made her appreciate the sacrifices of martyrs like the Berrigans she didn't want to be a martyr herself.

Kieran had come to get them in the van that belonged to the folk singer, who used it to transport his group to engagements. The singer had given Kieran permission to use the van for the summer, but it had sat idle until about a week ago when Kieran started using it for trips to New Jersey. Where or for what purpose he didn't say.

He had luckily found a parking place for the van not far from the jail, so it took them only a few minutes to walk to it. The van was old and somewhat battered, with a sticker on the bumper that said: MAKE LOVE, NOT WAR.

Laura opened a back door and left the passenger seat for Brigid so that she could sit next to Kieran. Among her other feelings toward him she was thankful to him for rescuing her. He had done what her father would have done for her but without asking how she had gotten herself arrested and thrown into jail.

The girls took the rest of the morning off. They had the apartment to themselves because Kieran had gone to a meeting, so they took showers and returned to their bedroom with only towels around them. It felt so good to be clean and safe at home again. After drying themselves they rolled into bed and lay there luxuriating in the prospect of a badly needed nap. It didn't take them long to fall asleep.

When they woke up they lay in bed for a while talking. They assessed their experience of demonstrating at the induction center, getting arrested, and being jailed. They did feel proud of what they had done, but they agreed that once was enough. They would resume the purely nonviolent tactics they had used in the Catholic Peace Fellowship.

At one point Laura changed the conversation by saying: "I talked with Owen yesterday. He's doing all right, but he misses me. I was thinking of going to see him for a few weeks in August, before the fall semester begins."

"That sounds like a good idea. How would you get there?"

"I'd take the train to Montreal and then another train to Nova Scotia. The only obstacle is my parents. I mean, they can't stop me, but they won't want me to go."

"So you haven't told them about it."

"No. I'm working up the courage. It's not my mother," Laura explained, "it's my father. He calls Owen a cowardly deserter."

Brigid knew that Laura's father had fought as a marine in the Pacific during World War II and later in Korea, and he had been awarded a Purple Heart, so he had strongly condemned Owen for avoiding the draft. "But doesn't your father understand that your boyfriend's acting on his beliefs as a Quaker?"

"No. He doesn't respect Owen's beliefs."

"So he wouldn't approve of what you're doing."

"Lord, no. If he knew, he'd call me a traitor."

"Well, I guess I'm lucky to have a father who's against the war."

"You *are* lucky. I hate being in conflict with my father."

They lay in silence for a while, and then feeling the urge to share a secret with her friend, Brigid said: "If I tell you something, will you keep it to yourself?"

"Of course I will."

"Well, I know that Kieran's almost a priest, but—" She had trouble coming out with it.

"You're in love with him."

"How did you guess?"

"I can tell by the way you act with him."

"Do you think he can tell?"

"No, I don't think so. Guys don't notice things like that."

"So what do you think?"

"I think it's awesome. He's so smart, and he's so attractive, it would be a waste for him to be a priest."

"But I don't see how I could change his mind."

"If he loves you," Laura told her, "you can change his mind."

"I think he loves me in a way, but I don't think he loves me the way I love him."

"If he doesn't, then you have to get him to love you that way."

"So how would I do that?"

"Just let him see what you have to offer."

Though she understood what Laura was suggesting, she couldn't imagine doing it. "Well, he's so caught up in his project, it's very hard to get his attention."

"Yeah. When I see him in that mode I feel like he's above us.

And he's put a barrier between him and us by not telling us about his project. I know he's protecting us, but he's acting like a parent to us. If he just told us what he's doing, we'd have a more equal relationship with him."

"I'm not sure if I want to know what he's doing."

"I'm not either," Laura told her. "But if you don't find out, then he'll have a secret from you, and he'll keep acting like a parent to you."

Brigid rolled over and lay on her back, reflecting on their exchange. She and Laura had both shared secrets with each other, which showed that they trusted each other. But trust wasn't the issue with Kieran. The issue was his wanting to protect them, and in that respect he *was* acting like a parent to them. So if she wanted to get him to love her the way she loved him, she would have to break through the barrier he had put between them.

For the next several weeks the girls resumed their efforts to turn public opinion against the war. In Dag Hammarskjold Plaza they ran into the girls from Mount St. Vincent and exchanged information about their activities, not mentioning what had happened to them at Whitehall Street because they felt they might have strayed from the values they shared with these girls. They were comfortable back in the routine of going from the plaza to the Isaiah Wall, and to the Empire State Building, and to Rockefeller Center, and to Times Square. Brigid still got satisfaction from talking to people, explaining why the war was wrong, but her view of the world had been changed by what had happened at Whitehall Street. It was as if she had gained some knowledge from that experience which caused a loss of innocence.

One Sunday evening when they were all seated at the kitchen table after a dinner of Chinese takeout, Laura asked Kieran to tell them at least the basic idea of what he was doing. Brigid still wasn't sure if she wanted to know, but she didn't stop Laura from asking the question because she wanted to see how Kieran would respond to it.

"I explained why I don't want you to know," he said patiently.

"Yeah, we get it. You want to protect us. But we don't want to be treated like children."

"I'm not treating you like children. I only want to prevent you from being accessories to my action. I don't want you to go to prison."

"And we don't want to go to prison," Brigid said. "We know what it's like."

"Well, prison is worse than a night in jail."

"You don't have to give us the details," Laura said. "Just tell us the basic idea."

"Are you sure you want to know?" he asked them.

Brigid hesitated. "I'm not sure, but I think we should know. I mean, in case something happens to you."

"She's right," Laura said. "We should know."

"Okay," he said, sitting back in his chair. "The basic idea is to put a major spoke in the wheels of their machinery. It's to take out a regional center of the draft board."

"How would you take it out?" Brigid asked him.

"With bombs. We'd completely destroy it."

"If it's a regional center," Laura said, "then a lot of people must work there."

"A lot of people do work there during the day. We'd blow it up during the night."

"But they must have watchmen at night."

"They do. So we'll lure the watchmen out of the building with a diversion."

"You're working with other people?"

"Oh, yeah. I couldn't do this by myself. For one thing, I don't know anything about bombs, but these people know how to make them."

"Who are they?" Brigid asked.

"They're people who believe that violence against things is justified."

"You mean people like the Berrigans."

"Yeah. But it's not them."

After a silence Laura said: "So you're going to completely

destroy the building. But how will you know if there's no one in it?"

"We'll go through the building to make sure."

"What if you miss someone?"

"We won't miss anyone."

After another silence Laura said: "I assume this building is in New Jersey."

"I'm not going to tell you where it is."

"But you've been taking trips to New Jersey, so it must be there."

"I'm not going to say."

After yet another silence Laura said: "Well, I don't think you should do this. You can't be absolutely sure that there's no one in the building."

"Yes, we can," Kieran argued.

"No, you can't. And I don't care if the Berrigans use violence. It's against our principles. We believe that violence only leads to more violence."

"Violence against people does, but violence against things doesn't. Things don't want to get revenge."

"You can't completely separate people and things."

Kieran turned to Brigid and asked: "What do you think?"

"I think," she said, not knowing exactly what she thought, "that if there's any chance of hurting a person, you shouldn't do it."

"What if there's no chance of hurting a person?"

Her bond of loyalty to her friend conflicted with her feeling for Kieran, which made her hesitate, but she finally said: "I still don't think you should do it."

"Thanks for your opinions," he said from a higher level. "But I'm going to do it anyway. We're not going to end this war by talking."

At that he left them and went out for a walk.

After cleaning up from dinner the girls sat in the living room and talked. They were both against Kieran's plan, though Laura was more strongly against it. In fact, she decided it was time for her to leave and go to Canada. It was late in July, and she would have the whole month of August to be with Owen.

They talked about whether Brigid should stay in the apartment alone with Kieran, and Laura felt she should. It would give her an opportunity to get him to abandon his plan to bomb the records center and to get him to love her the way she loved him. Brigid was dubious, but she decided it was worth a try.

SIX

BRIGID COULD SEE that Kieran wasn't happy about Laura's decision to leave. At first he tried to talk her out of it, but then he relented, saying it would better for her if she wasn't around when he carried out his plan. If she was in Canada at the time she wouldn't have any risk of being implicated.

The night before Laura left they had dinner at the pub they frequented, and as usual they had burgers. They talked around the subject that was most on their minds, and they did a little happy reminiscing about the summer, but it was still a sad occasion, and they couldn't pretend otherwise. Even Laura, who was glad she would get to see her boyfriend after being apart for so long, had a wistful look in her pure blue eyes.

The next morning after breakfast Kieran said goodbye to Laura and wished her well and then departed on an errand. Brigid stood by while Laura packed her things, and she followed Laura down the five flights of stairs. In front of the building she offered to go to Penn Station with her, but Laura said it wasn't necessary. They hugged each other for a long time, with tears in their eyes, and then Brigid watched her friend walk slowly toward Avenue A, carrying her suitcase. For the first time in her life she had a such a deep feeling of loss that she couldn't bear it, and standing on the sidewalk she cried and cried, until a passing woman stopped and asked her if she was all right.

To rise from her despondency she decided to go and join a demonstration, so she went back upstairs and put on the tee shirt that said PEACE and got a bag of fliers and went back down the stairs. She took the subway from Astor Place to Grand Central, and then walked up Second Avenue to Dag Hammarskjold Plaza, where she found the two girls from Mount St. Vincent. They asked where her friend was, and she told them that Laura had left for

Canada to see her boyfriend, who had fled there to avoid the draft. They sympathized, and they gave her some comfort. At least she wasn't alone that day.

But she was alone that night. Around five she got a call from Kieran who said he was in New Jersey, and since he had a meeting the next morning he would spend the night there. So she would have to eat alone. Since there were no leftovers in the refrigerator she decided to eat out, and not wanting to sit at a table alone, she went to the pub and sat at the bar. A glass of wine helped, and another glass of wine helped more, and she was able to numb her pain enough to finish a cheese sandwich. A guy sitting next to her tried to pick her up, but she rebuffed him with so much disdain that he left her alone.

That night she had the bed to herself, but she was so used to sleeping with Laura that she stayed on her side and left the other side empty as if she was saving it for Laura.

She didn't see Kieran until late the next afternoon, and he looked as if he had been up all night. She didn't ask what he had been doing because she knew he wouldn't tell her. Though he was obviously exhausted, he suggested that they go to the pizza place. It had a few tables, so instead of taking it home they could sit and eat the pizza there. They ordered the usual pizza with sausage, but it wasn't the same. Kieran was mostly silent, and she could tell that he too was affected by the departure of Laura. Munching on the hard edge of a crust, she realized that things wouldn't be the same without Laura.

For the next week she went to demonstrations at the usual places, but she didn't run into the girls from Mount St. Vincent again, and she felt lonely standing in a crowd without Laura. In fact, the only thing that stopped her from going home was the possibility of getting Kieran to love her the way she loved him, though it wasn't much of a possibility. He was hardly ever there, so they were together only for dinner, and instead of lingering at the table he got up immediately and went to the living room without inviting her to join him.

One afternoon she came back from a demonstration and took a shower and dried herself and for some reason got into bed naked, maybe because she was too tired to bother putting on her nightgown. She was lying there when she heard Kieran return to the apartment. As he walked through her bedroom on the way to the bathroom she pretended to be asleep. He didn't pause but went directly to the bathroom. Remembering what Laura had said about letting him see what she had to offer, she pulled the sheet down from her shoulder and exposed a breast.

Still pretending to be asleep, she waited for him to come back through her bedroom. When he stopped she knew he had noticed her breast and was looking at her. She could tell that he was being tempted by what he saw and by what he would see if she pulled the sheet down further. She held her breath, and she hoped that he would approach the bed and take advantage of the situation. But after a long, long time she heard him continue walking toward the front of the apartment, and even though he must have assumed that she was asleep and that her display of a naked breast was accidental, she felt humiliated because she knew what she had done. She had used her body in an effort to seduce him, and he had rejected her.

The next morning while they were having bagels and coffee for breakfast at the table in the kitchen she announced that she was going home.

"You are?" He looked surprised. "Why?"

"It's no fun demonstrating alone."

"Is it supposed to be fun?"

"No. But when you don't have someone with you, it's not the same. In fact, it's lonely."

He nodded. "Yeah. You're used to having company."

"And without Laura it's not the same in this apartment. I feel like I'm alone here."

He was silent for a while, and then he said: "I miss her too."

"I feel I've accomplished our goals. I've gone to more than fifty demonstrations, and I've given our message of love and peace to more than a thousand people."

"Yeah. You've done important work for our cause. You should feel very proud of yourself."

It helped to hear him say that. "So I think it's time for me to go home. I haven't seen my family in almost two months."

"Well, after I wrap things up I'll be leaving too."

"You mean after you bomb that building?"

He took a long, deep breath and slowly let it out. "I decided not to do that."

"You did? Why?"

"I decided that you and Laura are right. If there's any chance of hurting someone it would be wrong. And after reassessing the situation, I realized that I couldn't absolutely guarantee that there was no one in the building."

She was glad he had made this decision, but at the same time she was disappointed because by calling off his action he had come down from the level at which from the very beginning she had placed him. Remembering something Laura had said, she felt he was no longer so far above her, and while that change in their relative positions might have cleared the way for a different kind of relationship with him, her failure yesterday to seduce him made her unwilling, at least for now, to try again.

Immediately after breakfast she called her parents to let them know she was coming home. She had called them once a week to let them know she was all right, but talking on the phone wasn't the same as being with them, and now that she was going home she realized how much she had missed them. She packed her things, and then she took a last look around the apartment, pausing at the bed where she and Laura had spent so many nights together. She felt that if she was going to have any happy memories of this experience they would be about Laura.

She found Kieran in the living room, and they said goodbye there. He wished her well, as he had with Laura. At breakfast he had admitted that he missed Laura, and she hoped that he would miss her too.

Though she was glad to be home with her family Brigid had to readjust to the situation because she had enjoyed two months of complete freedom and she had been doing things that she couldn't continue doing at home. Instead of going to demonstrations she worked at the local supermarket, checking out items whose prices she used to know by heart but now she often had to look up. But she easily fell back into the routine of having dinner with her family, talking about things that had nothing do with the war in Vietnam, and she readapted to sleeping in her own bed again, though at times, especially when she woke up in the middle of the night, she missed having Laura with her.

One evening, shortly after coming home, Brigid got a phone call from Laura's mother, who asked if she knew where Laura was. Despite her reluctance to betray Laura's confidence she didn't want Laura's mother to worry, so she told her that Laura had gone to Canada to see her boyfriend. Her mother, who didn't sound surprised, asked if Brigid knew how long Laura planned to stay in Canada, and Brigid told her that as far as she knew it was only a visit and Laura was planning to return for the fall semester.

Later, reflecting on the conversation, she wondered why Laura hadn't called her mother to let her know where she was, but she concluded that it was because Laura was afraid that the call might be traced by the FBI, who could find out where Owen was and have him arrested. So she didn't think further about it.

In early August she went to a meeting of the CPF. Since there weren't many students taking classes at that time there weren't many members at the meeting. As requested by Megan, she reported on hers and Laura's activities in the city, highlighting the fact that they had been arrested and jailed for demonstrating at the Whitehall induction center. Their exploit impressed the girls at the meeting, which made her feel proud of it.

She learned at the meeting that Megan and Teri and some other girls were planning to go to Chicago next week for the Democratic Convention, where they intended to oppose Humphrey and promote McCarthy. Megan asked her if she wanted to join them, but she declined, feeling she had done enough for one summer.

Instead of being there she watched the events on television, sitting in the family room alone in the morning and with her parents in the evening. According to the newscasters, thousands of people were gathered in Chicago to protest the war, and thousands of armed men from the police and the National Guard were stationed in key areas of the city to control the crowds. The amphitheater where the delegates were meeting was surrounded by a barrier of barbed wire. And there was tension in the city that Brigid could feel over the television.

The first task of the delegates was to write a party platform, and the main issue was the bombing of North Vietnam. The peace talks in Paris had been halted by the demand from the North Vietnamese that the U.S. unconditionally stop the bombing and the refusal of the U.S. to meet that demand. The antiwar delegates wanted a platform that called for suspension of the bombing, but the mainstream delegates opposed that, and there was a long debate between the two sides. When a platform that didn't include a suspension of the bombing was finally passed by a narrow margin, the delegates from New York protested by putting on black armbands and singing: "We Shall Overcome." Which made Brigid proud to be a New Yorker.

The next task was to nominate the party's candidate for president. McCarthy was still in the race, and his supporters made valiant efforts to overcome the tide that was flowing toward Humphrey, who hadn't run in any of the primaries but had collected votes behind the scenes from the mainstream delegates. In the end, Humphry won the nomination, and there were cries of "No! No!" from the antiwar delegates.

Meanwhile, on the streets the police were brutally repressing the protesters, firing tear gas into the crowds and beating them. From what Brigid could see on television there were instances of violence by the protesters, but the overwhelming majority of them were peaceful. At a peaceful demonstration in Grant Park the protesters were singing along with Peter, Paul, and Mary, and that made her proud of them. She wondered if Megan and Teri were among that crowd, along with people like the girls from Mount St. Vincent.

The newscasters estimated that there were around ten thousand protesters in Grant Park when for some reason the police broke into the crowd and started beating a protester. The crowd reacted by pelting the police with unidentifiable objects and shouting epithets at them. The police fired tear gas into the crowd and chased the fleeing protesters, beating them with clubs and rifle butts. Some of the protesters broke away and marched down Michigan Avenue to the Conrad Hilton, where they were stopped by more police and were indiscriminately beaten. By then from what Brigid could see, the crowd had turned into a mob whose mission had changed from antiwar to antipolice, shouting "Kill the pigs!" And that didn't make her proud of them.

All the time she had been scanning the crowds, trying to spot Megan and Teri, and at one point she thought she saw them being beaten by the police, but since they wouldn't have been doing anything violent she saw no reason for the police to attack them, and she remembered how well the New York police had treated her and Laura. So she doubted that the girls she had seen being beaten were Megan and Teri.

That night she went to bed feeling depressed. With Humphrey as the Democratic candidate it didn't matter who won the election. Either way, the war would continue, and boys her age or even younger would continue being sent to die in Vietnam.

A week later she returned to St. Catherine for the fall semester. She was looking forward to seeing Laura and to hearing about her trip to Canada. When she didn't see Laura in any of her classes she assumed at first that they were assigned to different sections, but then she began to wonder if Laura had decided to stay in Canada.

That evening she called Laura's parents. Her father answered, and after Brigid identified herself as a friend of Laura's he gruffly said: "You can talk with her mother."

Brigid waited, and finally Laura's mother got on the line.

"I'm sorry to bother you," Brigid said, "but I haven't seen Laura in any of my classes. Did she decide to stay in Canada?"

"We don't know," Laura's mother said in a strained voice. "We haven't heard from her."

"She hasn't called you or written to you?"

"No, she hasn't. And I understand why she wouldn't want to tell her father what she's doing, but she has no reason not to tell me. I'm on her side."

"Well, maybe she's afraid that the FBI could trace a phone call or a letter."

"Yeah, I know. She explained that to me, and I told her not to worry about it. The FBI has more important things to do than to go after a draft dodger in Canada."

"From what she told me before she left, she didn't plan to stay in Canada. She planned to return for the fall semester. But she could have changed her mind."

"Yeah. She could have."

Feeling sympathy for the woman, Brigid said: "I wish I could help you contact her, but she only told me that Owen was in Nova Scotia. She didn't say exactly where."

"I believe she's all right, but I wish I *knew*. I just don't like the uncertainty."

"I understand. Well, I'll let you know if I hear from her, and please let me know if you hear from her."

"I will," Laura's mother said. "And thanks for calling."

On Tuesday of the following week Brigid went to the meeting of the CPF, where Megan reported on their experience in Chicago. Megan had a bandage on her forehead as a result of being beaten by the police. Though she and Teri had been demonstrating peacefully, they had both been arrested and put into jail. Looking at Brigid, Megan said with a wry smile that she and Teri were now members of the jail alumnae.

After the meeting Brigid joined Megan and Teri at the pub, and they talked about their experiences. When Megan asked her where Laura was she told her that Laura had gone to Canada to be with her boyfriend for a while, and that she might have decided to stay there. They agreed that if Laura had decided to stay there she was in a better place.

A few days later Brigid got a phone call from Laura's mother who told her she had gotten a call from Owen. He said he hadn't seen Laura or heard from her since she had told him she was coming to Canada, and he wondered if she had decided not to come. Since it was beginning to look like Laura was missing, her mother asked Brigid if she and Mr. Hughes could meet with her on Saturday. They would drive down from Poughkeepsie and meet wherever Brigid preferred. They arranged to meet at Brigid's house.

By now Brigid felt it was time to tell her mother about the situation, which she did in the kitchen while they cleaned up after dinner that evening. Brigid's mother asked her some questions, which were the same questions she was asking herself. Could Laura have decided simply to run away from everything? Could she have met someone on her trip who lured her away? Could she have been the victim of a predator?

Brigid lay awake that night speculating on the answers to these questions, and in the morning they were still buzzing around in her mind like hornets.

Laura's parents arrived at eleven. Her father was a big guy with buzz-cut blond hair and belligerent blue eyes. Her mother was petite and delicately pretty. Brigid invited them to come into the living room, where they sat down together on the sofa.

"Thanks for seeing us," Mrs. Hughes said.

"I hope I can help you," Brigid said.

"As I said on the phone, I got a phone call from Owen, who said he hadn't seen Laura or heard from her since she told him she was going to Canada, and he thought maybe she had changed her mind. Do you think that's possible?"

"It's possible," Brigid said, "but if she did, she would have gone home. Where else could she have gone?"

"Could she have had another boyfriend?" Mr. Hughes asked.

"I don't think so. She never mentioned another boyfriend."

"Maybe she didn't want you to know about him."

"Maybe. But we shared everything with each other."

"Do you think she could have met someone on her way to Canada?" Mrs. Hughes asked.

"That's more likely than her having another boyfriend. It's a long trip, and she could have met someone on the train."

"Someone who could have talked her into going somewhere else?" Mr. Hughes said.

"Yeah. But I can't imagine her going off with some guy she met on the train. She loves Owen, and she's completely loyal to him."

"I don't know why," Mr. Hughes growled. "He's a cowardly deserter."

"Please, Mike," Mrs. Hughes said. "He's not a deserter, he's a conscientious objector."

"You mean like that boxer who took a Muslim name."

Interrupting their family argument, Brigid said: "It's possible that she simply decided to run away from everything."

"What would she want to run away from?" Mr. Hughes asked.

"I don't know." As she confronted his dour face it occurred to her that Laura might have wanted to run away from her father, but she didn't say it. "There are always things that people might want to run away from."

"Did something happen to her this summer?" Mrs. Hughes asked.

"No, not that I know of." Brigid refrained from mentioning the night they had spent in jail.

"What were you doing anyway?" Mr. Hughes asked.

Since she could no longer pretend that they were doing an internship, Brigid admitted: "We were demonstrating against the war."

"Like you were doing with that lefty group at the college?"

"It's not a lefty group, it's a Catholic group."

"Well, I'm a Catholic, and I'd never take the side of a commie country against our country."

"We're not against our country," Brigid said. "We're against the war."

"You don't know anything about war."

"I know what this war has done to people."

"No, you don't. You've never been in a war yourself."

"I haven't, but my father has."

"Where did he serve?"

"In Italy."

"Italy," Mr. Hughes said scornfully. "What happened there was nothing like what happened at Guadalcanal, Okinawa, and Iwo Jima."

"This isn't helping us find Laura," Mrs. Hughes interjected.

"I'm sorry," Brigid said.

"It might help us," Mr. Hughes said. "If she spent the summer demonstrating against the war, she might have gone to Chicago and joined the demonstrations there."

"Do you think she could have?" Mrs. Hughes asked Brigid.

"Some members of our group went to Chicago, but I'm sure she wasn't with them. At our meeting two days ago they asked me where she was."

"Okay. So let's assume that she was planning to go to Canada. When was the last time you saw her?"

"The morning she left. I said goodbye to her in front our building. I offered to go with her to Penn Station, but she said it wasn't necessary."

"How was she getting to Penn Station?"

"She was taking the subway from Astor Place to Grand Central, and then the shuttle to Times Square, and then the subway downtown to Penn Station."

"Maybe something happened to her on the way."

"Yeah, but if it happened in the city you would have been informed about it."

"Then maybe it happened on the train. How long would it have taken her to get to Montreal?"

"I think she said about eleven hours."

"Where would it have stopped along the way?"

"At Poughkeepsie," Mr. Hughes said. "And also at Albany. I don't know where else."

"Then at some point she could have gotten off the train," Mrs. Hughes said.

"For what reason?" Brigid asked. "As far as I know, the only purpose of her trip was to go and see Owen in Nova Scotia."

"When she arrived at Montreal, how was she getting to Nova Scotia?"

"She was taking a train to Halifax."

"Do you know how long that would have taken?"

"I have no idea, but she said the whole trip would take about a day and a half."

"So there was plenty of time for something to happen to her."

"Yeah, there was."

After a silence Mrs. Hughes said: "Then whatever happened to her, it must have happened on the way from New York to Nova Scotia."

Brigid agreed, but she could only imagine what it was.

Kieran attended the next meeting of the CPF, and he led a discussion about the just war doctrine. In his studies for the next stage of Jesuit formation he had thought a lot about the doctrine and he had revised his position on it.

Seeing him at the meeting, Brigid had to contain her feelings. She was still in love with him, more than ever, maybe because of his absence from her, and she still wished that somehow she could get him to love her the way she loved him. As he talked to the group she listened to him and followed his arguments as if they were a trail that would lead her to his heart.

"I've concluded," he said, winding up, "that the just war doctrine isn't valid."

"As I understand your position," Megan said, "we shouldn't use the doctrine to show that the war in Vietnam is wrong."

"Exactly. If you use it for that purpose, you can also use it to justify another war, and I don't believe that war can be justified for any reason."

"What about World War II?" a girl asked.

"At first glance, it looks like a just war if there ever was one. But if we examine what we did in that war, it undermines our justification. I mean the bombing of civilians, especially our use of nuclear weapons. There's no way you can justify that."

"So we should have let the Germans and the Japanese take over the world?"

"We could have found another way to stop them. We didn't have to go to war."

"But the Japanese attacked us."

"They did, but do you know why they attacked us?"

There was a silence.

"They attacked us because we cut off their oil. Instead of cutting off their oil, we should have talked with them and tried to understand their needs."

"You mean like we should be doing now with the North Vietnamese," Megan said.

"Yes. We're bombing them, not talking with them. So we don't want peace. We only want to prolong the war."

"Then we should focus our efforts," Sister Audrey said, "on getting our government to stop the bombing and to talk with the North Vietnamese."

"You should," Kieran said. "And you should avoid using any kind of violence."

"That wasn't your position the last time you were with us," Father Justin pointed out. "You argued in favor of using violence against things, not against people. You supported the action of the Catonsville Nine, and yesterday a group of activists that included one of our founders, Jim Forrest, did a similar action in Milwaukee by taking files of draft records and setting them on fire with homemade napalm. Do you still support the action of the Catonsville Nine, and do you support the action of the Milwaukee Fourteen?"

"I don't support either of those actions."

"So you're against using any kind of violence to achieve our goals?"

"That's my position now."

"What changed your mind?"

"It was my experience with two members of your group last summer," Kieran said humbly.

"You mean Brigid and Laura?" Megan said.

Kieran nodded, looking at Brigid in a way that made her feel special.

"Have you heard from Laura?" a girl asked her.

"No, I haven't," Brigid said.

"I assume she's in Canada with her boyfriend," Megan said.

"I hope she is. But I don't know."

When the meeting ended, Brigid went out into the hall. She paused for a moment, and then she realized that Kieran had come after her.

"Can you go to the pub with me?" he asked her.

"Yeah, sure." She guessed he wanted to talk about Laura, and she headed for the pub with him alongside her.

As soon as they had the privacy of a booth he said: "You said you don't know if Laura's in Canada with her boyfriend."

"Yeah," she said. "Her boyfriend called her parents and told them he hadn't seen her or heard from her."

"When was that?"

"A week ago. And she left for Canada a month ago."

"By now she should be there."

"Yeah. But her boyfriend says she's not there."

After a fraught silence Kieran asked: "Do you think something happened to her?"

"I don't know what to think. I talked with her parents last week, and they think something happened to her on the way from New York to Nova Scotia."

"What could have happened?"

"Well, she could have met someone on the train and gone off with him."

"That doesn't sound like Laura."

"It doesn't. But it could have happened."

"I guess it could have. Or she could have been assaulted."

"I thought of that possibility, but I don't see how it could have happened on the train."

"She could have been forced to get off the train."

"But someone would have seen that happen and reported it to the police."

Kieran stared at the table in silence, and then, raising his head, he said: "She could have gone somewhere on her own."

"Like where?" Brigid asked.

"Laura's religious, and she could have gone on a retreat before joining her boyfriend."

"She didn't mention anything like that."

"Maybe she met someone on the train who encouraged her to do it. There are monasteries near Montreal, and maybe she went to one of them."

Brigid liked this idea because it would mean that Laura was alive. "But if she decided to do that, why wouldn't she tell her parents or her boyfriend?"

"Maybe she wanted them to worry about her."

"Why would she want them to worry about her?"

"So they'd value her more when she reappeared. You never did that with your parents?"

"No, but I can see Laura doing that. She doesn't have a lot of self-confidence."

"Of course it's only a speculation."

"Yeah, I know." She looked across the table at him, wishing she could get through the barrier that kept them apart. "How are things at Fordham?"

"They're going well. I'm advancing toward my goal."

She knew what that goal was, and she didn't see how she could compete with it. Offering her body hadn't worked, and her mind wasn't at the same level as his. So all she could say was: "I'm happy for you."

For the next few weeks she put the summer behind her and focused on her work in the nursing program. During that period she attended a meeting of the CPF at which the main subject for discussion was the involuntary redeployment of twenty-four thousand troops in Vietnam, which suggested that at the upper levels of government there were people who still believed they could win the war. It made Brigid remember how she and Laura had at least temporarily stopped those boys from going into the induction center, and she wished they could have stopped them permanently. Imagining what would happen to them, she felt that it might have been a good thing after all if Kieran had gone ahead with his plan to bomb the building that held the records for the boys who would be drafted next.

When she got home one afternoon there was a message for her from a detective in the Poughkeepsie police department. Her mother, who had the day off from her nursing shifts, had taken the message, and giving it to her, she said she thought it was about Laura, though the detective hadn't said what it was about. From their conversation before the visit by Laura's parents her mother knew about Laura's disappearance. In fact, her mother knew what they were really doing in the city, though she still didn't know that they shared the apartment with the man who was their mentor or that they spent a night in jail.

Brigid returned the call of the detective and arranged to meet him two days later at her house. Their meeting was short because Brigid had nothing to add to what she had already told Laura's parents, who presumably had given this information to the police. She had the feeling that the detective was only following the procedure for a missing person, and that he believed that Laura, like so many young people, had simply decided to run away.

A month later she got a call from a private detective whose name was Bill Leonard, and she arranged to meet him at her house. When she opened the door she saw a big man, older than her father, with roughly combed gray hair and weary blue eyes. She invited him into the house and led him into the living room, where they sat in chairs.

"I was hired by Laura's father," the detective said with a heavy Bronx accent. "He said the police aren't giving the case enough attention. And they probably aren't. They have so many cases of missing persons that they don't have time to investigate them."

Brigid nodded in agreement. "I had a feeling that the detective who questioned me was only following procedure."

"Well, I have time to investigate this case. So tell me about your relationship with her."

"My relationship with her?" It wasn't the question that she had expected him to begin with. "We were friends."

"Were you close friends?"

"I think we were. We shared secrets with each other."

"Tell me a secret that she shared with you."

Brigid hesitated, not wanting to betray her friend's confidence but at the same time wanting to help the detective find her. "She shared with me the secret that she was in love with a guy who went to Canada to avoid the draft."

"You mean Owen Webster?"

"Yeah, Owen. I didn't know his last name."

"Did she ever tell you where he was in Canada?"

"She told me he was in Nova Scotia, but she didn't tell me exactly where."

"As far as you know, she was going there to see him?"

"That's what she said. She was going there to see him but not to stay. She was planning to return and complete her degree."

"She could have decided to stay there."

"She could have. But Owen called her mother and told her he hadn't seen Laura or heard from her."

Bill smiled faintly. "Yeah, I know. That's what he told her mother, but it doesn't prove she isn't with him. He could have lied to her mother."

"Why would he lie?"

"So her father wouldn't go to Nova Scotia and bring her home."

"Laura's twenty. Her father couldn't make her come home."

"No, he couldn't. But he could make things difficult for her boyfriend." Bill paused. "You've met her father, so you know how he feels about Owen. He can't stand the idea of her living with a cowardly deserter, as he calls him. If he found them, he could report Owen to the police and have him deported."

"I guess he could."

"If I was Owen, I'd call her parents and tell them I hadn't seen their daughter. I'd want them to believe she wasn't with me."

"But why would Laura go along with him?"

"Why do you think? You just told me that she's in love with him."

Brigid considered. "I think it would be hard for her, but I can see why she'd want her father to believe she isn't with her boyfriend. If he believes it, then he won't go to Nova Scotia and look for her there."

"Right," Bill said. "But if he believes she *is* with her boyfriend, then he'll hire a private detective to find her."

"Is that why he hired you?"

"Yeah, that's why he hired me."

"So how are you going to find them?"

"I'm going to Nova Scotia tomorrow, and I'll look for them until I find them."

Encouraged by his confidence, Brigid said: "So you believe she's with her boyfriend?"

"I believe she is," Bill said. "I don't know where else she could be, do you?"

"I don't know, but she could have gone on a retreat."

"You mean a retreat in the religious sense?"

"Yeah. So if you're going to Montreal, you could ask the monasteries about her."

"I'll ask them, but I still believe she's with her boyfriend."

"I hope she is," Brigid said softly.

With a look of suspicion Bill said: "You haven't heard from her, have you?"

"No, I haven't."

"Are you sure you haven't?"

"Yeah, I'm sure. Why would I lie?"

"For the same reason that her boyfriend would lie," Bill said. "So her father won't go to Nova Scotia and bring her home."

"I wouldn't do that to her parents," Brigid assured him.

"You wouldn't? You said you were close friends. So you could have a secret that you're not sharing with her parents."

"I wish I did, but I don't. Believe me."

For a while the detective scanned her face as if he was trying to determine whether she was being truthful, and finally he said: "I believe you."

After he had gone she went out into the backyard and sat on the picnic table. Since it made sense, and since it gave her hope that Laura was alive, she was receptive to Bill's theory that Laura wanted her parents to believe she wasn't with her boyfriend so that her father wouldn't go to Nova Scotia and bring her home. Of course if Bill was right, then Brigid had to admit that Laura hadn't trusted her with this secret, and they no longer had a bond of sharing secrets. That was a loss, a painful loss. Yet as she lingered in the autumn sunlight the hope that Laura was alive prevailed over the feeling of loss.

SEVEN

ON ELECTION DAY she voted with her parents, and she watched the results with them on television. It was a close election, and she finally went to bed without knowing who had won. When she learned the next morning that Nixon had won she wasn't surprised but she was depressed. It was a big letdown from the wave of enthusiasm that had carried her and Laura from door to door in New Hampshire asking people to vote for McCarthy.

The next meeting of the CPF was like a wake, and while they talked about continuing their efforts to make people realize that the war in Vietnam was wrong, without the prospect of a real change in government they lacked an objective. And they were discouraged by the fact that although they and others like them had succeeded in turning most people against the war, their country had elected a president who embodied the crusade against communism that had led to intervention in a colony's war of independence, abandoning the principle of self-determination and embracing the policy of projecting power in world affairs through the use of war.

Brigid could usually hide her feelings when she had to, but in this situation she didn't feel any need to hide them from her mother, and one evening while she was helping her mother clean up after dinner she revealed them. It began with her mother asking if there was something wrong.

"Yeah, there is," she said, drying a plate.

"What is it?"

"Everything."

"What in particular?"

"Well, the war is wrong. We're killing people for no good reason."

"The war *is* wrong," her mother agreed, washing a plate.

"The boys we send to die in Vietnam are poor, and they're

111

mostly black and brown. We saw them going into the induction center."

"That's wrong."

"We kill people like Martin Luther King who want social justice. If anyone tries to change things, we assassinate him."

"And that's wrong."

"I understand why people get so frustrated that they resort to violence. But they shouldn't have to resort to violence. There should be a better way."

"Isn't that the mission of your group? To show people a better way?"

"Yeah, that's our mission, but after all our efforts most people voted to continue the war."

"You think they did? I thought both candidates talked about ending the war."

"They talked about ending the war, but they didn't offer a way of doing it. We haven't stopped bombing North Vietnam, and now we're also bombing Laos."

"And that's wrong," her mother said.

"But there's something else—" She hesitated, wondering if her mother would understand. "It's Laura. I told you her father hired a private detective to find her. Well, he went to Nova Scotia to look for her, and that was more than three weeks ago."

"You haven't heard from him?"

"No, I haven't. Of course if he found her, I wouldn't hear from him. I'd hear from Laura."

"Nova Scotia's a big area. He's probably still looking for her."

"I hope so." She took another plate. "The detective believes she's with her boyfriend, even though her boyfriend called her mother and told her Laura wasn't with him."

"If she *was* with him, why would he lie about it?"

"So her father wouldn't go to Nova Scotia and bring her home. He doesn't approve of the boyfriend," Brigid explained. "He was a marine in World War II and he calls the boyfriend a cowardly deserter for going to Canada to avoid the draft. He doesn't accept that her boyfriend's a Quaker, acting on his religious beliefs."

"Then Laura could be with him?"

"Yeah, she could be. The detective believes she's going along with her boyfriend's story so her father won't know where she is. Her father could make things difficult for her boyfriend. He could report him to the police and have him deported."

Her mother sighed. "Well, that's not a good situation, but there's nothing you can do about it. They have to work it out as a family."

"I know they do. But Laura's my friend, and if she's with her boyfriend now she should trust me with that information. She shouldn't hide it from me."

"How would she tell you where she is?"

"She could call me. She could use the phone that her boyfriend used to call her mother."

After a silence her mother said: "You want to believe the detective's theory that she's with her boyfriend because you hope she's still alive, but you don't believe it because you think she'd tell you where she is. So you're worried about her."

"I am," she admitted. She put down the plate and went into her mother's arms.

In early December the detective called her and told her the results of his investigation. He had traveled around Nova Scotia, going from town to town and asking people if there was a young American man living among them. He didn't have a photo of Owen, but he described him based on what Laura's mother had told him. He learned that there were a number of Americans in Nova Scotia who fit the description of Owen, and he met with them, one by one, until he found Owen, who was living in an apartment above a garage in a small town. Owen denied that Laura was with him, and Bill didn't see any signs of a female living in the apartment, but to make sure the girl wasn't hiding or hadn't dyed her hair to disguise herself, he stayed in the town for almost two weeks and spied on Owen, watching him do his daily routine, and he didn't see Owen with a girl at any time. From the way Owen looked and talked and acted he was heartbroken by the absence of Laura, and he had no way of knowing if she had fallen out of love with him and decided not to come and see him. Bill reassured him that she wasn't at home, and she wasn't at college, and she was officially a missing person, but that didn't seem to help the poor guy. Before ending the phone conversation Bill said he had asked about Laura at the only monastery he could find near Montreal, and Laura hadn't been there. So he concluded that something had happened to her on the way to Canada.

Brigid told her mother what the detective had reported, and her mother tried to comfort her. But now her sorrow wasn't over the loss of a bond with her best friend, it was over the apparent loss of her friend. If something had happened to Laura, then it must have killed her or incapacitated her, or else they would have heard from her. Imagining what might have happened, Brigid recoiled from her lurid thoughts and tried to believe that Laura would turn up some day alive. In this state of mind she was tempted to call Kieran and ask him to meet with her, so she could share her feelings with him, but she finally decided not to because it would stir up other feelings, which would make things even worse. Instead, she went alone to St. Brigid and lit a candle and prayed for a miracle.

For the next two weeks she focused on studying for her final exams. Most of the time her effort to learn the course material took her mind off the mystery of what had happened to Laura, and she put everything she had into doing well. After finishing her last exam she went to the pub with some classmates who wanted to celebrate, but she didn't feel any joy, she only felt relief from the ordeal of final exams.

At home she went to her room and flopped on her bed and closed her eyes, exhausted. Her mother had to wake her up for dinner, which she sat through like a zombie. After dinner, for a distraction, she agreed to play a game of chess with Brady, who usually beat her. She didn't mind losing to him because he was a bright kid.

After three games, which he easily won, she said goodnight to her parents and went to bed. She slept until nine the next morning, and she spent most of her vacation sleeping. She attended the obligatory family events like Christmas Eve dinner and Christmas Day mass, but she didn't do much else. And her parents didn't annoy her by trying to rouse her out of her stupor. Her mother must have told her father about the disappearance of Laura and explained how it had affected her. So they let her alone, though they didn't ignore her.

She was glad when the spring semester began. She had been assigned to St. John's Hospital for a clinical practicum, and she was looking forward to that because it would get her out of the classroom and into the real world of nursing. She would be at the hospital on Tuesdays and Thursdays, under the supervision of a nurse who had received her degree from St. Catherine and had a good reputation among the students.

As Brigid was getting up from her desk after her first classroom meeting in medical-surgical nursing, a girl came over to her and said: "Hi. I'm Dana. I see that we're both assigned to St. John's for the clinical in this course."

"Hi, I'm Brigid. I'm glad to meet you." Of course she had seen this girl before in classes, in the hallways, and in the cafeteria, but they didn't really know each other. Brigid had been occupied by her relationship with Laura, and Dana evidently had so many friends that she didn't need another. She had short brown hair and brown eyes that bubbled over with energy. And she had a laugh that carried over the din of the cafeteria and made people want to join the fun that she and her friends were having.

"If you need a ride there, I can give you one. I have a car."

"Well, I was going to walk there, but it would be nice to have a ride. Thanks."

"We're supposed to be there at eight in the morning," Dana said. "I could pick you up. Where do you live?"

"On Greenvale Avenue, between Palisade and Broadway." She gave Dana the house number.

"Oh, that's perfect. I live on Portland Place, so you're right on my way there."

She remembered that Teri lived on Tower Place, which was one street over from Portland Place. "Do you know Teri Ryan?"

"Yeah. I've known her forever," Dana said, her eyes lighting up. "When we were kids we used to play baseball on Tower Place. But I haven't seen much of her in a while. She got into music, and then she joined that antiwar group."

Brigid could tell that the Catholic Peace Fellowship wasn't a group that Dana would join, but it wasn't a putdown, it was only something she wouldn't do. "Teri has an amazing voice. Have you heard her sing?"

"Yeah, I have. On special occasions she sings at our church."

"You mean Sacred Heart?"

Dana nodded. "I have to go there with my family. If I ever missed a holy day of obligation, my father would kill me."

"Did you go to Sacred Heart High School?"

"Yeah, but I lasted there only three weeks. I was kicked out for unruly behavior, and I've been in the doghouse ever since."

"So where did you go to high school?"

"Gorton. And I survived."

After they parted in the hallway Brigid felt better than she had in a while. She was glad to have met Dana, who was different from anyone she had known before. In a way she admired this girl for getting kicked out of Sacred Heart and surviving at Gorton. She concluded that Dana must be wild, and she must be tough, but she also must be serious enough to have been admitted to the nursing program at St. Catherine.

The next morning Dana arrived to pick her up at quarter of eight, as she had promised. She was driving a car that was old and battered. While idling in front of Brigid's house its engine rattled. But it was a car, and when Brigid got into the passenger seat Dana assured her that it was safe and reliable. She said her father had bought it for her as a reward for good behavior, and he knew cars. He had worked as a mechanic before he joined the Yonkers police force.

They got to the hospital a few minutes early, and they checked in with their supervisor, a stout woman who could have been their mother. From the way she treated them Brigid could tell that she was a strict disciplinarian, but she understood that they were young and inexperienced. At the same time it was also clear that she had high expectations of them.

In a room for nurses they changed into the scrubs that would identify them as students, and they followed their supervisor, whose name was Joyce, to the surgery floor, where they were assigned to work with nurses.

The day was long but also fulfilling, and when it ended at four o'clock Brigid wanted to go home and rest. But Dana talked her into going to a bar on Lake Avenue near where she lived. It was called O'Malley's, and when they got there it was filling with people who looked like they were coming from work. There were a lot more guys than girls. Some guys at the bar made room for them, and they sat on the stools with guys all around them. Dana called to the bartender, whom she obviously knew, and got him to come and take their order. Since Dana had a beer on tap, Brigid had one too, instead of the bottled beer she had at the college pub.

"This is one of my regular places," Dana told her. "I've been coming here since I was fifteen. Of course I had a fake ID."

"I like this place," Brigid said, looking around.

"It's the best place around here. It's a neighborhood place, but people come here from everywhere."

She spotted Teri seated in a booth with her twin brother. "There's Teri. Did you come here with her when you were fifteen?"

"Oh, yeah. She was a wild girl then."

"Is she different now?"

"She's more serious. She has a boyfriend, which makes a difference."

Brigid had met Teri's boyfriend. His name was Andre, he played the piano professionally, and he was very nice. "Do you have a boyfriend?"

"No. I don't go out with guys for long. I get tired of them quickly, so I move on to another guy. It's much more interesting that way."

"I guess it would be."

"Do you have a boyfriend?"

"No, I don't. In fact, I don't have much experience with guys."
Dana looked at her closely. "You like guys, don't you?"

"Oh, yeah. I just never met one that turned me on." Of course
that wasn't true. From the moment she first saw Kieran he had
turned her on, but she didn't know Dana well enough to share this
secret.

"I understand. It's better to be picky. I mean, there're so many
guys in the world you can always find a better one."

At that moment a guy, who had approached from behind them,
said to Dana: "You seem to know the bartender. Could you get
him to come over here?"

"Sure," Dana said after turning around to look at him. The guy
had friendly brown eyes and broad shoulders. Another guy was
standing next to him. This guy was taller, with fair hair, a finely
chiseled face, and wild blue eyes.

Dana yelled at the bartender, whose name was Pete, and got
his attention.

Talking between Brigid and Dana, the guy with brown eyes
ordered two beers. With the guys standing there, the girls had to
pause their conversation, and in the awkward silence the guy who
had ordered the beers said: "Thanks. We've never been here
before."

"You haven't? Where are you from?"

"We're from Yonkers."

"Where in Yonkers?"

"We live on Warburton Avenue, a few blocks north of the
museum."

"In one of those old Victorian houses?"

"Yeah. We have an apartment in one of them."

"I knew a guy who lived in one of those houses. He was going
to Manhattan College at the time. He had several roommates, and
those guys really knew how to party."

"We went to Manhattan," the guy said. "We graduated two
years ago, and now we're working at Otis Elevator."

"You must be engineers."

"Yeah. We work in the design area."

"So if I get stuck in an elevator, I can blame you?"

"You can if you ever get out."

The guys finally introduced themselves. The guy with the friendly brown eyes was Glenn, and the guy with the wild blue eyes was Tommy. By now the girls had turned their stools around so that they were facing the guys.

They had another round of beers, and they continued talking, exchanging information about each other. When the guys learned that the girls were nursing students it seemed to heighten their interest in them. Aware of the perception that girls in nursing, because they were familiar with the human body and all its functions, were less uptight about sex than other girls, Brigid raised her guard.

When they had finished the second round Dana motioned to the bartender, making the sign of a check in the air. The guys made an offer to pay their tab, but Dana declined it. She paid the bartender, and then slid off the stool, saying: "It was nice to meet you. We'll see you around. You can have our seats."

"Thanks," Glenn said. "Are you sure you don't want to stay?"

"We can't. We have an engagement."

They left the place and walked to Dana's car, which she had parked down the street. They got into the car, and Dana said there was a restaurant on Saw Mill River Road where they could have dinner. It was almost six, and Brigid was expected home for dinner, but wanting to stay with Dana and talk, she decided to call home from wherever they were going and tell her mother she was eating out with a friend.

The restaurant was in a commercial block in the middle of an industrial area. Knowing where to look for a parking spot, Dana found one, and they walked from there to the restaurant, which was Italian. They found a table for two in the corner, and before sitting down Brigid called home from a pay phone near the entrance.

Explaining that she didn't have room for any more beer, Dana ordered a carafe of white wine, and they perused the menu.

"Do you know Italian food?" Dana asked her.

"Oh, yeah. My mother's Italian."

"So is my mother. But you look Irish, so your father must be Irish like my father. I guess there was something going on between Irish guys and Italian girls."

"They were both Catholic, so they went to the same churches and schools."

"Yeah, they did. Well, they have good Italian food here, though it's probably not as good as your mother's."

They ordered pastas, and while they were waiting for their food, sipping wine, Dana asked: "So what do you think of those two guys?"

"I don't know," Brigid said. "What do you think?"

"I think they're attractive, and they're smart enough to get engineering degrees at Manhattan."

"And they have good jobs."

Dana smiled. "We sound like we're evaluating them as potential husbands."

"I wouldn't go that far."

"I wouldn't either. But we could have a good time with them."

"Maybe we could."

"I could tell that Tommy likes you. Did you notice how he kept looking at you?"

"No, I didn't."

"He couldn't take his eyes off you."

"Well, I could tell that Glenn likes you."

"So why don't we go to O'Malley's on Thursday and see what happens."

"You think they'll be there?"

Dana nodded. "I know they'll be there. Want to bet?"

"Okay," Brigid said. "I'll bet a round of beer."

Dana won the bet. The guys were sitting at the bar, and they both got up to offer their seats. They had a round, and then they went to a booth where they had another round. The guys suggested that they eat there, and Brigid let her mother know she wouldn't be home for dinner. After eating burgers they hung out in the booth for a while, and then the guys suggested that they go to their apartment on Warburton and have a drink there. Dana declined, saying they had to go because they had a lab test early the next morning. The guys then asked them if they could meet on Friday or Saturday, and Dana said they weren't free on those days, but they were free next Tuesday. Brigid understood her friend's strategy of playing hard enough to get so that the guys would feel deprived but not so hard that they would be discouraged.

For the next two weeks they met with the guys on Tuesdays and Thursdays. They kept declining the invitation to go to the guys' apartment for a drink until finally on Thursday of the second week they said that they were free that Saturday. By then Brigid felt at ease with Tommy, and she appreciated the fact that instead of always talking about himself as most guys did, he asked questions about her, and he showed a fair amount of interest in her as a person. She learned that he had grown up in the Bronx and gone to a Catholic high school there. His father was a fireman, and his mother had a clerical job at a Catholic elementary school. So he had been raised with the same values as she had. Yet occasionally she caught a flash of something wild in his eyes, which she had noticed when she met him, and she wondered where it came from and what it meant.

The guys had offered to pick them up at their homes on Saturday, but at that point Dana wasn't ready to let the guys know where they lived, so they met at O'Malley's and had a drink there, and then they paired off, with Dana and Glenn in her car and Brigid and Tommy in his car. They drove to a restaurant on Central Avenue called Candlelight Inn, where they drank beer and ate wings that were truly awesome. After hanging out there for a while they drove back on Underhill Road to the Saw Mill River Parkway and exited at Hastings, where they got onto Warburton Avenue and headed south. The house was a mansion which must have been built by a wealthy family and now was divided into several units. The guys' apartment was on the second floor, and it had a living room, a kitchen, and two bedrooms.

They sat in the living room with Dana and Glenn on the sofa

and Brigid and Tommy in the two easy chairs. Glenn had mixed some drinks, which he got out of the refrigerator, and brought a tray with four glasses on it, saying: "I hope you like Manhattans."

"I love them," Dana said, reaching for a glass.

Brigid hesitated, but finally took a glass. There were red cherries in the glasses, and she didn't know what you were supposed to do with them. She watched Dana, who popped her cherry into her mouth and smiled contentedly, so Brigid did the same with hers. The drink was strong, and it went to her head.

Tommy had put on the radio, which was playing "I Can't Get Next to You" by the Temptations, and Brigid immersed herself in the music. Glenn brought another tray of drinks, which went down faster than the first batch.

When Glenn and Dana went off to his bedroom Tommy got up and asked Brigid to join him on the sofa. It didn't take him long to kiss her, and since it felt good she kissed him back. They were deep in kissing when she became aware of the cries of pleasure coming from Dana. Like her laugh, they carried and made Brigid want to join the fun that her friend was having. So when Tommy took her hand and raised her from the sofa and led her toward his bedroom, she more than willingly went with him, feeling that the time had come.

Later, when he saw the blood on the sheet Tommy said: "I'm sorry. You should have told me you were a virgin."

"It's okay," she assured him.

"I hope it didn't hurt."

"It didn't," she lied. At least maybe it wouldn't the next time.

He put his arms around her and held her.

She was awakened by Dana, rapping on the door and yelling: "Come on. We gotta go. It's eleven thirty."

Knowing that Dana would be in serious trouble with her father if she wasn't home by midnight, Brigid got up and gathered her clothes and put them on while Tommy dragged himself out of bed with a sheet wrapped around him.

Dana was waiting for her in the living room, anxious to leave. With her hair brushed and her clothes neatened, she looked as if nothing had happened.

Brigid paused long enough to kiss Tommy goodnight, and then she followed Dana out of the house and down to the street. They got into the car, and Dana turned into a street that did switchbacks up the hill to Broadway.

As they rounded another corner Dana asked: "How was it?"

"It was okay," Brigid said. "It was my first time."

"It was? Oh, no, you're not on the pill?"

"No. I'm not." It was only a few days since her last period, so she figured that her risk of getting pregnant was minimal. "But I'll have to get on it."

"I can help you," Dana said. "I have a great doctor. I'll refer you to her."

"Okay. Thanks." She was glad that the doctor was a woman.

It was eleven fifty when Dana dropped her off at her house. She watched the car drive away, hoping that Dana would make it home by midnight.

She found her mother in the family room, watching a talk show on television.

"How was your date?" her mother asked.

"Oh, it was okay," Brigid said, afraid that her mother might somehow detect that she had lost her virginity. "We went to a place called Candlelight Inn and hung out there."

"Did you get something to eat?"

"Yeah. They had awesome wings."

Her mother looked at her closely. "Were you there the whole evening?"

"No. We stopped at O'Malley's afterward and had drinks there."

"Is that the place on Lake Avenue?"

"Yeah. We go there after work at the hospital."

"Your father knows the owner. He's a good customer."

It occurred to her that her father could check to see if she had been at O'Malley's late in the evening, but she decided it wasn't likely. Her parents trusted her.

"Well, you should go to bed," her mother concluded.

"Yeah, I should." She kissed her mother goodnight and headed upstairs, conscious of having moved to another level of deception: from hiding the fact that she and Laura were sharing the apartment with a man to hiding the fact that she had just had sex with a guy.

As she lay in bed that night she examined her feelings for Tommy and compared them with her feelings for Kieran. She liked Tommy, and she looked forward to having some good times with him, but she didn't love him the way she loved Kieran. In fact, there was no comparison between her feelings.

For the next six weeks she and Dana double-dated with Tommy and Glenn. They would go to a place for drinks and dinner and then go to the guys' apartment, where they almost always ended up in bed. In the meantime Brigid had stopped attending the CPF meetings, partly because she didn't have the time and partly because they made her think of Laura.

A high point during this period was their discovery of The Upstairs Room, which a girl had told Dana about. It was down on South Broadway in an area that was deteriorating. As its name suggested, it was on the second floor of a building above a store. It was just a big room with a bar and a disk jockey who played songs that were perfect for dancing. On the floor, which felt like a trampoline with all those people bouncing up and down on it, Brigid discovered that she loved to dance, and Tommy was a good partner. As they moved to the thumping beat of the music the wild look in his eyes flickered, and something was released in him that made him dance like a crazy man. It turned her on, and she responded like a crazy woman. At times other people on the floor stopped dancing in order to watch them.

From then on they went to The Upstairs Room every Saturday, and they stayed there until after eleven, giving Dana enough time to get home by midnight. Dana always took responsibility for watching the clock, so Brigid didn't have to worry about it. In fact, when she was out on the floor dancing with Tommy she didn't have to worry about anything. For once in her life she was simply having a good time.

One night during spring break they had drinks and dinner at

O'Malley's and then went to the guys' apartment, where along with the usual cocktails Glenn offered joints. Remembering the time at the Fillmore East when the guys next to her and Laura had given them a joint, Brigid felt that at least this was something she had done before, and she had no problem with it.

From the combination of Manhattans and joints she got higher than a kite, and so did the others. The sex with Tommy was like a dream, but when Dana woke her up it wasn't eleven thirty, it was almost three in the morning.

"I'm in deep shit," Dana told her as they got into the car.

"Could you tell your father your car broke down?"

"No way. He knows about cars."

"Well, maybe you could blame it on me."

"How? Tell him you locked me in a closet and wouldn't let me out?"

"Tell him I had a breakdown, and you took me to the hospital."

"He could check on that. And he'd never believe you had a breakdown."

Brigid had met her friend's father a few times, and she had evidently impressed him as a sane girl. "But I *could* have had a breakdown."

"You're not crazy enough to have a breakdown, even though you dance like a crazy girl."

"So you don't want to make up an explanation?"

"No. It's bad enough getting home this late, but if he ever caught me lying to him—" Dana shuddered. "I'll just have to face him and tell him the truth."

"But you won't tell him about the joints."

"No. I'll tell him I had too much to drink. I'll tell him I didn't want to drive in that condition, so I decided to sleep it off. I think that might work for me."

Brigid thought it might work for her too. "I could tell my parents we both had too much to drink, and we didn't want to drive in that condition."

"I guess we have to tell them we fell asleep at the guys' apartment. But nothing happened. We were too drunk."

They agreed that it was a plausible story.

Dana's father believed it, and Brigid's parents believed it too. But Dana's father took away her car privilege for the rest of the semester, which limited their social activities. In any case, by then Dana was tired of Glenn, and though Brigid wasn't yet tired of Tommy she decided to stop seeing him before she got tired of him. Also, since they had always double-dated it would have been awkward for Brigid to keep seeing Tommy. Not only that, but without Dana's car she would be dependent on Tommy to go anywhere. And with classes resuming after spring break it was time for them to focus on their work in the nursing program.

She continued seeing Dana at the hospital on Tuesdays and Thursdays, and on other days they often met at the college pub after class, where among other subjects they talked about their plans for the summer. Dana's father wanted her to work at a nursing home in South Yonkers, believing it would be a suitable penance for her. Since Brigid didn't have plans for the summer, and since she didn't mind doing penance with her friend, they both applied for jobs at the nursing home, and they both got jobs, which they started in June.

As she was doing the paperwork for her summer job at the nursing home Brigid remembered that a year ago she was planning to spend the summer in the city with Laura and Kieran, and feeling the losses of that summer, she wondered if her life would be all downhill from then on.

EIGHT

BRIGID COMPLETED THE nursing program the following May, and she sat with Dana during the graduation ceremony that the college held on the big lawn. It began with four Irish pipers, a tradition established by the Sisters of the Redemption, whose order originated in Ireland back in the 19th century. The pipers were big guys, wearing kilts in a green plaid, and they played a tune that Brigid had heard at the St. Patrick's Day parades in Yonkers, which her family always attended. The pipers were followed by the faculty, wearing academic regalia with different colored robes that indicated where they had earned their doctorates. A number of faculty wore robes of maroon, the color of Fordham University. And then came the students, wearing their simple regalia with gold tassels arranged on the right side of their caps.

The faculty sat up on a stage while the students sat in rows of chairs on the lawn. They stood for the national anthem, sung by a student with a voice influenced by Diana Ross, and they remained standing for the invocation, delivered by Father Justin, who wore a maroon academic robe. Then the president, in a light blue robe, welcomed the students and their families and friends, who were seated in rows behind the students. She was followed by a list of speakers, who talked and talked, but the students put up with it because their big moment was coming, the conferral of degrees. About a thousand students were graduating, and guided by ushers, they formed a line, they climbed the stairs, and they walked across the stage as their names were called out by the provost. They stopped at the president, who shook their hands, congratulated them, and gave them a piece of paper while cameras flashed and families cheered. Like most of the students, Brigid and Dana were the first in their families to get college degrees, and back at their seats, they hugged each other in a glow of pride at their accomplishment.

127

Brigid's parents had a party at their house to celebrate, and there were more than forty people in the backyard, including grandparents, aunts, uncles, and cousins. Her father procured the food from a deli on Saw Mill River Road, and it was supplemented by pans of meatballs as well as pans of sausages with peppers from her Italian grandmother. The meatballs were a succulent mixture of ground beef, pork, and veal in a hearty red sauce, and they quickly disappeared. The sausages with peppers were also popular. Of course there was beer, supplied by the company that employed her father, drawn from a keg in a washtub of ice. It was a great party, and when it was over her mother insisted that because she was the guest of honor Brigid didn't have to help clean up, but she did anyway, grateful for the party.

The last hurdle for Brigid and Dana was to pass the test for certification in nursing, which they both did about two weeks later. They had already been looking for jobs, and with their certification in hand they had a lot of opportunities. After considering several hospitals Brigid took a job at St. John's because it was familiar, and Dana took a job at Lawrence because it was different. Lawrence was in Bronxville, where rich people lived, and since Dana had never met any rich people she thought it might be interesting to meet some.

After her period of orientation Brigid requested assignment to the emergency room, which she felt would be challenging. And she was right. It was the most challenging work she had ever done. For all her education, she had to deal with situations that hadn't been covered by her textbooks, courses, or clinical work, and she had to ask the doctors and experienced nurses what to do. Of course she was learning, but she didn't want to learn at the expense of her patients, so when she didn't know what to do she always asked questions. Unlike the floors where according to her colleagues it could sometimes get boring, especially on the night shifts, the emergency room was never boring. All kinds of people came there, with all kinds of problems: the old guy who couldn't stop his nose from bleeding, the boy who held on to a lighted firecracker too long, the girl who swallowed a toothpick, and the guy who got his finger stuck in a bottle. Of course there were the usual cases of broken bones, abdominal pains, heart attacks, knife wounds, births, and appendectomies. Knife wounds were common on Saturday nights, and births were common early in the morning. Among the variety of patients there were those who appreciated what you did for them, those who couldn't handle being in a hospital, and those who did nothing but complain.

At that time nurses were still working eight-hour shifts, and as a junior nurse she had a schedule that was obviously designed to accommodate the senior nurses, randomly alternating from day shifts to night shifts and from weekdays to weekends. She didn't mind the lack of a pattern, but every month she had to give her mother a copy of her schedule so that meals could be planned accordingly. Her mother was still working as a nurse at St. John's but being senior she had a more regular schedule, which provided a basic structure for planning. At times Brigid wished she had a schedule like her mother's, but most of the time, after four years of being constrained by the rigidly structured nursing program, she liked not having a regular schedule. For some reason her schedule made her feel free.

Though they worked at different hospitals she and Dana stayed in touch by meeting about twice a month at O'Malley's. Instead of sitting at the bar they always took a booth now, which gave them privacy. Dana was working on the maternity floor, as she had requested, and so far she had few regrets. The good part was seeing healthy babies come into the world while the bad part was seeing babies who were born with problems.

One night they were in a booth at O'Malley's when Dana noticed a guy at the bar whom she recognized.

"You see that guy?" Dana said. "I met him at the hospital."

"Is he a doctor?" Brigid asked.

"No, he's the husband of a woman who delivered a baby last week. And the girl he's talking to isn't his wife."

"Maybe they're friends."

"No, I can tell he just met her, and he's chatting her up."

Brigid looked at the guy, who was tall and blond and haughty looking. Unlike most of the guys in the place, who were in their work clothes, he wore an expensive-looking suit. "So is he a rich guy from Bronxville?"

"Yeah. He makes a lot of money on Wall Street."

"Good for him. But what about his wife?"

"She's at home with the baby."

"Then he's definitely not the kind of guy you wanted to meet in Bronxville."

"No, but from what I've seen, they're not all like him."

After a pause Brigid said: "You know I haven't been on a date since we got wrecked with Tommy and Glenn."

"I haven't either. I don't have time for guys now."

"I don't have time for anything but work. But I love what I'm doing, so for the time being I don't need anything else."

"I don't either."

They sipped their wine, and they talked about the possibility of moving out of their family homes and renting an apartment together. There were pros and cons, the pros being that they wouldn't have to report to their parents, and the cons being that they would have to pay rent. They decided to wait until they were earning more money.

"There they go," Dana said, looking toward the bar, where the guy from Bronxville was leaving with the girl he had been chatting up. "He wants sex, and he can't get it from his wife now, so he's going to get it from that slut."

"Where would they go?"

"To a motel. There's one on Saw Mill River Road that has mirrors on the ceiling, so the person on the bottom can look up and see the other person's butt."

"That's gross."

"I've never been there," Dana hastened to say, "but I know a girl who went there. She said it made her want to be on top."

They both laughed.

"So he's cheating on his wife," Brigid said, feeling sorry for the poor woman.

"The wife who just delivered his baby."

"What a creep. If my husband did that to me, I'd kill him."

"You'd get life for that," Dana said. "You'd only get a year or so for cutting off his balls."

They stayed and ate burgers. Brigid had already told her mother she wouldn't be home for dinner, so she didn't have to call her. But the obligation to let her mother know what she was doing all the time made the idea of sharing an apartment with Dana seem attractive. They only had to wait until they earned more money.

A year later they were still living at home with their families. They had gotten raises, but after looking at apartments in areas of Yonkers that would be convenient for both hospitals, they still didn't think they could afford the rent. They still liked their jobs, and they still had no time for guys.

In early May, at the request of her supervisor, Brigid had gone to St. Catherine to meet with students in the nursing program for the purpose of recruiting. As usual there was a shortage of nurses, and the hospitals were eager to hire people right out of college. Her supervisor thought she would be perfect for recruiting at St. Catherine because she was a graduate of the nursing program there and because she was an excellent employee, though that appraisal hadn't been fully reflected in her salary. After making her pitch to a roomful of students Brigid decided to drop by the office of Sister Maura, whom she hadn't seen since graduation. Though she had only taken a religion course with Sister Maura she felt more connected with her than with any other faculty member at the college, maybe because she had gotten to know her through meetings of the Catholic Peace Fellowship.

Sister Maura was in her office, and she welcomed Brigid happily and invited her to sit down in the chair in front of her desk.

"Tell me what you're doing," Sister Maura said.

"I'm working in the ER at St. John's," Brigid said.

"Do you like it?"

"I love it. I mean, at times it gets crazy, but I feel like I'm helping people."

"That's our mission, to help people." Sister Maura paused.

131

"Since you were so enthralled by Daniel Berrigan, you might want to go to the play he wrote."

"He wrote a play? What's it about?"

"It's about their action at Catonsville. It was performed last January at the Good Shepherd Church, and I saw it there with Sister Audrey. It was very powerful, though I still have questions about his tactics."

"Is it still playing there?"

"No, it's opening on Broadway on June 2nd, at the Lyceum Theater."

Brigid had never attended a Broadway show, but she knew it was a big deal to have a play performed on Broadway. "Will it be hard to get a ticket?"

"I don't think so. I mean, the audience is people like us. But if you want to go, you should call and reserve a ticket."

"Okay, I will. Thanks for telling me about it."

"We saw Kieran O'Donnell at the play," Sister Maura said as if she knew that Brigid would be interested. Nothing escaped the notice of the nuns.

"I haven't seen him in almost three years. Is he still at Fordham?"

"Yes, he is. He's advancing through the second stage of Jesuit formation. We talked for a while, and I was impressed. He'll make a perfect Jesuit." The way Sister Maura said this, it wasn't entirely complimentary, though it could have been only the usual tension between nuns and priests.

"He's a very bright man," Brigid said.

"Oh, by the way," Sister Maura said, "did you ever find out what happened to your friend Laura?"

"No, I didn't. Her family hired a private detective, but he never found a trace of her. It's a mystery."

"It's like so many things that happen in this world, for which we have no explanation. God knows what happened to her."

Brigid felt like saying that since God knew what happened to Laura, then He should reveal it, but she didn't want to be disrespectful, so she thanked Sister Maura for telling her about the play, and she promised to stay in touch with her.

Since she knew that Dana wouldn't want to see the play she tried to think of someone she could ask to go with her, but in the end she called the box office of the theater and bought one ticket for the Saturday matinee on June 5. Around noon that day she took a train to the city, allowing plenty of time to get to the theater. She walked from Grand Central uptown to 45th Street and then crosstown to Sixth Avenue. She wound her way through the eddies of people, enjoying the vibrancy of the city after not being there for three years.

At the corner of Sixth she looked up and down the avenue for a place where she could grab a bite to eat, but there were only giant office buildings, so she kept walking, and she found a place on Seventh, where she ate a slice of pizza standing at a counter.

When she got to the theater there were people waiting outside because the doors weren't open yet. She waited with them and finally went into the lobby. It was twenty minutes before curtain time, so she visited the bathroom, waited in a line there, and returned to the lobby, where right in front of her, in clerical clothes, she saw Kieran. Controlling her excitement, she approached him.

"Well, hello," he said with a friendly smile. "I didn't expect to see you here."

"I heard about the play from Sister Maura," she said, not knowing what else to say.

"I saw her and Sister Audrey at a performance in January. When the play came to Broadway, I decided to see it again."

"You must have liked it."

"I did." He paused. "If you're free afterward, we could go and have dinner."

Since she was alone he must have assumed that she was free, and she was glad she hadn't found anyone to come with her. "Yeah, I'm free."

They arranged to meet in front of the theater, and then they went to their separate seats in the orchestra. Before the play began she had time to scan the program, and reading the description of the action at Catonsville, she was transported back in time.

The play made a compelling case for what the nine activists had done to publicize their cause against the war. The high point for Brigid was the speech given by the actor who played Daniel Berrigan, which began with an ironic apology for burning paper instead of children, explained their rationale, and proclaimed: "And so we stretch out our hands to our brothers throughout the world. We who are priests to our fellow priests. All of us who act against the law turn to the poor of the world, to the Vietnamese, to the victims, to the soldiers who kill and die for the wrong reasons, for no reason at all, because they were so ordered by the authorities of the public order which is in effect a massive institutionalized disorder. We say: killing is disorder; life and community and unselfishness is the only order we recognize. For the sake of that order we risk our liberty, our good name." By the end of that speech Brigid was in tears, not only moved by the fervor of the words but also crushed by the loss of illusions that had led her to believe she could change the world.

She met Kieran in front of the theater, and he suggested that they have dinner at a restaurant on 46th Street between Eighth and Ninth Avenues. It took them a while to walk there, and on the way they really couldn't talk with all the people around them.

The restaurant was Italian, in an elegant brownstone with a courtyard in back, where they got a table. Around the courtyard were potted trees illuminated by filtered spotlights, and in the middle was a fountain which emitted the barely audible sound of splashing water. A formally dressed waiter gave them menus as well as a wine list for Kieran.

"Would you like white wine?" he asked her.

"Sure. Whatever you want."

He ordered a bottle of wine, and then while they perused the menus he said: "If you like veal, I can recommend the veal scallopini."

She did like veal, which her mother cooked in stews, so she said: "Okay."

He ordered for both of them.

When the waiter had left them she asked: "How do you know this restaurant?"

"My uncle used to bring me here when I was in high school."

"Where did you go to high school?"

"Loyola," he said as if it was a given.

"That's a good school. Where were you living?"

"With my uncle and aunt. They had an apartment on the Upper East Side. They didn't have children, so they sort of adopted me while I went to high school."

"What did your uncle do for a living?"

"He had a faculty position at Hunter, teaching philosophy and religion. He started his career at Fordham, but he had a calling to serve a different population."

"How could he afford to live on the Upper East Side?"

"His wife had money. She came from a family that went back to the time of the Dutch colony in New York. But you'd never know it," he added. "She's very nice, and she's involved in a lot of charities."

"So you went to a Jesuit high school. Is that when you decided to be a priest?"

"I was thinking about it before high school. I didn't have an epiphany like Thomas Merton, but by the time I was a junior I knew I wanted to be a priest."

"A Jesuit priest."

"Of course," he said, again as if it was a given.

She paused before asking: "Have you ever had any doubts about it?"

"We all have doubts. I had doubts during that summer," he admitted. "But I overcame them."

"What about now?"

"I have occasional doubts. For example, when I have to listen to a boring lecture."

She laughed, as she was supposed to.

"Now, what about *you*?"

"I have doubts."

"I didn't mean that. I meant what are you doing now?"

"I'm working as a nurse in the ER at St. John's Hospital in Yonkers."

"Do you like it?"

"Yeah. I really do."

"What do you like about it?"

Without hesitation she said: "I like being able to help people."

"That's the right motivation," he said. "How long have you worked in the ER?"

"It's a little over a year now. It keeps me out of trouble."

He smiled. "Were you ever in trouble?"

"Yeah, I was in trouble that night in jail."

"I'm sorry I didn't rescue you sooner, but they waited until the next morning to call me. They must have wanted to teach you a lesson."

"It must have worked. I haven't been in jail since then."

"Speaking of jail," he said, "they finally caught Daniel Berrigan, and they sent him to prison, making him a martyr."

"So what did you think of his play?"

"I liked it, and I learned from it."

"What did you learn?"

He took a long deep breath and then exhaled. "I learned that I was naive to think that I could top him by blowing up a records center. What the Berrigans did at Catonsville was theatrical, and it dramatized the evils of the war. But my action wouldn't have been theatrical, it would have only been a bombing."

"Why was their action theatrical?"

"Because they got caught doing it. They deliberately got caught, so they'd get publicity. But how would I have gotten caught in the act of bombing a records center? By telling the police in advance what I was going to do?"

"So is that why you decided not to do it?"

"That's one reason. There were other reasons. But I know I made the right decision."

"I think you did," she said for what it was worth.

They talked until their food arrived. Her veal scallopini was wonderful—it was something she could tell her mother about.

They lingered at the table, finishing the bottle of wine and sipping espressos. They talked about a lot of things, including his program at Fordham and her work at the hospital, and they returned to the subject of the war, which was still going on under Nixon with emphasis on bombing civilians. At the end of their conversation Kieran shared with her his mission to teach at Fordham and to write about issues of peace and justice in order to educate the public so that when this war was finally over their country would never wage war again.

They left the restaurant and headed east. They parted at Times Square because he was taking a subway to the Bronx and she was taking a train to Yonkers. As she walked toward Grand Central she realized that he hadn't once mentioned Laura. His apparent lack of interest in the lost girl led Brigid to speculate that if he had been accessible for a relationship, he would have preferred her to Laura. And she had heard that Philip Berrigan left the priesthood and got married, so there was hope.

After five years of working in the emergency room she began to feel symptoms of burnout, and she decided it was time for a change, so she looked for another job in nursing. In the meantime she and Dana hadn't rented an apartment together because Dana had met a guy at the hospital whom she liked a lot. He wasn't a doctor, he was a visitor, and she met him in the elevator that he was taking to visit his mother on the surgery floor, where she was recovering from a procedure. Every day he came to see her around six in the evening and he stayed until eight, when visitors were supposed to leave. He was a good-looking guy who dressed in conservative suits, though when he took off his jacket it revealed that he wore red suspenders. Dana also noticed that his shirts had pinned collars. So she suspected that he was a WASP.

It turned out that he was a WASP, with a last name for a first name, Grayson. He lived in the city on the Upper East Side, and he worked at a prestigious law firm on Park Avenue. But those things didn't impress Dana as much as the fact that every day while his mother was in the hospital he took a train from the city to Bronxville and then took a train back to the city. They talked in the hall as long as Dana could get away with it, and they continued seeing each other after his mother was discharged, but it wasn't easy to get together. Either he had to take a train to Yonkers, where she would pick him up at the station, or she had to go into the city, where she would meet him at a bar in his neighborhood. Since Dana was still living with her parents, there was nowhere in Yonkers other than a motel where they could have sex, and if she went to his apartment she had to take a late train home. So after about six months of dealing with this situation Dana rented an apartment on East 80th Street, which Grayson had found for her, and she got a job at New York Hospital. From then on Brigid saw Dana only about once a month, at a place on Second Avenue called Bar Harbor. It was a different world from Yonkers or the East Village: instead of the carpenters, plumbers, and mechanics who hung out at O'Malley's, or the artists, writers, and musicians who hung out at Rigoletto, the people at this place were young professionals who worked at banks, law firms, and advertising agencies. It was interesting, but Brigid preferred the worlds of O'Malley's and Rigoletto.

Also in the meantime the war in Vietnam had ended. As she watched the television footage that showed a helicopter lifting from the U.S. Embassy with the last people rescued, leaving behind the Vietnamese who had helped them and would pay for it, she had mixed feelings of relief that the war was finally over and regret that she hadn't been able to end it sooner. It was such a waste of human life for no good purpose, an unjust war if there ever was one. And she felt the weight not only of the casualties in Vietnam but also of the casualty in her own life, the inexplicable loss of Laura.

A month after her decision to get out of the emergency room she interviewed for a position at Phelps Hospital in North Tarrytown, a village about twenty miles north of where she lived. The position was to work in the operating room as a member of a team led by a pioneer in hip and knee replacements. She knew it would be challenging, but instead of treating patients for random events on a variable schedule of days, nights, and weekends, she would treat patients for predictable events on a regular daytime schedule. Another attractive feature of the position was that it would give her a reason for leaving home and getting her own apartment.

For her interview with the head of the nursing department she took a bus to the Yonkers station, a train to Tarrytown, and a taxi to the hospital. From that experience she realized that for this job, instead of being able to walk from her house to the hospital, she would need a car. The interview went well, but she had to come back the next day for an interview with the doctor who worked for the leader of the team. She was nervous about this interview because although she had a lot of experience dealing with a variety of problems in an often chaotic environment, she had no experience working in an operating room.

The doctor's office was in the orthopedics department, and she was led there by a girl who answered phone calls and did clerical work. There was no one in the office, but the girl told her to have a seat, the doctor would be with her in a minute. While she waited, sitting in a chair in front of the desk, she looked around and noted the framed diplomas on a wall: a bachelor's degree from Princeton and a medical degree from Cornell. There were also two framed certificates in areas of orthopedics.

When the doctor finally came into his office Brigid was surprised by how young he looked, even though from the date on his bachelor's degree she had calculated that he was thirty-one. He looked even younger, maybe because there were no marks of suffering on his face.

"Hi, I'm Parker Ralston," he said breezily, extending his hand. "No, don't get up."

From her seated position she shook his hand, which was smooth and pliant. "I'm Brigid McBride. I'm glad to meet you."

He moved gracefully around the desk and sat down and faced her. He was wearing a blue button-down shirt with a striped tie, and the cuffs of his sleeves were rolled up. He looked at the top paper of her application, which someone had placed on his desk. "I see that you've worked for five years in the ER at St. John's, so you must be tough."

"I've survived," she said.

"Well, I can guess why you want a different position, but you tell me."

"I want a position where I can learn about a specialty," she said, repeating what she had rehearsed to herself. "Where the work is more predictable than what I'm doing now."

"There's a lot to learn about what we're doing. So what makes you think you could learn about joint replacements?"

"I did well in college, as you can see from my transcript."

He shuffled the papers. "Oh, yeah. You got straight A's, so you must know how to learn. But the work we do requires perfection. Our team leader has zero tolerance for errors. Do you think you could handle that kind of pressure?"

"I handled the pressure in the ER, as you can see from my recommendations."

He found them. "Yeah. The head of ER says that you can deal with any kind of situation. Have you ever screwed up?"

"Not in my work."

That made him smile. He had perfect teeth, and he smiled not only with his mouth but also with his steady blue eyes. "Now, the other thing our leader expects is absolute punctuality. You live in Yonkers, so how would you get here?"

"If I get the job, I'll rent an apartment in Tarrytown, and I'll drive here."

"You have a car?"

"I'll get one."

"Okay. I have a last question." He paused, not taking his eyes off her face. "What was your best experience working in the ER?"

After thinking she said: "I had a lot of good experiences, so it's hard to say which one was the best, though the one that stands out is helping to prevent a miscarriage by a woman who came to the ER hemorrhaging. It made me feel like I'd saved two lives."

He nodded as if she had said the right thing. "Okay. We'll contact you."

She stood up, believing that the interview had gone well but not knowing if she would get the job. She shook hands with the doctor and found her way out.

The next day the head of the nursing department called her and told her she was hired. She just had to come to the hospital and go through a process with personnel. After being switched to personnel she made an appointment for the next day.

Her parents, who reluctantly agreed that it was time for her to live on her own, helped her find an apartment in Tarrytown. It was in a garden apartment complex on Broadway, a few blocks south of the town center. It had a living room, a bedroom, a kitchen, and a bathroom. The rooms were small, but for a single person they would be fine. And with the higher salary she would earn in her new job, Brigid could afford it.

Her parents also helped her buy basic furniture: a bed, a chest of drawers, a sofa, a table, and two chairs. Her father knew a place on Tuckahoe Road where they got a good deal on the furniture. Her mother knew where to buy sheets and towels.

The hardest thing to find was an affordable, reliable car, but one of her father's customers had a Chevy Malibu that was five years old with less than thirty thousand miles on it, so they made a deal and registered it in Brigid's name. She had a driver's license, which she had gotten while she was in high school along with other kids her age who took a driver's training course, but she hadn't driven much, so she needed practice.

Meanwhile, she had given notice to St. John's, and the staff in the emergency room had given her a sendoff party at a place that had recently opened near the hospital called The Rehab Room. She had ten days off before starting her new job, so on one of those days she went into the city and met Dana at Bar Harbor. Dana was already there, and she was occupying a booth when Brigid arrived, just ahead of the evening rush.

Though she had told Dana over the phone about her new job, they hadn't yet had an opportunity to talk about it, and their conversation began with Dana's questions about what she would be doing at Phelps, and Brigid's responses.

"So you're going to learn how to do hip and knee replacements," Dana said, impressed.

"I'm going to learn how to help the doctors do them," she corrected her friend.

"Did you ever think about being a doctor?"

"No, I never did. I like being a nurse. What about you?"

"I'd never want to be a doctor. And I'd never marry one."

"Why would you never marry a doctor?"

"I'd never see him." Dana paused. "Though that could be an advantage."

"Yeah, if you didn't want to see him."

"Now, tell me about the guy you're going to work for."

"There's not much to tell. I only had an interview with him."

"What's his background?"

"He went to Princeton and then to Cornell."

"So he's Ivy League, just like Gray."

"Where did Gray go to college?"

"Dartmouth and Columbia. What's your boss's name?"

"Parker," she said.

"So he's a WASP too."

"I guess he is. He was wearing a blue button-down shirt with a striped tie."

Dana laughed. "You know, they're from a different world."

"Yeah, they're rich, and they're Protestant."

"And they go to Ivy League colleges."

"Well, we went to a good college."

"For nursing, yeah. But those colleges give them an advantage. I mean, Gray's smart, and he's good at his job, but I'm sure that having his law degree from Columbia helped him get a position at that firm."

"He still has to be good at his work."

"Yeah, and in two years he'll have a chance to make partner. But in the meantime they make him work like an animal."

"Does he have to work late?"

"Yeah, almost every night, so during the week I only see him a few times. But he usually doesn't have to work on weekends."

"Don't you have to work on weekends?"

"Only once a month." Dana was working on a surgery floor where most of the procedures were scheduled.

"I'll have a better schedule in this job. It's from eight to four, during the week. Unless there's an emergency, they don't do procedures on weekends."

"I think you made a good decision."

"I think I did, but we'll see."

They ordered burgers, and while they were eating, Dana asked: "Is Parker single?"

"I don't know."

"Was he wearing a ring?"

"I didn't notice. I was concentrating on the interview."

"Well, next time you see him, notice. Okay?"

"Okay," she said. "But either way, it's not a vital piece of information."

Giving her a look, Dana said: "You never know."

On the train going home Brigid pondered what her friend had said. Her boss was attractive, and if he was single, with all his prospects he would be a good catch. But there were many reasons why Brigid couldn't even think about having a relationship with him, starting with the fact that he was her boss. And though it wasn't unusual for a nurse to marry a doctor, she couldn't see that happening with her. Right now, her only objective was to do a good job and become a valuable member of the team.

NINE

ON HER FIRST day of work at Phelps she met the team leader, Dr. Hartmann. He was a big man with functionally cut blond hair and forbidding blue eyes. His handshake welcoming her to the team was a bone crusher.

It was Monday, so they were preparing for the procedures that they would do on Tuesday and Wednesday. Except for occasional emergencies, they operated only on those two days, and they used Thursdays and Fridays for follow-ups and consultations. Today there was little for Brigid to do other than become oriented. Late in the morning Parker gave her a manual on preparations, procedures, and follow-ups, which he told her to study and learn.

For the next month she observed him examining patients, assisting Dr. Hartmann with procedures, attending to patients in the recovery room, and doing follow-ups. She also observed the senior nurse in the operating room, a woman in her mid-thirties whose name was Nancy. She was impressed by the way that Nancy had everything needed for a procedure laid out in perfect order, and when Parker confided that Nancy was OCD she understood that he meant it as a compliment. But one time during a hip replacement after Nancy had handed a tool to Dr. Hartmann, he told her in a withering voice: "When I ask for something I want it right away. I don't want it two seconds later." Brigid suspected that indirectly Dr. Hartmann was teaching a lesson to the newest member of his team, and she recalled what Parker had said about their work requiring perfection. But she felt bad for Nancy for being used for this purpose.

During her period of observation she read and reread the manual that Parker had given her as if she was preparing for an exam, and she felt good when she was able to relate something she had learned from the manual to what they actually did with the patients. By early July she was assisting Nancy, and they were working well together.

Meanwhile, she was getting used to living alone, away from her family, but she didn't have much social life. After three weeks on the job she met Dana at their usual place in the city, and they got caught up. On Fridays she occasionally went out with three fellow nurses to a bar on Main Street in Tarrytown. On Saturdays she had dinner with her family, and back at her apartment she stayed up late watching "Saturday Night Live" on television. On Sundays she attended mass at St. Teresa of Avila in North Tarrytown, though not always because there were times when she needed sleep more than church.

One Friday in late July she was sitting in the office that she shared with Nancy when the receptionist, whose name was Estela, appeared in the doorway and told her that Dr. Ralston wanted to see her. Of course she was nervous, afraid that she had done something wrong, and she sat down in front of his desk, bracing herself.

"You've been with us almost two months," he said, leaning back in his chair and looking relaxed, "and I wanted to tell you, Dr. Hartmann is very happy with you."

That made her feel good.

"And so am I. You realize that I took a chance hiring someone who had no experience in an operating room, but you've done even better than I hoped."

"Thank you," she said, for some reason valuing his opinion even more than Dr. Hartmann's.

"If you're free this evening," he said tentatively, "I'd like to buy you a drink and celebrate your surviving almost two months with us."

She hesitated, caught off guard.

"Of course if you're not free this evening, we can do it some other time."

"No, I'm free," she managed to say.

He grinned. "Great. Then let's get out of here at five, okay?"

They left the office together and walked to the parking lot. He told her they were going to a place on the river in Dobbs Ferry, she told him where she lived, and he suggested that instead of taking two cars she leave her car there and go in his car.

He followed her, and after she had parked her car she got into his car, a Chevy Impala, and they drove south on Route 9 to Dobbs Ferry, where they went through town and down a hill to a pricey-looking restaurant. They got a table outside with a view of the river and the Palisades. A gentle breeze came across the water, stirring the fronds of the potted palms, and the rays of the summer evening sun were long and benign.

He ordered a gimlet, which she had never heard of, and she ordered a glass of white wine. As they waited for their drinks he said: "I know you're good at the job, but I don't know how you feel about it. Do you like it?"

"Yeah. It's challenging."

"You like being challenged?"

"I guess I do. I don't like doing things that are easy."

"What have you done besides nursing?"

"I went to school. and I went to college, and I also worked in a supermarket."

"What else have you done?"

"Do you really want to know?"

He inclined his head toward her. "Yeah. I do."

Feeling as if she had nothing to lose, she said: "I spent a summer living in the East Village, demonstrating against the war in Vietnam."

"Were you a member of an organization?"

"Yeah, I was a member of the Catholic Peace Fellowship."

He shook his head. "I don't know that organization. Is it connected with your church?"

"No. It's a lay organization, but up to a point it has the blessing of our church. Some priests and nuns are members of it."

"You mean like the Berrigan brothers?"

Surprised, she said: "You know who they are?"

"I read about them in the papers. I was doing my residency at the time."

"So what do you think about what they did?"

146

"I think they showed the courage of their convictions, and I admire them for that. And just so you know, I always thought that the war in Vietnam was wrong."

She was glad to hear that. For some reason, it mattered that they were on the same side.

When their drinks arrived she asked him what was in a gimlet, and when he told her she made a face. And then he said: "So you're Catholic. Did you go to Catholic schools?"

"I went to a Catholic elementary school, a Catholic high school, and a Catholic college."

"Wow. After all that do you still go to church?"

"When I can get up in time, I do."

"Well, I was raised as an Episcopalian, and I admire what our clergy are doing to promote peace and social justice, but I don't have time for church."

"Where did you grow up?"

"In Irvington." It was the village immediately north of Dobbs Ferry.

"Did you go to high school there?"

"Yeah. It's a good school, so I had no problem getting into college." He tossed this off as if Princeton was any old college.

"What made you decide to be a doctor?"

"My father's a doctor. But of course I threatened to do other things before I came around."

"Like what?" she asked.

"Like playing the piano for a living."

"What kind of music?"

"Classical. My teachers told me I had enough talent to play professionally. But my father introduced me to a successful concert pianist who told me about the endless travel, the one-night stands, and the tone-deaf audiences. So I changed my mind and majored in biology and went to medical school."

"Do your parents still live in Irvington?"

"Yeah. And my father's still practicing. His specialty is internal medicine."

"My parents are still working."

"What do they do?"

"My father's a beer distributor, and my mother's a nurse."

He smiled. "So you followed in your mother's footsteps just like I followed in my father's."

"Yeah," she said. "My mother was my role model. As far back as I can remember, I wanted to be a nurse like her."

"Well, be sure to tell her that Dr. Hartmann is very happy with you."

"I will," she said, reaching for her wine.

They had dinner there, and over dessert they watched the sun go down over the Palisades.

When she got home she lay down on the sofa and closed her eyes, savoring her memory of the evening. She wondered if he was only being a nice boss or if he liked her. She didn't know what he could see in her because they were from such different backgrounds, but she had noticed something in the way he looked at her that gave her encouragement.

Her instincts proved to be correct because the next Friday he asked her if she was free, and they went to the same restaurant on the river. Then, and over the weeks that followed, she learned more about him, including the fact that he was the oldest of three children, with a younger brother and a younger sister. The younger brother had also gone to Princeton, as their father had, so the family had money that went back another generation. He let her know that Ralston was an old Scottish name, not an English name, so that they had in common the fact that they were Celtic. He told her how his sister had the nickname Purina in high school because of her last name's association with the breakfast cereal Ralston Purina. Actually, he said, the name of the company didn't come from a family name but from an acronym of a social movement that was founded in the 19th century by a man who believed in white supremacy. The acronym, which spelled Ralston, was from Regime, Activity, Light, Strength, Temperation, Oxygen, and Nature. The man was a nut about purity, which led him to become a racist. So the money in Parker's family didn't come from breakfast cereal but from the shrewd dealings of his great-grandfather on Wall Street.

Brigid shared with Parker the history of her own family: how her father's parents had immigrated from Ireland and settled in the Bronx, with her grandfather supporting his family by doing construction jobs, and how her mother's parents had immigrated from Italy and settled in Yonkers, with her grandfather supporting his family by selling fruits and vegetables. So instead of being a member of the third generation of her family to go to Princeton, she was the first in her family to go to college. Still, though they had such different backgrounds, Brigid was finding that they had the same values, including the fact that their purpose in their chosen careers was to help people and the fact that their vision of the world was based on justice.

After having dinner with him over several weeks she accepted his invitation to go to his place for an after-dinner drink. He lived in a relatively new condo development on the river side of Broadway, about a quarter of a mile south of her apartment. His condo had two bedrooms, a living room with a view of the river, and a decent kitchen. One of the bedrooms was used as a study, and its walls were lined with medical textbooks on the lower shelves and novels on the upper shelves. A bookcase near the desk was packed with journals. A stereo system was perched on top of a cabinet, with racks of records below it. And near the window, in a place of honor, was an electronic keyboard.

After the tour they settled on the sofa in the living room and sipped wine from a bottle that he had brought from the refrigerator. He had put on the radio of his stereo system, and from hidden speakers at both ends of the sofa she could hear the soothing sounds of stringed instruments playing something classical. Since he didn't tell her the name of the composer he must have assumed she knew it, but she didn't know it, and she didn't ask because she didn't have to know it. She only wanted to enjoy the music.

She was ready for the inevitable kiss and for what followed in the bedroom. There were many good things about it, but maybe the best was that, unlike the times with Tommy, she didn't have to get home by a deadline. She could spend the night there.

Now that they had made love they had a different relationship, and the challenge was not to let their personal intimacy affect their professional behavior. Without being told, Brigid knew that Dr. Hoffmann would not approve of their being lovers, so they couldn't do anything in his presence that would make him suspicious.

One thing that helped them manage this risk was the rigor of their work schedule. For starters they couldn't even think about spending the night together on Mondays or Tuesdays because they had to get up early the next morning and be ready for the complex, demanding procedures they would undertake in the operating room. On Wednesdays they were too exhausted for anything other than a drink after work, though they had to avoid the bar in Tarrytown where Brigid had gone with her fellow nurses, and on Saturdays she was committed to having dinner with her family. So that left Thursdays, Fridays, and Sundays, and for the time being she only spent the night with him on Fridays.

Another thing that helped them was the fact that Dr. Hartmann was completely focused on his work, so he only noticed what happened in the operating room, and there were no reasons for them to be together with him anywhere else. In fact, she didn't see him much outside of the operating room, other than passing in a corridor, though once she had to share the elevator with him, and he was even more awkward than she was. So they were able to compartmentalize their personal and professional lives, and they continued working together on the team as if nothing had happened between them.

In late August, on a Thursday, she went into the city and met Dana at Bar Harbor. There were fewer people than usual at the bar, presumably because a lot of the regulars were on vacation. After glancing around she saw Dana in a booth with a perfect tan.

"Were you at the beach?" she asked, sliding into the seat across from Dana.

"We spent two weeks at Cape Cod," Dana said. "Gray's family has a place in Dennis."

"That must have been nice."

"His family wasn't there, so we had the place all to ourselves."

Dana already had a glass of white wine in front of her, so Brigid waved to the server and ordered the same for herself. "So things are going well with you guys?"

"Oh, yeah. I'm not getting tired of him. What about you? Has anything happened between you and that doctor?"

"Yeah. We're seeing each other."

"That's great. Now, what's his name again?"

"Parker," she said. "Parker Ralston. And he's no relation to the breakfast cereal."

"Good. I hated that stuff. My mother made us eat it during the winter. It was supposed to keep us warm."

"His family has money. Not that it matters, but it doesn't hurt."

"As long as he wasn't spoiled."

"He wasn't."

Dana sipped her wine. "Did you ever think we'd have WASP boyfriends?"

"I never knew a WASP before, at least that I was aware of."

"They have their good points."

"Do they have bad points?"

"Well, they don't have experience in the real world like we do. But that's why they need us. We complement them."

She wondered if that might apply to Parker and her, though she hadn't yet identified anything she had that he didn't have, other than her experience in antiwar activities. "So things are going well with us, but there's one thing I worry about."

"What's that?"

"If anything happens to our personal relationship, it would affect our professional relationship."

"What could happen to your personal relationship?"

"I don't know. I guess he could decide that I'm not the girl he wants or needs."

"It sounds like you're looking ahead."

"I am, aren't you? We're twenty-seven, so we should be close to finding someone we could spend our lives with."

"How long have you been seeing this guy?"

"About a month."

"Then you hardly know him."

"I know him well enough to wonder if he might be the right guy for me."

"Well, don't rush things. I've been seeing Gray for more than a year, and even though I'm sure he *is* the right guy, I'm not going to rush things. He still has another year before he has a chance to make partner."

"What if he doesn't make partner?"

"I believe he will, but I don't know, and if he doesn't it would change things. I mean, it wouldn't change things for me, but it would for him."

"So let's assume he does make partner. What do you think will happen then?"

Dana beamed. "He'll ask me to marry him."

"And you'll say yes?"

"I'll make him wait for a day or two, but then I'll say yes."

She reached over and clasped Dana's hand, letting her know she was happy for her. At least one of them was moving ahead with her personal life.

On a Saturday night late in the fall when they had returned to Parker's apartment after having dinner, Brigid followed him into the study where he was going to put on some music. Spotting the keyboard near the window, she asked: "Do you still play?"

"Oh, yeah. But only for myself."

"You never play for other people?"

"No, I don't want to inflict it on them."

"I wouldn't mind if you inflicted it on me."

He gave her a long, searching look. "You really want to hear me play?"

"I really do," she assured him.

"Well, all right. But don't say I didn't warn you."

She sat down in the chair at his desk, and he went over to the keyboard, which had a chair in front of it. He sat down and did nothing for a while as if he was deciding what to play, and then he began playing softly.

The melody was slow and sad. It was like a lament for something lost, and it made her mourn for that lost summer. It moved her to a point beyond tears, and then suddenly it was fast and furious, with loud chords pounded on the keys. It was like a protest against the injustices of the world, and it raged against them, moving up and down the keyboard as if it was seeking a victory over the forces of evil. Then finally it was slow and peaceful, like a reconciliation, a forgiveness of sins, a hope for peace. It ended with a chord that was so soft she could barely hear it.

Speechless, she sat there, wiping away the tears that had run down her cheeks.

He turned around and asked: "Did you like that?"

"I loved it," she said with a catch in her throat. "What was it?"

"A nocturne by Chopin. At the time he wrote it he was living in exile from Poland, and he put into it his feelings of loneliness, rage, and hope."

"I got those feelings."

"Good," he said. "It's easier to communicate feelings with music than it is with words."

"Would you play another one?"

"Yeah, sure. I'll play another nocturne."

While listening to this nocturne she was moved as much as by the first one, and she realized that it wasn't only the music, it was the way he played it, putting into it the feelings that the composer had wanted to communicate. It showed that he had such feelings himself, and it made her appreciate him even more.

He played for about an hour, and then he turned off the keyboard and got up and came to her and leaned over and kissed her on the forehead. "Thanks for listening."

"Thanks for playing."

They continued seeing each through the holidays, which they spent with their respective families. He hadn't introduced her to his parents, who lived only a few miles from the hospital, and it bothered her because if he was serious about her, wouldn't he want his parents to meet her? But she kept reminding herself of Dana's advice not to rush things, so she accepted the situation.

She also kept thinking about what Dana had said about their complementing their boyfriends. She could see how that might apply to Dana and Gray because she was a nurse and he was a lawyer, so they were in separate worlds professionally. But she and Parker were in the same world professionally, and though she might complement him as a member of their team she was still only a nurse and he was a doctor, so they were at different levels in that world. Still, she imagined that there were a lot of good marriages between doctors and nurses.

One night in January they were having dinner at an Italian restaurant in Dobbs Ferry when she noticed two of the nurses that she had gone out with seated at a table opposite them. She tried to avoid making eye contact with them, but when it happened accidentally one of them made a hand sign that it was cool to be dating Dr. Ralston. At the time she didn't mention it to Parker, but later when they were at his apartment, sitting on the sofa and sipping wine, she told him that two nurses on their floor had spotted them having dinner together.

"Don't worry about it," he assured her. "They're not going to tell anyone. And for all they know, we were only having dinner together."

"Don't be so sure," she told him. "Women can tell if a couple is having a relationship."

"They can? Just by looking at them?"

"Yeah, just by looking at them."

"Well, our boss can't tell just by looking at us, and he has no use for gossip."

"I still wish we didn't have to hide what we're doing."

"What do you want us to do?" he said with a smile. "Announce our engagement?"

Since she could tell he wasn't joking she was at a loss, and finally she said: "We've only been seeing each other for six months, so I don't think we're at that point."

"You don't?" He looked disappointed. "Then maybe as a next step we can stop hiding it from our parents. What do you think?"

"I think that would be a good idea."

"How about next Sunday we have dinner with my parents?"

"Fine," she said casually, handling the situation as she imagined Dana would.

His parents had Sunday dinner at one, a family tradition that enabled them to go to church. They went to St. Barnabas, an old church on Broadway that Brigid had passed many times. Since it was an Episcopal church she assumed that it was for rich people.

Parker's parents lived in a house that was at least three times larger than the house Brigid's parents lived in. It was made of stone, and it looked as if it was built in the previous century when titans like J.P. Morgan were making fortunes on Wall Street. She expected his parents to be snooty, but they were the opposite. They welcomed her with hugs, and they made her feel at home with them. His father was an older version of Parker, with silvery hair and kind blue eyes. His mother was a natural blond, though she must have been coloring it to hide the gray. For a while they sat in the living room, which had a big stone fireplace and a view of the river, and then they went into the dining room, where four places were set at a table that evidently had the capacity to be lengthened.

Brigid assumed that the house had a staff, including a cook, but when Parker's father went into the kitchen and returned with a platter of roast beef, surrounded by roasted potatoes and carrots, she guessed that the staff had Sundays off. He set the platter in front of him and then asked Brigid to pass her plate. "Do you like it rare, medium, or well done?"

"Medium," she said, giving him a margin for error.

Moving quietly around the table, Parker's mother served the wine. It was red, though it was nothing like the hearty wine her grandmother served with spaghetti and meatballs. It was a wine that urbane people drank with fine dining.

During the dinner Parker's parents mostly paid attention to her, asking about her family, her education, and her career. Then, with a sympathetic wink, his father asked her how she liked working with Parker, and with a deadpan look she said it was all right, which got a laugh, as it was meant to. And finally his father asked how she liked working with Dr. Hartmann.

"It's a privilege," she told him seriously.

"You know, Dr. Hartmann was a pioneer in joint replacements. Doctors come from all over the country, all over the world, to learn from him."

"I've learned a lot from him," Parker said.

"The man is brilliant," his mother said. "But he can be gruff, to put it mildly."

"When I made my first error in the OR he beat me to a pulp verbally. I'll never forget it."

"I'll bet you never repeated that error," his father said.

"I never did. As I told Brigid when I interviewed her, Dr. Hartmann has zero tolerance for errors."

"Do you think Dr. Hartmann ever made an error himself?" his mother asked.

"He must have made errors," his father said. "Developing joint replacement procedures was a process of trial and error."

"Like everything in medicine," Parker said.

"Like everything in life," Brigid said.

"Young woman," his father said, "you have a lot of wisdom for your age."

"I got that from my parents."

"You're wise to give them credit."

As they drove away from Parker's house she felt that the dinner had gone well. From the questions his parents asked her she knew he had told them he was serious about her, and from the way they had treated her she knew they liked her.

A year later they were still seeing each other, still developing their relationship, and still hiding it from Dr. Hartmann. By then they had become so adept at compartmentalizing their lives that they were like two different pairs: a doctor and a nurse who worked together during the week on a surgery team, and a man and a woman who lived together on weekends. Also by then she had introduced Parker to her parents, and they alternated having dinner with their parents, hers on Saturday and his on Sunday, about once a month. Out of caution they decided not to have their parents meet each other until they got engaged.

Meanwhile, Gray had made partner in his law firm, he had asked Dana to marry him, and she had said yes. The wedding was scheduled for late May with Brigid as the maid of honor and Parker invited as a guest. The night before the wedding a party was given by Gray's parents for the bride and groom, the bride's parents, the maid of honor, and the best man. It was held in the private room of a restaurant in Bronxville, where Gray's parents lived. It was the first time Brigid had met Gray, who honestly said he had heard so much about her and treated her as if he appreciated her friendship with Dana. It was a fun party, and Brigid drank more than she should have, so instead of driving home to Tarrytown she crashed at her parents' house, which brought back memories of the time when she and Dana were nursing students.

The wedding was held at Sacred Heart. Since Gray wasn't Catholic it wasn't a mass but it was a nice wedding. Dana was a beautiful bride, and Gray was a handsome groom, and they looked joyful going down the aisle as a married couple. Like the wedding, the reception had been organized by Dana's parents, so it was held at the Polish Center in downtown Yonkers, which had facilities for weddings, anniversaries, birthdays, and other events. With the families and friends of the bride and groom there were more than two hundred people at the reception, with food and music and dancing. It was the first time Brigid danced with Parker, and she was impressed by how well he danced. He wasn't crazy like Tommy, but he had the moves.

When it came time for Dana and Gray to leave the reception the girls assembled for the bride to toss out her bouquet. Of course Dana threw it straight at Brigid, but a girl who couldn't have been more than twelve intercepted it.

Before leaving, Dana hugged her and told her. "Don't worry. It's only a superstition."

"I know." She didn't care about the bouquet. "Have a great honeymoon!"

Participating in Dana's wedding unearthed the question in Brigid's mind of whether she and Parker should get married. They had buried it after he asked prematurely if they should announce their engagement, but now it was revived. They had known each other for more than two years, and everything felt right about their relationship. They could have continued as they were, but there were advantages in getting married. The biggest advantage was that instead of being together only on weekends they could be together all the time. And they would no longer have to hide their relationship from Dr. Hartmann. So it didn't surprise her when on a Saturday night, as they were lying in bed after making love, Parker asked her to marry him.

Unsure of how to answer, she bought time by asking: "When would the wedding be?"

"I don't know. How about October?"

"Would that give our parents enough time to prepare for it?"

"I think so," he said. "It's three months away."

"Well, let's sleep on it," she finally said.

"Do you have doubts?"

"Not about you."

"You mean you have doubts about yourself?"

"I always have doubts about myself."

"Okay, we'll sleep on it," he said, sounding disappointed but also hopeful.

Instead of sleeping on it she was kept awake by it long after he was in dreamland. She wanted to say yes, and she couldn't find any good reason for not saying yes. But something that she didn't understand was holding her back.

When they got up the next morning he didn't press her on the question. He gave her space, which was one of the many things she liked about him. They had brunch at the restaurant on the river in Dobbs Ferry, they went to an afternoon movie at the art theater in White Plains, they had dinner at a local diner, and then he left her at her apartment, where she lay awake for another night wrestling with the question.

The next day after work she drove to her parents' house in Yonkers, and she found her mother in the kitchen making dinner. After hugging her mother and asking her if she could help, she sat down at the kitchen table.

For a while she watched her mother stirring and tasting, and then she said: "Guess what. Parker asked me to marry him."

Her mother turned from the stove. "He did? That's great."

"Well, it didn't surprise me. I mean, we've talked about it before."

"So when do you want to have the wedding?"

She hesitated. "I don't know. The thing is, I haven't said yes."

"You haven't?" her mother said, gazing at her with those dark eyes that didn't miss a thing. "Do you have doubts?"

"That's what he asked me," Brigid said. "I don't have doubts about him, I have doubts about myself."

Her mother set down the wooden spoon and came over and sat down at the table with her. "Do you have doubts about how you feel toward him?"

"I know I love him, so that's not it."

"Do you have doubts about whether you're the right person for him?"

"I know he believes I'm the right person for him, and that's what counts, isn't it?"

"Yeah. But do *you* believe you're the right person for him?"

"I think I am. We have a good relationship."

"Then it's not something between you and him, it's something in you," her mother said. "Do you know what it is?"

"I think I know."

Her mother waited.

"I'm in love with someone else."

"Well, that could be a problem. Do I know this person?"

"No. It's someone I knew when I was in college."

Her mother frowned. "I don't remember a serious boyfriend."

"He wasn't a boyfriend. He was—a mentor."

"A mentor? Oh, no. I hope you're not in love with one of your professors."

"He's not a professor," Brigid said. "He's someone I met through the Catholic Peace Fellowship."

"I hope he's not married."

"No, he's not married. That's not the problem."

"What *is* the problem?"

Without revealing what it was she said: "He has something more important to do than to have a relationship with me."

"Do you have any hope for a relationship with him?"

"I don't have much hope, but I have enough to give me doubts about whether I should marry Parker."

Her mother frowned again. "Well, if you don't have much hope for a relationship with this person, it doesn't sound like a good reason not to marry Parker."

"Maybe it's not a good reason. But what if it stops me from loving Parker the way he loves me?"

Her mother sighed. "Your father and I didn't have that problem. We dated other people, but we didn't fall in love with anyone until we met each other."

"You were lucky."

"We were blessed."

"So I don't know if I can love Parker the way he loves me."

"I understand. But you don't have to love him that way to have a good marriage. You only have to love him."

"Then I should take a chance on marrying him?"

"From what I've seen of him," her mother said, "he's a good man, so you wouldn't be taking a chance on him, you'd be taking a chance on yourself. And you know yourself, so you have to decide if you should take that chance."

She thanked her mother for listening. She hadn't expected her mother to help her make a decision, but her mother had helped her understand her situation.

As she drove home to her apartment she thought about the reasons why she should marry Parker. He was patient with her, he was kind to her, he was interested in her, he respected her, and he loved her. He worked in a profession that she understood and valued. He helped people in a major way, restoring their ability to walk, run, and even dance without pain or fear. He was everything she could want in a husband, except for one thing: he wasn't Kieran. And it wouldn't be fair to marry Parker if she was still in love with Kieran. It wouldn't be fair.

TEN

AFTER TURNING PARKER down she knew it wouldn't be good for either of them if she continued working on the team, so she took a vacation, which she had saved for a trip with him, and she looked for a job. Since there was a shortage of nurses it didn't take her long to find a job at White Plains Hospital on a surgery floor. She didn't have to explain to Parker why she was leaving, but she had to find a plausible explanation for Dr. Hartmann, who still didn't know about her relationship with Parker. She ended up telling him she liked working for him, and she had learned a lot from her experience on his team, but for reasons that had nothing to do with work she couldn't handle the pressure right now. It was essentially true, and he evidently believed it because he told her she had served him well, and that if she needed a letter of recommendation he would happily give it to her. She accepted his offer, which her new employer needed to complete her personnel file.

It was an easy commute to White Plains from her apartment in Tarrytown, so she decided not to move. In her new job, instead of working eight-hour shifts from Monday through Friday she would work twelve-hour shifts three days a week, at times on weekends. Since she didn't have a social life that the weekend shifts would interfere with, and since she liked the idea of fully immersing herself in work for twelve hours straight, with four days off for resting and sleeping, she embraced her new schedule. Also, with the twelve-hour shifts she would avoid the rush-hour traffic to White Plains, so she could drive to work in about a half hour.

When she told her mother about her decision on Parker's proposal her mother supported her and understood why she couldn't continue working with him. At the time her mother was still working at St. John's, but she wondered aloud to Brigid if after so many years it might be time for her to find a new job herself, ideally in a clinic instead of a hospital.

Brigid started her new job after Labor Day weekend, which she celebrated with her family in the backyard, drinking an imported beer that her father's employer was introducing and eating burgers that he grilled. She liked the nurse managers on her floor at White Plains Hospital, and she adapted easily to her position. After five intensive years in an emergency room and two demanding years in an operating room there weren't many situations on a surgery floor that she couldn't handle. But during her second week on the job she encountered a situation that she couldn't handle.

The patient was a man about her father's age who had come out of surgery and started complaining as soon as he regained his senses. The problem was he only spoke Spanish, and Brigid didn't understand Spanish. To help her, she found Yolanda, a fellow nurse whom she had just met, and she asked her to translate the patient's complaint. Yolanda readily joined her at the man's bedside and addressed him in a way that sounded formal and respectful. They conversed for a while, and then Yolanda turned to her and explained that the man wasn't complaining about the effects of his surgery or about the services of the hospital, he was complaining about the absence of his son, who was supposed to be there attending to him. Yolanda explained that in her culture members of the family were expected to perform the functions of nursing assistants for loved ones. She solved the problem by going to the phone at the nurses' station and calling the man's son and ordering him to come to the hospital.

This experience and the fact that there was a sizable Hispanic community in White Plains convinced Brigid that in order to be effective at her job she would have to learn Spanish, so on the way home she stopped at the library in Tarrytown and found a course in Spanish on tapes. She checked it out of the library and took it home and after trying it decided to buy it. She called the phone number on the back of the book that came with the tapes, and she ordered courses for all three levels: beginning, intermediate, and advanced, paying for them with her credit card.

Over the next several months her spare time was occupied by learning Spanish, but after completing the advanced level she realized that she wouldn't become fluent in the language unless she practiced it and used it. In the meantime she and Yolanda had become friends and when they were on the same seven-in-the-morning to seven-in-the-evening shift they had drinks after work at a bar on Mamaroneck Avenue, which helped them unwind.

One night a young woman paused at their booth and had a brief exchange with Yolanda in Spanish before moving on.

"*Esa joven, es amiga tuya?*" Brigid asked.

"*Sí, fui a la escuela secundaria con ella. Tu acento no es malo.*"

"*Gracias. Lo he estudiado mucho.*"

"If you want to practice with me, we could talk in Spanish now and then."

"That would be great."

So after that they went back and forth between the languages, sometimes in the middle of a sentence, which made Yolanda laugh and say they were beginning to speak Spanglish.

Yolanda was single and lived with her family in a neighborhood of White Plains where there were Hispanics, mostly Cubans and Puerto Ricans. One night after work she took Brigid to a Cuban restaurant on Quarropas Street which had a line of steam trays as well as table service. There, after a round of mojitos, Brigid was introduced to roasted pork shoulder with black beans and rice and fried bananas, which in Spanish was *pernil con frijoles negros y arroz y plátanos fritos.* In perusing the menu she learned a lot of useful words in Spanish.

As time went by her Spanish improved, so she was better prepared for the next challenging situation. It was a young man who had come up from the emergency room via the operating room with a broken shoulder, a concussion, and face lacerations. He had short dark hair and coffee-colored skin, and when he opened his eyes they were filled with torment. From the nurse manager Brigid learned that he had run into a bridge abutment with his car, going fast, and the police suspected it was a suicide attempt. So she was instructed to watch him carefully.

It was after eleven at night when he arrived on her floor, and with lights out he went to sleep. But around two in the morning Brigid heard him screaming, and she rushed to the room, where she found him huddled in the bed with his knees up and his arms wrapped around his legs, shaking and sobbing. Instinctively, she went to him and put a comforting hand on his shoulder, saying: *"No te preocupes. Estoy aquí para ti."*

He raised his tear-filled eyes to her, looking grateful that she spoke his language.

Since there wasn't much happening at that hour she pulled up a chair and sat with him for the rest of the night, except for a few interruptions to do her rounds. And talking in Spanish he told her why he woke up screaming. He had a nightmare about the ambush in which he had lost two of his buddies, unable to help them. It was a nightmare that he kept having, along with flashbacks of how they had died. It had happened in the last year of the war. Since Brigid knew from his chart that he was twenty-three now she figured that he had been drafted and sent to Vietnam when he was only eighteen. And it broke her heart.

Her shift ended at seven that morning, but instead of leaving she stayed until the young man's parents arrived, shortly after the breakfast hour. They were both short, and the young man looked like his father, who had straight black hair, high cheekbones, and an aquiline nose. Conversing in Spanish, she learned from his mother that they were from Ecuador and they lived in the Bronx. The boy, Amato, was their only son, and their three daughters were all younger. Without being told, his mother knew that Amato had tried to kill himself, and she wept as she told Brigid that he hadn't gotten any help from the Veterans Administration. He had come home with both his arms and legs, so as far as they were concerned there was nothing wrong with him.

Brigid wanted to help him, but since she had no experience with mental disorders she got his mother's phone number and promised to call her. She left the hospital and went directly home, where instead of lying down to rest as usual she got on the phone and called the only person she could think of for a recommendation. It was

Thursday, so Dr. Hartmann would be in his office, seeing patients. She left a message for him, and within a half hour he got back to her. She knew him well enough not to apologize for calling him, she simply asked him if he could recommend a psychiatrist to treat a veteran with a mental disorder caused by the war. Without hesitation he recommended a man who was affiliated with the New York Hospital mental health center in White Plains and also, it happened, with White Plains Hospital. She called Amato's mother and gave her the name and phone number of the doctor, and then she lay down, exhausted from her lengthened shift. But she didn't sleep, she lay in bed thinking, envisioning a mission for herself that would tie together the different strands of her life.

The next day, which luckily was a day off, she called the head of the nursing department at St. Catherine and asked her if the college had a program in mental health. Indeed it did, a master's program in mental health that could be completed in two years. So that afternoon she drove to the college and got the brochure on program, which she read in the library. Since the program seemed to fit her needs she went and talked with an admissions counselor and enrolled in the program. There was no financial aid for graduate programs, but she figured that if she controlled her expenses she could pay for it herself. And since the program had rolling enrollment she could start it in the spring.

In the meantime Dana and Gray had bought a house in Bronxville, and Dana was back at Lawrence Hospital. Since O'Malley's was about midway between where they each lived they met there for lunch in late October. They hadn't talked since the end of July when Dana and Gray were about to go to Cape Cod for their vacation, so Dana began the conversation by asking Brigid how she liked her new job.

"It's fine," she said. "I mean, it's a normal job."

"So you don't miss working in the OR."

"No. The only thing I miss is the level of learning. But guess what." She paused for effect. "I've enrolled in a master's program in mental health."

"Really? You're a masochist."

"Well, I don't think it'll be as bad as the nursing program. At least it doesn't have courses in chemistry and microbiology."

"I hated chemistry," Dana said. "I never saw the point in learning that shit."

"I'm going to start the program this spring."

"Well, I'm sure you realize that going back to school will interfere with your social life."

"I don't have much of a social life. But I have a friend at the hospital who helped me learn Spanish and introduced me to Cuban food."

"Is she Cuban?"

"Yeah. She lives with her family in White Plains."

Dana sipped her drink. "Do you ever run into your ex-boyfriend?"

"No. We live and work in different worlds."

"Do you ever regret not marrying him?"

"I did at first, but I don't anymore. I've moved on with my life, and I have a new mission."

"Let me guess. You want to help veterans who were fucked up by the war."

"Yeah. You know me," she said, impressed.

"Of course I know you. We've been friends for how long?"

She counted. "I think it's ten years."

"Now, that's something."

"It's longer than I've had a relationship with anyone. I mean, except my parents and my little brother."

"What's he up to?"

"He's working for an engineering firm that does environmental impact statements for developers."

"Does he have a girlfriend?"

"Not that I know of."

After a silence Dana asked: "Do you have a boyfriend?"

"I don't have much time for a boyfriend, and after I go back to school I won't have any time for one. And I don't feel like I need a boyfriend."

"Well, having a husband isn't the answer for everything, but it goes a long way."

"You haven't gotten tired of him," Brigid kidded her.

"No, I haven't. I keep discovering new things about him. You know, being a WASP he's very different."

She understood, but she asked anyway: "How is he different?"

"He's more reserved. He keeps his feelings under control, but when he lets go—" Dana smiled beatifically. "But you must have found that with your WASP."

"Yeah, he had more passion than you'd ever guess."

"So maybe they're only different on the surface."

"Maybe they are. Maybe people of all backgrounds are only different on the surface."

For a while Dana pondered that statement, and then she said: "Well, I'm glad I married him, and I hope you find someone who'll make you feel the same way."

"Right now," Brigid told her, "I just want to get through this master's program so I can pursue my mission."

"You will. You were by far the best student in our nursing program."

That made her feel good. "Thanks. So how do you like living in Bronxville?"

"I like it a lot. I didn't think I would, but it's like the Upper East Side. It's the same kind of people, with the same kind of jobs, except they're taking the train to work instead of the subway. And you have more space living in a house."

"So we go in a circle, from houses to apartments and back to houses, and when we get old we go back to apartments."

"I don't want to think about getting old. We're only thirty, so we're still young."

"Yeah, it wasn't such a big deal turning thirty."

"The only thing is," Dana said, "I became more aware of the clock ticking."

Though she didn't think often about the clock she could understand why Dana would, being married and living in a house with rooms for children.

They had one for the road, and then they parted with a hug.

Brigid began the master's program in January, and from then on her time was completely occupied by studying for her courses, attending classes, and working at the hospital. She was challenged by the courses on physical assessment and pathophysiology, but she was able to build on what she had learned in the nursing program, and the new material helped her develop a greater understanding of her patients.

The most challenging course was advanced quantitative research methods, and it required her to review the math she had learned as an undergraduate, but once she understood the processes she felt empowered by her ability to use data for analyzing problems. For this work the college had a lab filled with Apple II computers, and along with word processing they were equipped with VisiCalc, a spreadsheet for working with data. Brigid had to learn how to use the computers and the spreadsheet because they hadn't existed when she was in the nursing program, but she had learned in high school how to touch type, and this skill was invaluable for using computers.

After she had completed the first year of the program her courses in the spring semester included a clinical practicum in therapeutic management, and at her request she was assigned to the Veterans Administration medical center in the Bronx. Though she had grown up in Yonkers, which bordered the Bronx, she had rarely been there, so she had to rely on directions from a fellow student to find her way to the VA medical center, which was on West Kingsbridge Road. With her pass she was admitted to a parking area, and she entered the massive building with doubts about whether she should have requested this assignment. She was supposed to work with Dr. Garrett, a psychiatrist, and with help from the receptionist she found his office. The door was open, so she walked in and saw a man with round shoulders behind a desk, studying a paper in front of him.

Reluctant to break his concentration she waited a few moments before saying: "Dr. Garrett?"

He looked up with perplexed gray eyes.

"I'm Brigid McBride." Since she could tell he had no idea why she was there, she explained: "I'm in the mental health master's program at St. Catherine College, and I've been assigned to you for a clinical practicum."

"Oh, yeah," he said as if that rang a distant bell. "Please sit down."

She sat in a chair in front of the desk and politely waited for him to speak.

After clearing his throat he finally said: "I hope you don't expect me to teach you. I'm very busy, so you'll have to learn by watching and listening."

"That's fine," she said.

"I'll explain to my patients that you're a nurse assisting me. You *are* a nurse, aren't you?"

If he had bothered to read her resume he would have known her experience. "Yes. I've worked as a nurse for nine years."

"Where did you work?"

"I worked for five years in the ER at St. John's, for two years in the OR at Phelps, and for almost two years on a surgery floor at White Plains."

He nodded. "Good. And why did you go into mental health?"

"I want to help veterans with mental disorders caused by the war."

"Well, you picked the right area. It's estimated that half of our veterans have mental disorders, so you won't have any lack of patients."

"You must see a lot of patients."

"We do. We're overwhelmed by them."

"What do you do for them?"

"We do what we can to treat their symptoms, but we don't have the resources to deal with their underlying problems."

She understood. "So how do you treat their symptoms?"

"With drugs. It's the only way we can deal with the volume. And the drugs help them. At least they enable them to function."

For now she didn't ask any more questions.

She spent the day watching and listening. Most of the time was spent in an examining room, where he saw one patient after another. By five o'clock she had lost count of the number of patients, almost all of them black or brown.

Since he left for the day shortly after five she left along with him, and they walked to their respective cars. As she drove home she reflected on what they had done for the patients. With returning patients the doctor began by asking how they were doing, and he listened to their disjointed answers. He had a nurse take their vital signs, and then he asked them questions about their specific problems. He concluded by renewing their prescriptions for whatever they were taking. To Brigid it didn't seem like he did very much for them, but she knew she shouldn't judge him because he obviously had more patients than any doctor could possibly handle. Still, she wondered why her master's program included nonpharmacological treatments when in the real world the treatments mainly consisted of drugs.

By the second week it occurred to Dr. Garrett that being an experienced nurse she could take the vital signs of his patients, which would release the regular nurse for other duties, so from then until the end of the semester she had more interaction with the patients, who while she was taking their temperature, their pulse, and their blood pressure would sometimes tell her things they didn't tell the doctor. One of them, a smooth-talking cute Dominican who discovered that she spoke Spanish, even asked her out on a date.

On her last day of the practicum she thanked Dr. Garrett and told him she had learned a lot from him, which was essentially true, though it didn't mean she had learned how to treat patients with mental disorders caused by the war.

About a month later, during the summer, she was attending to a man her father's age who had undergone gall bladder surgery, when his doctor came into the room. With a jolt she recognized Parker's father, whom she hadn't seen since she had broken up with Parker.

Smiling as if he was genuinely glad to see her, Dr. Ralston said: "I saw your name at the nurses' station, and I hoped it was you. How are you doing?"

"I'm doing fine," she said, overcoming her shock. "How are you doing?"

"We're all doing fine," he said, evidently including Parker.

She stepped back while he examined his patient and asked him questions. Of course she had a professional reason for staying in the room, but she also had a personal reason because she liked Dr. Ralston, and she hoped he hadn't been too upset by the breakup.

After making some notes in the patient's chart he invited her to follow him out into the hall, which she gladly did. She began the conversation by saying: "I didn't know you were affiliated with this hospital."

"I am, but I hardly ever come here. I have affiliations with other hospitals that keep me busy."

"Well, it's good to see you. I'll always remember how nice you were to me. And I'm sorry if I upset you and Mrs. Ralston."

"I respect your decision. And don't worry about Parker. He's a big boy." He paused and then changed the subject. "So what are you up to? I mean in your professional life."

"I've almost completed a master's degree in mental health."

"That's wonderful. What do you plan to do with it?"

"I plan to help veterans with mental disorders caused by the war."

"That's a fine mission. Do you have any specific plans?"

"No. I just did a clinical at the VA medical center in the Bronx, and the only thing I learned is that we're not doing enough for veterans with mental disorders."

"What are they doing for those veterans?" he asked as if he knew the answer.

"They're giving them drugs. And I understand why. From what I could see, they don't have the resources to do anything but treat the symptoms."

"So what would you do?"

"I'd deal with the underlying problems."

Dr. Ralston nodded. "I know a doctor who does that, and he's looking for a psychiatric nurse to assist him. Would you be interested?"

"Sure, I would, but I have one more semester to complete, and I have to pass the certification."

"If you're the right person, it might not be a problem. Of course he'd expect you to complete everything."

"Of course," she said.

He gave her the name and phone number of the doctor, and he said he would recommend her to him. She thanked him, and they parted in the hall.

The doctor's name was Wesley Osborne, and his office was in a medical building on Broadway across from St. John's. She made an appointment to see him, and two days later she was sitting in the reception area, waiting for him to return from an emergency. From the framed certificates on the wall she learned that he had his medical degree from Yale and his residency at Columbia Presbyterian Hospital, which together with his name suggested that he was another WASP. She smiled at the thought of what Dana would say if she got the job, that she was destined to spend her life working for WASPs.

A man in his forties with iron-gray hair and kind brown eyes rushed into the office, took one look at her, and said: "You must be Brigid."

"Yes," she said, rising from the chair.

"I'm Wesley Osborne. I'm sorry I kept you waiting but I had an emergency."

"I understand."

"Well, come into my office. Clara, please hold all calls."

She followed him into an office whose walls were lined with prints of Hudson River scenes. Besides a desk it had a sitting area with a sofa and two easy chairs. Motioning to one of them, he asked her to sit down, and he took the other one.

Instead of asking her about her experience he began by saying: "Tell me about your family."

"Well, my parents live in Yonkers," she said, unable to guess how much he wanted to know. "My father works for a beer distributor, and my mother's a nurse. She works at St. John's Hospital. And my younger brother's a civil engineer."

"How much younger is your brother?"

"Three years."

He nodded as if this was a satisfactory answer. "What about your grandparents?"

"My grandparents on my father's side live in Highbridge in the Bronx, and my grandmother on my mother's side lives on Nodine Hill in Yonkers."

"Were any of them immigrants?"

"They all were."

He nodded as he had before. "Where did they come from?"

"My father's parents came from Ireland, and my mother's came from Italy."

"So you got it from both sides."

Not understanding, she asked: "Got what?"

"Catholicism. I didn't get it from either side, but I married into it, and I converted. It was one of the best things I ever did."

She looked at him more closely, realizing that she had seen him and a woman on Sunday at St. Teresa. So he wasn't a WASP after all.

"Your resume says you did a practicum at the VA medical center in the Bronx. Did you learn a lot from that?"

"No. I only learned that they're not doing enough for veterans with mental disorders caused by the war."

"They're not," Dr. Osborne said, "but I don't blame them. They don't have the resources to do what needs to be done."

"What do you think needs to be done?"

"I'll tell you, but first tell me what *you* think needs to be done."

"I think we need to deal with the underlying causes of the disorder. I don't know how to do that, but if there's good way of doing it, I'm ready to learn."

Again he nodded, making her feel that she was giving the right answers to his questions. "Okay, I'll tell you what needs to be done. First, we need to name the disorder, describe it, and categorize it. You're familiar with the DSM?"

"Yes." She had learned about the Diagnostic and Statistical Manual of Mental Disorders in her program. It was the handbook published by the American Psychiatric Association that was used by psychiatrists and clinicians to diagnose mental disorders. It was also used to classify patients for billing purposes under healthcare plans.

"Well, back in 1952 the DSM had a name for it. Not a good name, but at least a name. They called it 'gross stress reaction.' But for some reason they took it out of the manual in 1968, and they didn't have a name for it until this year. I assume that the committees working on the DSM couldn't agree on what it was, so they decided not to deal with it, leaving us all to our own devices. During that period of limbo we had to call it depression or manic depression so that the patients would be covered for treatment under their healthcare plans. But we had a working name for it. We called it 'post-traumatic stress disorder.' Of course it's not a new disorder. It's been around since human beings started fighting wars. The name changed from 'shell shock' to 'battle fatigue' to 'combat exhaustion' and now finally 'post-traumatic stress disorder,' but the disorder didn't change. It's the same disorder that has always affected veterans of war, going back to the earliest wars in pre-history, and while there were ways of treating the symptoms there wasn't an effective way of dealing with the underlying causes. Until recently." He paused. "Based on our clinical experience, we think an effective way of dealing with the causes is cognitive behavioral therapy."

She had learned about cognitive behavioral therapy in her program, so she knew what it was.

"We believe that the disorder is caused by a traumatic event. The patient's behavior is a reaction to that event, and it's driven by fear. He usually has nightmares or flashbacks reliving the event, which can lead to violence either against a perceived threat or against himself. Which helps to explain why there are so many suicides by veterans."

"I treated a patient at White Plains Hospital who tried to kill himself by crashing his car into a bridge abutment."

"Then you know what I'm talking about."

"Yeah. That's what made me decide to go into mental health."

He nodded approvingly. "Our objective is to enable the patient to live with the memory of the event, and a promising approach that we're using now is a type of therapy in which the patient is exposed to the event in a controlled, safe situation. So the patient's fear is mitigated, and he learns to manage it."

"I understand," she said to let him know she was following him.

"But it takes a while for the patient to benefit, so we have to continue the therapy, and of course some patients take longer than others. For example, the emergency I had today was a patient who I thought was making progress. But this morning he tried to kill himself. He shot himself, aiming at his heart. He missed his heart, and he did some serious damage to his sternum, but he'll recover from that wound. The wounds he'll have trouble recovering from are invisible. The politicians who sent those boys to war don't see those wounds, so they don't believe in them and they don't provide enough money for proper treatment. When the boys who were drafted and sent to war return with severe mental disorders, the politicians don't care."

"I care," she told him with feeling. "I tried to stop them from being drafted."

He looked at her with interest. "You did? How?"

"When I was in college I joined the Catholic Peace Fellowship, and I was involved in antiwar activities. The high point was the summer I spent in the East Village with a friend and our mentor. We went out every day and demonstrated against the war. We stood in the streets wherever a lot of people could see us, but our most important target was the Whitehall induction center. One time we formed a human chain to stop the boys who had been drafted from going into the induction center."

"Did you succeed?"

"We succeeded in getting our pictures taken and published in the newspapers. But we were arrested, and we spent a night in jail."

"How did they treat you?"

"Not badly, but I wouldn't want to do that again."

"You don't have to. The war's over. But now we have to repair the damage."

"I'm sorry I got off the subject."

"No, that was helpful for me to understand your mission."

176

She collected her thoughts. "You were telling me about a therapy in which the patient is exposed to the traumatic event in a controlled, safe situation. So the patient's fear is mitigated, and he learns to manage it."

"There's more to it, but that's the basic idea."

"Okay. I think I understand how it works." From what she had learned in her program she saw how it could be more effective than just giving the patients drugs. And that thought led her to ask: "Do you use drugs?"

"I only use them if necessary to stabilize patients in the short term so that they can benefit from therapy. I don't use them in the long term. They don't help patients deal with the underlying causes." Abruptly changing the subject, he said: "According to your resume you're fluent in Spanish. How did you learn it?"

"By taking courses and talking with people. I found that I needed it for my work at White Plains Hospital."

"You'll need it for your work here."

For a while they sat in a comfortable silence, and then he told her: "After I read your resume I contacted Dr. Hartmann, whom you gave as a reference. I asked him about you, and he said you were the best nurse he ever had. So if you could work with that tough old German, I believe you can work with me. Do you want the job?"

Elated, she replied: "Oh, yes, I do. It would fit perfectly with my mission."

"Then you got it. And you can call me Wesley."

They agreed that she would start the job right after Labor Day, which would give them both a chance to take a vacation in August. She would still have to complete the final semester of her program, but the classes were in the evening, and now she wouldn't have to work around a schedule of twelve-hour nursing shifts. Her schedule would be like it was when she worked at Phelps, eight hours a day from Monday to Friday. Though she didn't have any social life, it would still be nice to have weekends off.

She gave notice to the hospital, and a woman in personnel who handled her departure told her she had three weeks of vacation coming, so her last day of work there was the first Friday in August. The following week she met Dana for lunch at O'Malley's, and she told Dana about her new job and her new boss. When Dana made her expected remark about his being a WASP, she corrected her and told her Wesley was Catholic, a convert to the faith, which made him a WASC. She also told her that based on the ring she had noticed on the third finger of his left hand, he was married, so her relationship with him would be strictly professional. Dana invited her to spend a week at Cape Cod with her and Gray, but she was afraid she would be a third wheel for them, so she graciously declined. She spent the week cleaning her apartment, thankful that the air conditioning worked because the weather was extremely hot, even for August.

During the last week of August she was walking along Main Street in Tarrytown, window shopping, when she was stopped by two girls wearing red tee shirts that said PAX CHRISTI. She had heard of this organization but she didn't know much about it, so she asked them about it, and they told her it was founded in France after World War II for the purpose of promoting peace and justice. Its members were mostly Catholic, as were the two girls, who went to Marymount College up on the hill. They told her their actions for peace and justice mostly consisted of peaceful demonstrations in the county and in the city. One of their current targets was the buildup in nuclear weapons, which they took every opportunity to oppose. They also had events with speakers. In fact, they were on the street that day to promote an event to be held at their college in late September. They gave her a flier for that event, and Brigid was startled by the name of the speaker: Fr. Kieran O'Donnell, a Jesuit priest and a professor at Fordham University, who would talk about his book *Our Unjust Wars*. The girls were selling tickets to the event as a way of raising money for Pax Christi. The event was on a Saturday evening, which wouldn't conflict with any of her classes, so she bought a ticket. The girl who took her money put her name and address on a list, evidently for the purpose of recruiting her for Pax Christi.

She hadn't let on that she knew the speaker, but after she got home she could no longer contain her feelings. It was eleven years since she had spent the summer in the East Village with Kieran and Laura, and it was eight years since she had met Kieran at "The Trial of the Catonsville Nine." Over those years while she was building a career in nursing, Kieran was advancing through the stages of Jesuit formation. While she played around with one guy and developed a serious relationship with another guy, Kieran must have remained celibate. So now he was a professor at Fordham, he had published a book, and he was going to give a speech at Marymount, a Catholic college for women. But most importantly Kieran had professed his final vows, and he was a priest, so now she had less hope than ever of getting him to love her the way she loved him. And feeling as if she had finally lost him, she sat down on the sofa and wept.

ELEVEN

AS USUAL HER family had a cookout in the backyard on Sunday of Labor Day weekend. Her grandparents from Highbridge were there, and her grandmother from Nodine Hill was there, still looking fit. In addition to her famous meatballs and sausages with peppers she had brought the cannoli that everyone loved from the surviving Italian bakery in her neighborhood. For the first time ever Brady came with a girlfriend, a pretty Latina whose name was Aleda. From talking with her in Spanish while Brady stood there at a loss, Brigid learned that she was Dominican, had grown up in Alto Manhattan, and now lived in White Plains. She worked at the White Plains campus of Mercy College, where she was getting a degree in business with free tuition as an employee. She had met Brady in the same bar where Brigid had gone with her fellow nurses at White Plains Hospital.

Switching to English so Brady could join in the conversation, they talked about the bar and the people who went there. It turned out that Aleda knew Yolanda, though not well because Yolanda was several years older and she was Cuban. That was something Brigid had learned from her patients: speaking Spanish might be the only thing Hispanics had in common, though Dominicans and Cubans did have other things in common, including the fact that their countries of origin had been ruthlessly exploited by the United States. In fact, their countries had both been occupied by the U.S. military.

As Brigid mingled with other members of her extended family, including her cousins on both sides, they wanted to know about her new job. She gave them a general summary of what she would be doing because she didn't know enough about it to give them any details. After hearing about the veterans who returned from Vietnam with mental disorders, they smiled and looked happy for her, and they didn't ask about her personal life.

She started the job the day after Labor Day. Clara, who served as receptionist and did the paperwork, which was in the process of being moved to a computer, gave her the forms she needed to fill out as an employee and also gave her an orientation. From Clara she learned that Wesley hoped to open an office in the Bronx so that they could serve patients for whom the Yonkers office wasn't convenient. Since most of their patients lived in southern Westchester or in the Bronx, and since most of them didn't have cars, the offices of the clinic had to be located where they could easily be reached by bus or subway. So the Bronx location was likely to be on Fordham Road near a subway station.

Clara was delighted that Brigid spoke Spanish, and from their conversation in that language Brigid learned that Clara was Dominican and lived with her family on Nodine Hill. It helped them get off to a good start when she told Clara that her grandmother lived on Nodine Hill and that her brother had a Dominican girlfriend.

When they were done she met with Wesley, who outlined her responsibilities. At first she would work closely with him in treating patients so that she could learn by observing and assisting him. She would perform the regular nursing functions, which included taking vital signs and reviewing the patients' physical conditions. She would sit with him while he interacted with the patients, and she would take notes. Since a lot of them spoke Spanish her fluency in that language would be useful for understanding what they meant. He had found that if they tried to speak English, or if he translated what they said into English, important meanings were distorted or lost. He explained that he had learned Spanish by serving in Colombia for two years as a volunteer for the Peace Corps after graduating from Williams College. He had grown up in Petersburg, a small town in upstate New York not far from that college, and he had gone there on a scholarship. His service in the Peace Corps was his way of reciprocating for the scholarship, and that had exposed him to a world where healthcare services weren't available, which had made him decide to go to medical school.

For several weeks she followed the training program, and she noticed that their patients were like the ones she had seen at the VA medical center, except that with fewer patients they had the resources to provide treatment at a deeper level. It wasn't long before she had a chance to observe exposure therapy, in which Wesley used photographs of a wounded man to trigger a reaction of fear from the patient. With soothing words he told the patient not to worry, there was no present danger, only the memory of a past danger, so there was nothing to be afraid of. The patient calmed down and quietly wept while Wesley held him, repeating to him that there was nothing to be afraid of. It reminded Brigid of scenes in which Jesus told his disciples not to be afraid, and she was so moved that she had to wipe away her own tears. At that point she knew that helping people in this way was what she had been put on earth to do.

On the last Saturday of September she drove from her apartment to the event at Marymount College. It started at seven in the evening, and it was held in a lecture hall that looked like it could accommodate about a hundred people. It was completely filled, with the audience consisting mostly of students but also professors, parents, and people from town who must have been recruited by those girls in the red tee shirts. There were no reserved seats, so Brigid was glad she had gotten there early. She took a seat in the middle of the eighth row, not wanting to be in the front row, right in Kieran's face.

When he strolled out onto the stage, led by a girl who was listed in the program as the president of the student committee on international affairs, Brigid was startled. It wasn't because he looked older, which he did a little, but because he looked essentially the same. With its wavy dark hair, its fine features, and its dazzling blue eyes, it was the same face that years ago had literally taken her breath away.

While Kieran sat down in a folding chair the girl went to the podium and introduced him as a Jesuit priest, a distinguished professor at Fordham University, and the author of a book that would rewrite history. She thanked her committee for sponsoring him, and she welcomed him to the podium with a round of applause. In fact, a number of the girls did more than applaud, they whistled and even screamed like girls about to see a rock star perform. It reminded her of how Kieran was received by the girls in the Catholic Peace Fellowship.

Standing at the podium he began by thanking the girl who had introduced him, thanking the committee, and thanking the college, which he noted had a close relationship with his university. He then launched into his speech, which he said would cover the material in his book. His thesis was that all the wars fought by our country failed to meet the criteria of the just war doctrine, which he briefly reviewed. He began the list with our War of Independence, which he refused to call the American Revolution as the textbooks did because it wasn't a revolution like those in France, or Russia, or Mexico, in which the ruling class was overturned. Our War of Independence was led by rich merchants from New England and rich plantation owners from the South whose only motive for the war was to relieve themselves of the monetary burden of supporting Britain. In other words, it was for money, and though the men who fought the battles were farmhands and laborers, it was the rich who reaped the benefits of victory. And what they established wasn't a democracy by any stretch of the imagination. It was a republic in which the rights and privileges were reserved for white males who owned property. Women, nonwhites, farmhands, and laborers had no rights, and they couldn't vote.

The purpose of the War of 1812 was to annex parts of Canada. As usual farmhands and laborers fought and died in that war, and since it was a failure the only people who benefitted were the owners of companies that provided equipment and supplies to our armed forces. The next war, the Mexican War, was for the same purpose, and this war achieved its purpose because it enabled us to annex a third of Mexico and thereby expand our country to the west. But neither this war nor the previous war met the first criterion of the just war doctrine because we were not attacked, though our government tried to make it look like we were attacked. And only the Mexican War met any criterion, namely, the third: there must be serious prospects of success. The Spanish American War again had the purpose of territorial expansion, and it met the third criterion but none of the others. To justify that war our government made it look like we were attacked. With the help of an obliging press, the accidental explosion of the battleship *Maine* was amplified into a cause for war.

World War I wasn't about expanding our geographical borders but about projecting our power into an unstable Europe, and our government tried to justify it by saying that our purpose was to make the world safe for democracy, which was blatantly hypocritical because we didn't have a democracy at home. Women still didn't have the right to vote, and blacks weren't even considered citizens, not to mention the immigrants from Ireland and Southern Europe who were treated at best like second class citizens. We were still the white male republic that emerged from our War of Independence, and despite the government's attempts to justify it, World War I met none of the criteria for a just war.

The Korean War was about containing communism, which threatened the rights and privileges of our ruling class. But that war met none of the criteria for a just war, beginning with the fact that we were not attacked. The Vietnam War was also about containing communism, and it met none of the criteria. What made that war especially heinous was the fact that we interfered in the war of independence of a country that was trying to liberate itself from a colonial power. Kieran said he could talk all night about that war, but because of the time constraint of his speech he would move on.

At that point he paused and asked the audience if he had left out any wars. A student raised her hand, he called on her, and she asked about our Civil War. And another student asked about World War II. He was ready for them, and he explained that in the cases of both those wars we were attacked, so they met the first criterion of the doctrine. But in his judgment they didn't meet the next three criteria, especially not the last criterion: the use of arms must not produce evils and disorders graver than the evil to be eliminated—for example, our use of bombardments and nuclear weapons against civilians. He admitted that both of those wars had an ultimate justification. Our Civil War ended slavery in our country, and World War II ended the genocide practiced by the Nazis against Jews and Slavs. But those justifications didn't exist at the beginning of those wars, they arose out of them. And since other ways of ending slavery and genocide hadn't been shown to be impractical and ineffective, those wars were also unjust, whatever their positive results.

Kieran concluded by stating that wars were not a way of achieving peace, and that peace was not simply the absence of war. A true peace was based on social justice, so if we wanted peace we had to achieve social justice. There was no other way.

His message went over well with the audience. They applauded enthusiastically, again with whistles and a few screams. When he opened the floor for questions, hands went up all over the place. For Brigid the most interesting question was did he think that after Vietnam we would ever get into a war like that again. His answer was yes because as a country we never learned from our mistakes. Still, he hoped that his book would have some influence on our leaders if they were ever tempted to go to war.

After the speech there was a reception in another room, where they served cookies and a non-alcoholic punch. On the far side of the room Kieran was seated at a desk with a pile of his books for signing. The line of adoring girls was long, so instead of going to the end of it Brigid walked around it, got his attention, and suggested that they meet afterward. He nodded definitely before opening a book to sign it for the next girl.

They went to a bar on Main Street and got a booth and ordered beers. A few silent men were installed at the bar and a group of boisterous college students were clustered at a round table in back. The sounds of "The Rose" by Bette Midler were coming from the jukebox. As they waited for their drinks he lifted a paper shopping bag and set it on the table, saying: "This is for you. I hope you like it."

185

Knowing what it was, she reached into the bag and pulled out his book. She opened it and saw on the title page an inscription, which said:

> Brigid,
> This is what I'm doing now instead of
> bombing draft centers.
> Peace,
> Kieran

"How did you know I'd be there?" she asked him.

"You live in Tarrytown, only five minutes from Marymount. If you hadn't been there, I'd have been pissed."

"But how did you know I live in Tarrytown?"

"They gave me a list of the people attending. Your name and address were on the list."

Silently thanking the two girls in the red tee shirts, she thumbed through the pages of the book, intending to start reading it that night.

"It's been a long time," he told her after she had raised her eyes from the book.

"Yeah," she said. "It's more than eight years since we met at Daniel Berrigan's play."

"You look good. What have you being doing?"

"I've been changing careers. I'm still a nurse but I went from the emergency room to an operating room to a surgery floor to a clinic that treats veterans with mental disorders."

"So now you're a psychiatric nurse?"

"Yeah. I have a master's in mental health."

"Do you like your present job?"

"I love it," she said. "I finally found my mission."

"I'm glad for you," he said, gazing at her with affection.

"Well, what about you?"

"As you saw in the program, I teach at Fordham, I write books, and I give speeches."

"What do you teach?"

"Philosophy and religion."

"Do you like teaching?"

"I love teaching," he said "It's the thing that gives me most satisfaction."

"I know you'd be a good teacher."

"It's nice of you to say that. I didn't teach you much."

"Yeah, you did. You were our mentor."

He shook his head. "I almost led you astray."

"Almost. But after all you made the right decision."

He stared at the table as if he had lingering doubts about it.

Changing the subject, she said: "I liked your speech. I wanted to ask a question, but those girls were all over you."

"What was your question?"

"Has there ever been a just war?"

"No, there hasn't. War is never justified. If you go back in history you see that every war was about territorial expansion. The wars of the Old Testament, the wars of the Greeks, the wars of the Romans, the wars of the Middle Ages—they were all about territorial expansion. They were started by men who needed to satisfy their egos."

"Did women ever start wars?"

"Yes, but not very often, and when they did they were usually influenced by a man."

"So what is it about men that makes them want to go to war?"

"You're the psychologist. You tell me."

She thought about it. "I guess it's a feeling of inadequacy. It's what makes a boy hit another boy on the playground."

"Do you think his feeling of inadequacy might arise from his feeling of injustice?"

"Yeah, it might. The boy might feel it's not fair for him to be short, or fat, or dumb. For him not to have things the other boy has."

"I think you're getting to the crux of it. He feels he should have those things, so he starts a fight and takes them. It's all about territorial expansion."

"But how does that explain our war in Vietnam?"

"It was about our wanting to expand the realm of our ideology

187

and to stop the other side from expanding the realm of its ideology."

"So it was our feeling of inadequacy, our feeling of injustice over the fact that we didn't have the whole world in our realm."

He nodded. "Yeah. Instead of being thankful for what we had, we wanted more."

"For me," she said after a moment, "the most interesting question they asked you was, do you think that after Vietnam we would ever get into a war like that again. And you said yes because as a country we never learn from our mistakes. So you don't think we learned *anything* from the war in Vietnam?"

"No, I don't think we did," he said. "There are politicians who say that if we'd gone all out, we could have won it."

"By bombing the North Vietnamese into the stone age?"

"Or by using nuclear weapons."

"What are they thinking?"

"They're not thinking. They're acting from the lower part of the brain. And it shows how little they understand the situation. The people they say we should have destroyed were fighting for their independence, for their survival. We were only fighting for expansion of our ideology. So there's no way we could have defeated them."

"Well, I wonder what those politicians would feel if they saw the boys who return from Vietnam with mental disorders."

"They wouldn't feel anything."

"You mean they wouldn't feel responsible?"

"Not at all. In their minds the other side was responsible for what happened to those boys."

"But *they* should feel responsible," she argued. "I tried to stop those boys from being drafted, and still *I* feel responsible for what happened to them."

"I understand. You're doing penance."

She nodded. "Yeah. I'm not doing what I do purely out of the goodness of my heart."

"That's why I teach, and that's why I write. I feel responsible for not finding a way to end the war sooner. I want to change people's hearts and minds so we won't commit that sin again."

"So you're doing penance too."

"Of course. We're all doing penance. I mean, those of us who care about what happened to those boys and what happened to those civilians in Vietnam. Do you know how many widows and orphans we left there?"

"No," she said, "but it must be a lot."

"It's hundreds of thousands, and they're escaping from that poor ravaged country any way they can, but mostly by boat."

She was aware of the boat people, but she hadn't thought about them much. "Are many of them coming here?"

"Yeah. They're also going to countries in Southeast Asia."

"Widows and orphans. God help them."

"You know what the Scriptures tell us? Be good to widows and orphans. Over and over they tell us to be good to widows and orphans."

They continued talking about other things, but what he had said about widows and orphans stuck in her mind. She was thinking about them as she drove home, as she undressed for bed, and as she lay in bed awake into the night.

After working with Wesley for about six months he started giving her patients of her own, though he was always there to guide her. The office had a room for medical examinations and two rooms for therapy, one of which he assigned to her. As she met with her own patients she applied what she had learned from him, and she gained confidence from the way the patients responded to her. Most of them were a few years younger than her but close enough in age so that she could have been their older sister. At times she was conscious of being a white girl, but that didn't seem to bother them.

With preparation and guidance from Wesley she did her first exposure treatment late in February. The patient, Jadyn, was a young black man who lived in south Yonkers and worked in the mailroom of a major publishing company in the city. He was a good-looking, intelligent guy who had played quarterback for the

Yonkers High School football team before graduating and being drafted into the army. He did two tours of duty in Vietnam, which wasn't usual but for some reason his unit was sent back there, and on his second tour of duty his patrol was ambushed by the Viet Cong. His best buddy was wounded by a grenade that ripped open his belly. After driving the enemy away and calling for medics Jadyn stayed with his buddy and stopped the guts from spilling out. But he couldn't stop his buddy from dying.

He had the usual symptoms of PTSD. He had a recurrent nightmare about his buddy's guts spilling out and wrapping around him like the tentacles of an octopus. He had flashbacks and headaches and moments at work when he was startled by a coworker opening a package with a box cutter. One time he attacked a coworker who was ripping open a large box, which prompted his employer to recommend therapy. He had started with a general practitioner on Yonkers Avenue, who had sent him to the VA medical center in the Bronx, where he had seen Dr. Garrett. It was Dr. Garrett who had referred him to her. After meeting with him twice a week for several weeks Brigid felt that he needed more than talking about the traumatic event, so she discussed with Wesley the possibility of exposure therapy

Wesley agreed that they should try it, and he had the idea of using photos from a surgical operation that showed the intestines of a patient whose belly had been opened up. The photos were in vivid color, and even after all that Brigid had seen in the emergency room and the operating room she had to grit her teeth to look at them. Wesley assisted her in the therapy, and he was standing by when Jadyn reacted to the photos. Brigid assured him that there was nothing to be afraid of, and while he sobbed she held him as if he was her younger brother.

It wasn't a miracle, there were no miracles, but it helped him overcome a major obstacle. They kept meeting twice a week, and it wasn't long before he started talking about going to college, taking advantage of his veteran's benefit. She asked him what career he would like to pursue, and he told her he wanted to be a teacher as well as a coach. She suggested that he apply to St.

Catherine, and she offered to write a letter of recommendation for him. Within a month he applied to the college and was accepted.

Having made some progress, Brigid called Dr. Garrett and thanked him for referring Jadyn. She told him what had been accomplished so far, and Dr. Garrett said he would keep referring patients to her.

In the meantime Dana had gotten pregnant and delivered a baby boy, whom she named Matthew after her father. Brigid visited her friend in Bronxville a few weeks after the birth, and she found Dana happier than she had ever seen her. Dana let her hold the baby, which made her realize that even though she loved what she was doing in her work, there was something missing from her life, and it wasn't a man.

Through the week that followed she thought about it, and wanting to talk with someone about it, she drove to her parents' house on Saturday afternoon. It was a nice day, with the weather finally warming up, and she found her mother as expected on the patio in the backyard, reading a novel by an author who they both agreed wrote nothing but trash.

She sat down in one of the chairs that her father had repaired many times, and her mother put down her book as if she knew there was something Brigid wanted to talk about.

"You know," she began, "I'm thirty-two."

"I know your age," her mother said, smiling. "I just happen to be your mother."

"I don't have much time to find the right man, to marry him, and to have a baby. And anyway I don't want to be married."

"Being married has advantages."

"I know. But it also has disadvantages. And I can't think of anything I need a man for."

"They're good at fixing things and opening bottles of wine."

"Yeah." She smiled. "Seriously, I'm happy being single, except that there's something missing from my life."

"What's missing?" her mother asked.

"Well, last Saturday I went to see Dana, who just had a baby.

She let me hold him for a while, and that's when I realized there's something missing."

"So you want to have a baby. That's good. But how can you have a baby without a man?"

"I can adopt one. There're a lot of orphans in this world."

"Yeah, there are. And I know you'd be a good mother."

"How do you know?"

"I know you. In fact, I've known you for thirty-two years," her mother reminded her. "That's as long as anyone has known you. So I know you'd be a good mother."

She appreciated her mother's support.

"So where would you find a baby to adopt?"

"A while ago I was talking with someone, and he reminded me that there are hundreds of thousands of widows and orphans from Vietnam."

"And that would fit your mission."

"It would." She was impressed by her mother's making the connection.

After thinking for a moment her mother said: "If you want to find an orphan from Vietnam you should contact Catholic Charities. They're involved in resettling the refugees from there. They recently sent me a letter requesting a donation."

"Do you still have that letter?"

"No, but you can easily find them. Their main office is in the city."

"Okay. I'll contact them."

"Now, if you're serious about this, you have to think about how you'd manage as a single mother. It's hard enough being a mother, but being single would make it harder. And having a job like yours would make it even harder."

"I could take a leave of absence."

"You wouldn't be happy without that job."

She didn't ask her mother how she knew. "Well, I could adjust my schedule. I know that Wesley would understand."

"I believe he would, but you should discuss it with him."

"I will. I mean, I would have anyway."

"You know," her mother said after a silence, "we have an empty house here, with two bedrooms that we don't use. So if you adopt a baby it would make sense for you to move back here. You'd be closer to your office, and you'd have two built-in baby sitters."

"You think Dad would go for it?"

"I know he would. He's dying to have a grandchild, and Brady's not moving fast enough for him, though he finally got engaged to Aleda."

"Really? That's great."

"They haven't announced it officially, but he told me. It's supposed to be a secret, so keep it to yourself for now."

She didn't have to think about her mother's offer before she said: "If I adopt a baby I'll move back here. Where's Dad?"

"He went to the Yankee's game with two of his good customers. I won't tell him about this until it's definite, okay?"

"Okay. And thanks, mom. Thanks for everything."

"Thank *you*—for a conversation that was a lot more interesting than this trashy novel."

She got up and went to her mother and hugged her, and then she left.

She started the process with Catholic Charities, whose main office was in a large new building on First Avenue at 56th Street. It began with interviews to make sure that she was qualified to adopt a baby. It greatly helped that she was a nurse, that she had an extended family, and that she was a practicing Catholic. A competent woman was assigned to her case, and eight months later they found a baby whose father was killed in the war and whose mother drowned when the boat they were using for their escape overturned. The baby was saved by a boy who was a good swimmer but was no relationship to her. The survivors were taken to the Philippines, where the baby was put into the care of local nuns. The plan was to fly the baby to New York accompanied by a young woman who volunteered her services for the purpose of relocating refugees. And they were scheduled to arrive in early February.

Right after the conversation with her mother Brigid had talked with Wesley about her idea of adopting a baby, and he had supported it, offering to adjust her schedule in any way that would help her. Since she was seeing patients on her own now they talked about her having a split schedule from nine to one and from three to seven, which would accommodate patients for whom it would be more convenient to meet in the evening and would work for her because she would live within walking distance.

When she learned that the adoption was definite she brought him up to date. It was around six in the evening after they had seen their last patients for the day and Clara had left. Sitting in the chair in front of his desk, she told him about the baby's background.

After hearing it he said: "Of course you realize that this baby, or any baby you adopt, will have PTSD."

"A baby? How?"

"From the trauma of losing her mother."

"But she's only eleven months old. How can she know she lost her mother?"

"She knows, believe me. And that will give you challenges. She won't be like the men you're treating, but the trauma will be there, deep inside of her, and when it comes out you'll have behavioral problems to deal with."

"I have experience dealing with them."

"I know you do, and that'll make you an ideal mother for someone like her. Not every woman who adopts a child has your experience. But you'll be challenged."

"I understand. And thanks for telling me. It helps to know what I'm getting into."

"For a baby with her background," Wesley told her, "for all babies, the most important thing is to give her love, to give her love, and to give her love."

When she saw the baby it was very easy to give her love, she was so adorable. Wesley suggested that she take a leave of absence for at least three months so that she could bond with her baby and enjoy the experience. According to the adoption papers her name was Nhu, and she kept that name, though when she was baptized at St. Brigid she was given the additional name of Maria, which Brigid didn't use in practice but called to mind when she prayed to the Blessed Mother.

After she went back to work she adopted the split schedule they had talked about, and it was fine. She had the early morning with Nhu, who napped during the middle of the day, and then she had the early afternoon with her. She was usually done before seven, so she was home in time to put Nhu to bed, in a crib not far from her own bed. As her mother had predicted, her father loved the baby and held her and talked with her and played with her. She hadn't realized how happy both her parents would be to have a grandchild.

Not much later Brady and Aleda were married, and they settled into a large apartment in White Plains, which they could afford with their two incomes: from his job at the engineering firm and from her job at Mercy College.

Nhu was in second grade at St. Brigid School when Wesley decided that the time had finally come to open a Bronx office. By then Brigid was on a schedule from nine to five, and since Wesley spent two days in the Bronx she covered the Yonkers office on those days. It wasn't long before they agreed to take on another doctor, who could spend three days in the Bronx and two days in Yonkers. With their records on a computer now, Clara was able to hold the expanded practice together, and she was happy with her higher salary.

Nhu was doing well, though there were times when she had a flare-up. Since she didn't have nightmares or flashbacks about losing her mother, and since Brigid was prepared for behavioral problems, she was usually able to deal with these problems, and she continued doing the most important thing: she gave Nhu love, she gave her love, and she gave her love.

When Nhu was around ten an incident occurred that made Brigid wonder if love was enough. It happened on the playground of the school where a boy called Nhu a name, and Nhu hit him, hard enough to give him a bloody mouth. Brigid was called into the office of the principal, who had heard from both parties to the fight. The principal was inclined to take Nhu's side after hearing what the boy had called her, but she told Brigid that she expected her to deal with the problem and make sure that there was no more violence from her daughter.

As soon as Nhu came home from school that day Brigid had a conversation with her. They were in the living room with no one else around, sitting on the sofa side by side.

After listening to her daughter's version, Brigid said: "Now, tell me again why you hit that boy."

"He called me a gook."

"That's really nasty. You know what that means?"

"It means I'm a yellow Asian who doesn't deserve to be alive."

"Is that how you feel? That you don't deserve to be alive?"

"I do when people call me that name."

"Have people called you that name before?"

"I don't remember, but they must have because I've felt that way before."

"You don't remember when."

"No. I just remember how I felt."

"That you don't deserve to be alive."

Nhu nodded. "It also makes me feel I don't belong here. I don't look like anyone else. I don't even look like you."

"Well, you don't have to look like me to be my daughter."

"I know, I know, but sometimes I feel I never should have left Vietnam."

"You didn't have any choice about that. Your mother took you with her when she escaped from there."

"Sometimes I wish she hadn't."

"If she hadn't taken you with her you probably wouldn't be alive. So your mother saved your life."

"But she died saving it."

"Do you feel it's your fault that she died?"

"Sometimes I do."

Brigid understood that Nhu was feeling survivor's guilt, which explained why she felt that she didn't deserve to be alive. She had dealt with this feeling in patients, so at least she recognized it. "When your mother decided to escape from Vietnam she did it for herself as well as for you. She risked both your lives in trying to save them. She knew what she was doing. So it wasn't at all your fault that she died, and you deserve to be alive because that was what your mother wanted. If she could see you now she'd be happy. Your being alive makes her dream come true. And you know what? It makes *my* dream come true."

Nhu gazed at her with the doubts fading from her eyes. "You really mean that?"

"I really do. Come here, sweetheart." She opened her arms and Nhu came into them for the refuge she needed.

There were no further incidents like that one, and though Nhu would always have to live with the loss of her mother she gradually learned how to deal with it.

Nhu did well in elementary school, and she did well at Sacred Heart High School. By the time she went to college at St. Catherine she knew she wanted to be a physician assistant, so she took the science courses for that program, which were like the courses that Brigid had taken in the first two years of the nursing program, except that there were more of them.

Nhu was starting her senior year of college when two hijacked airplanes crashed into the twin towers of the World Trade Center. When it happened Brigid was sitting in the kitchen having her breakfast and listening to the morning news on public radio. She was alone because her parents had gone grocery shopping and Nhu was in the process of getting up. The news commentator was interrupted by the announcement that a plane had flown into one of the towers. It was presumed to have strayed off course and accidently hit the tower. They were still talking, speculating, when Nhu came into the kitchen with her hair wet from taking a shower. Brigid told her what had happened, and Nhu sat down at the table with a bagel, looking grim.

"They think it was an accident?" Nhu said as if she didn't believe it.

"They don't know. They're trying to find out more about it."

They listened to the conflicting reports until shortly after nine when a second plane hit the other tower, and then they knew it wasn't an accident.

Nhu left for her morning class, and Brigid went to work, where she learned from Clara that it was a terrorist attack. She would have liked to talk with Wesley about it, but he was at the Bronx office with the other doctor. When her first patient called to cancel his appointment Brigid got on the phone to assure him that there was nothing to be afraid of, but he was freaked out. She urged him to come and see her, but she lost the connection. Evidently his cell phone service had been knocked out by the explosions.

For the rest of the week the news was all about the attack: the casualties, the heroic actions by the first responders, and the impact on New Yorkers. It didn't take long for the politicians to talk about retaliation, and when they learned that the man who had planned the attack was hiding in Afghanistan they demanded that the government there hand him over. That didn't happen, and within a month we invaded Afghanistan.

Brigid remembered what Kieran had said about our country never learning from its mistakes, and she resolved to oppose the war, which to her looked like Vietnam all over again. When she called Sister Maura to ask what the Catholic Peace Fellowship was doing, she learned that it was no longer active at the college because there weren't enough students with a strong commitment to peace and justice. She recommended that Brigid contact Pax Christi, and remembering the two girls in the red tee shirts, she called Pax Christi and learned that they were planning a demonstration against the war on the next Saturday. She told Nhu about it, and Nhu wanted to join her, so they made signs and on Saturday morning they took the train into the city.

The demonstration was being held at the Isaiah Wall, which brought back poignant memories. As they stood with the group of protesters, with Nhu holding a sign that said LOVE and Brigid holding a sign that said PEACE, she felt as if nothing had changed since thirty-three years ago when she and Laura had worn tee shirts with the same messages in the same place. A man who looked like a relic of the Sixties was standing in front of them, facing them, and evoking that era with his protest songs. When he started playing "Where Have All the Flowers Gone?" the group joined him. Brigid remembered Teri leading the girls of the Catholic Peace Fellowship in this song, and of course she knew the words, but she was surprised that her daughter knew the words and joined the group in singing: "When will they ever learn?"

TWELVE

As OFTEN AS possible Brigid and Nhu went into the city on Saturdays to join a demonstration against the war in Afghanistan, and later also the war in Iraq. On the surface these wars were different from the war in Vietnam, but fundamentally they were the same. Unlike the young men who were drafted and sent to Vietnam, the young men and women fighting in these wars were voluntary members of our armed forces, but their situation was the same because they still mostly came from levels of society where families were poor and opportunities were limited, and they still risked their lives on behalf of people who lived comfortably and never served in the military. Since the troops deployed in Afghanistan and in Iraq were serving voluntarily the protests this time didn't target draft boards or induction centers, they targeted the wars. In the mind of Brigid, who had read Kieran's book carefully, while the government exploited the public's fear of terrorism to justify these wars, their real purpose was to expand the realm of our ideology.

Meanwhile, Brigid continued her education. In the following fall, encouraged by Wesley, she enrolled in the doctoral program in psychology at St. Catherine, which offered most of the courses online and allowed her to do her clinicals at their office. With her master's degree in mental health she was on a fast track, and she already had a topic for her dissertation. She would use data from her patients to analyze the effects of cognitive behavioral therapy on veterans with PTSD. The only obstacle, which she easily overcame, was the requirement of the institutional review board that she get permission from her patients to use their data for this purpose, and her patients were all amenable to having their cases used in a study.

Nhu completed the bachelor's level of the physician assistant program and advanced to the master's level. During that time she developed a relationship with a young man with a doctorate in physical therapy from Columbia who worked for a successful practice in Irvington. His name was Sergio, and his parents were immigrants from the Dominican Republic who had moved from Alto Manhattan to Nodine Hill, where he grew up. He was a nice, sensitive young man, and Brigid really liked him. Remembering her own behavior in her early twenties, she had no problem when Nhu occasionally spent the night with him on Fridays, though she expected Nhu to tell her in advance when she wouldn't be coming home for the night.

Dana and Gray celebrated their twenty-fifth wedding anniversary. By then they had three boys, the oldest of whom was graduating from Dartmouth and had been accepted at Harvard Law School, following in his father's footsteps. The next oldest was going to MIT that fall, and the youngest was still at Bronxville High School. At the party they held at their country club Dana made a short speech, which she delivered looking straight at Brigid, saying that the secret of their marriage was that she hadn't gotten tired of Gray, and amid the friendly laughter that followed, Gray said he hadn't gotten tired of her either.

Brigid completed her doctorate in three years, and she was preparing to publish a book from her dissertation when Wesley was diagnosed with pancreatic cancer. He lasted long enough to turn over the practice to her. And then, before the end of that year, her father died of a heart attack. She was still mourning the loss of Wesley and her father when Vijay Patel came to her house and told her about finding Laura's body. So it had felt like a triple whammy.

About a month later Vijay called her and asked to meet with her again. He told her upfront that there were no new developments, so he only wanted to give her an update out of courtesy. They agreed to meet on the Saturday after Ash Wednesday. As they had done for years, Brigid, her mother, and Nhu went to the early service on Ash Wednesday at St. Brigid. They sat in their usual pew, the third from the front, with no one around them because for some reason people avoided the left front pews and congregated in the back.

The service began with the entrance antiphon:

> You are merciful to all, O Lord,
> and despise nothing that you have made.
> You overlook people's sins, to bring them to repentance,
> and you spare them, for you are the Lord our God.

This was followed by the collect, the first reading, the psalm, the second reading, and the gospel. Then came the blessing and distribution of ashes. Brigid let her mother and Nhu get into the line ahead of her, and she watched them come away from Father Paul with black crosses on their foreheads. When it was her turn she lowered her eyes as the priest put the ashes on her forehead, saying: "Remember that you are dust, and to dust you shall return." It made her think of her own mortality, and it also made her think of her father, Wesley, and Laura, who had returned to dust, and kneeling in the pew, she prayed for them.

When she got to her office she noticed that Clara, who was still with them after more than twenty-five years, had ashes on her forehead. She was now in her late forties, with two children in high school, and a husband who had the valuable skills for fixing computers. They had moved from an apartment on Broadway to a house in the neighborhood where Dana had lived, and their kids went to Sacred Heart.

She stood and talked with Clara for a while, reviewing the day's schedule. She was glad that her appointments today were continuing patients because she didn't feel like she had the mental energy to start working with a new patient. Her mind was at least partly occupied by anticipation of her meeting with Vijay on Saturday.

When that day finally came she heard the doorbell from the kitchen, where she was making another pot of coffee. She went to the door and greeted Vijay and invited him in, observing that he had politely waited for her invitation before moving forward.

She asked him to sit in the living room while she brought coffee, and she found him in the same chair where he had sat at their first meeting. She handed him the mug that said LOVE and she kept the one that said PEACE. She watched him take a sip of coffee, marveling at the fineness of his fingers and the length of his eyelashes.

"Thank you for meeting with me," he said. "I wish I had more to report, but at least I can tell you about our efforts to find out what happened."

She nodded for him to go ahead.

"After reviewing the notes of the police and the notes of the private detective we concluded that whatever happened to Miss Hughes, it must have happened in one of three possible intervals: between her house and the Poughkeepsie train station, between Penn Station and Poughkeepsie, or between your apartment and Penn Station."

"Okay," she said. "What about the first possibility?"

"That was the one the police thought was the most likely. They even had a suspect for a while, a guy who prowled the area between her house and the train station. But it turned out that he had an airtight alibi. He was in jail at the time Miss Hughes disappeared."

"So what about the second possibility?"

"The police and the private detective checked at the stops where she could have gotten off the train between Penn Station and Poughkeepsie. It was an express train, so there weren't many stops. And none of the people at the station offices remembered seeing her. She was a strikingly beautiful blond, so if they'd seen her they would have remembered her."

"I think they would have," Brigid agreed.

"That doesn't rule out the possibility that she got off the train, or was forced off the train, at one of those stops along the way, but it doesn't seem likely."

"What about the third possibility?"

"That's the hardest one to investigate. There are so many things that could have happened to her between your apartment and Penn Station, and so many possible witnesses. As they say, it's worse than looking for a needle in a haystack. The private detective interviewed everyone at Penn Station who could have seen her board the train, and he didn't find anyone who remembered seeing her. Still, he determined that she did buy a ticket to Montreal, so he believed that she was going to Canada and that something happened to her on the way."

"As I recall, that's where he left it."

"He didn't know that her body would be found in Peekskill. And there's one more thing he didn't know."

"What's that?"

"Since I talked with you the first time our forensics people analyzed the remains of a piece of paper that was found in her pocketbook. Over the years the paper had deteriorated beyond recognition, but they were finally able to identify it as a train ticket to Montreal."

"So she never used her ticket."

"It looks that way."

"Then whatever happened to her, it happened between our apartment and Penn Station."

"Yes, that's what we believe now."

Brigid thought for a long moment. "If she didn't use her train ticket, then how did she get to Poughkeepsie?"

"We wondered about that. And we speculated that she could have been driven there by someone who picked her up in the city."

"She wouldn't have gotten into a car with a stranger. It had to be someone she knew."

"She knew people in your neighborhood, didn't she?"

"Yeah, she did." There were all those artists, writers, and musicians whom they had known casually. And being a trusting person, Laura could have gotten into a car with one of them. But most of them didn't have cars.

"I know it was a long time ago, but if you can think of anyone who could have offered her a ride, please let me know. Otherwise our department will have to end this investigation."

"I understand." She assumed that they had limited resources that were needed for other things. "If I can think of anyone, I'll let you know."

"All right. And thanks for your time."

She showed him to the door and went back into the living room and collected the empty coffee mugs, feeling disheartened.

Of course she fully understood that finding out what happened to Laura wouldn't have brought her back, but at least it would have provided closure.

That night she lay awake, remembering the conversation with Vijay, and what stood out was a fact that she hadn't known before, that Laura hadn't used her train ticket. And she was intrigued by the theory that someone had driven Laura to Poughkeepsie. The faces of the artists, writers, and musicians swirled around and around in her mind. Back then she knew some of their names, especially the ones who hung out at Rigoletto, and they were the most likely ones. But after all that time she couldn't remember any of their names. She doubted that the coffee shop was still in business or that Carmine, whose name she did remember, was still around. Before going to sleep she resolved to find out the next morning.

After searching through the internet and finding nothing about the coffee shop or about Carmine, she decided that the only way to get the names of people they had known that summer was to ask Kieran and see if he could remember anyone. She had followed his career but she hadn't actually seen him since the speech he gave at Marymount, and that was more than twenty-five years ago. Not knowing how to contact him, she went to the directory of Fordham University, and among the faculty in the theology department she found an email address for him. She wanted to keep her message simple, so she asked him if he was free for lunch this Saturday or the next. When she didn't hear from him by the next day she was worried that something had happened to him, or that he didn't want to see her. But the following day she got a message from him, and they arranged to meet on Saturday at O'Malley's because he said it would easier for her than going to Fordham and finding a parking spot.

He was in a booth when she arrived, and she sat down facing him. There were streaks of gray in his wavy hair and two parallel lines in his forehead but otherwise he hadn't changed, and the sight of him still made her heart beat faster.

"It's good to see you," he told her affectionately. "You look great."

"Thanks," she said, accepting the compliment. "So do you."

"Tell me what you've been up to."

"Okay. Since I last saw you I got a doctorate in psychology, and I have a clinic in Yonkers where I help veterans with PTSD. They're veterans from Vietnam, Afghanistan, and Iraq, and they keep coming. But the most important thing is, I adopted a baby from Vietnam."

"Wow, you've been busy. Tell me about the baby."

"She's not a baby any more, she's a young woman who just turned twenty-four. She's a physician assistant, and she works in the ER at St. John's Hospital."

"It sounds like she's following in her mother's footsteps."

"She's gone way beyond me," Brigid said. "When I worked in the ER back then I was only a nurse, but she can do almost anything a doctor can do."

"You haven't mentioned a father."

"She doesn't have one, except her biological father who was killed in Vietnam."

"It sounds like you've had a good experience being a mother."

"It's the best experience I've ever had. I mean, it wasn't easy. She had some baggage from losing her mother, but she learned how to live with it."

"I'm sure you helped her."

"I tried," she said. "But there are limits to how much you can help another person. At some point they have to help themselves. So I give her credit."

A waiter came and took her order for a glass of white wine.

"You know," Kieran said, "it's more than twenty-five years since we last saw each other. Can you believe it?"

"No, I can't. The time goes so fast."

"I measure time by semesters, in batches of students. They keep coming."

"So do your books. I counted nine of them since I saw you at Marymount."

"There's another on the way. I used to think I'd run out of material, but we keep going to war. We keep making the same mistakes over and over."

"That's a definition of insanity."

"You may remember what Daniel Berrigan said in his play, that the war in Vietnam was a symptom of a 'massive institutionalized disorder.' Which is insanity."

"Whenever I can, I go into the city and protest against the war in Afghanistan and the war in Iraq. My daughter goes with me, and we have signs with the same messages that Laura and I had on our tee shirts when we demonstrated against the war in Vietnam."

"Love and peace."

"Right," she said, seeing an opportunity to broach the subject. "Speaking of Laura, about a month ago a detective from Peekskill contacted me, and I met with him in our living room. He told me they'd found Laura's body."

"What?" He looked extremely upset. "Where did they find it?"

"Outside of Peekskill on an old estate. The land was being cleared for development, and when they opened the family mausoleum they found her body."

"How do they know it was her body?"

"Her suitcase was with her, and it had a tag with her name and address."

"Oh, my God," he said, closing his eyes and exhaling.

"They think someone killed her and took her there, but they don't know where or how it happened or who did it. They asked me to help them."

After a long silence he asked: "Where do they think it happened?"

"They think it happened after she stopped at her home in Poughkeepsie because there were winter clothes in her suitcase, which she must have gotten there. She didn't have any winter clothes at the apartment."

"Do you think she was planning to stay in Canada?"

"As far as I know, she was only planning to stay there for a while and then to return for the fall semester. But she must have wanted the option of staying there."

After another long silence he said: "So they think it happened on the way to Canada?"

"For a long time they did. But recently they identified a piece of paper from her pocketbook as a train ticket to Montreal, so they know she never used the ticket."

"Then how did she get to Poughkeepsie?"

"They think someone gave her a ride there, someone in the neighborhood who had a car. And that's where I need your help. I can't remember the names of the people who hung out at the Rigoletto. Do you remember any names?"

"I could probably dredge up names," he said, "but if someone gave her a ride to Poughkeepsie he had a car, and the only people who had cars were musicians who needed them to carry their equipment."

"Well, I remember a big guy who played the drums. He must have had a car."

"He did. And there were some others. But that was thirty-seven years ago, and even if we could remember a name, how would they find him?"

"I don't know, but musicians belong to unions, so there could be a record of him."

"There could be. Well, let's see if we can remember the name of the drummer."

She thought for a while. "I think his name was Stanley."

"Yeah, it was Stanley."

"I think Stanley is a Polish name, so what's a Polish last name? Kowalski?"

"That's the name of a character in 'Streetcar Named Desire.' He was played by Marlon Brando."

"Oh, yeah." She paused. "My mother grew up in a neighborhood that was Polish and Italian, so maybe she can suggest a last name."

"But there were other musicians who had cars."

"Well, whoever it was, it was someone she knew. She wouldn't have gotten into a car with a stranger."

They ordered burgers, and while they were eating, Kieran told her about his latest book. It was about the current wars in Afghanistan and in Iraq, and he explained how the purpose of these wars was to expand the realm of our ideology.

When she got home she found her mother in the family room watching an old movie on television. It was black and white, a crime movie with Humphrey Bogart, whom her mother adored. She sat down on the sofa with her mother and they watched the last fifteen minutes of the movie. Then, using the remote, her mother turned off the television as if she knew that Brigid had something on her mind and wanted to talk about it.

"I had lunch with Kieran today," she began.

"How's he doing?" Her mother had never met Kieran but she had heard enough about him so that the question came naturally.

"He's doing fine. He's going to publish another book."

"That's nice. He's at Fordham, right?"

"Yeah, he's at Fordham." She hadn't told her mother what she had learned from the Peekskill detective at either of their meetings because she didn't want to burden her mother with it, so she approached the subject in a roundabout way. "When you grew up on Nodine Hill, you said it was a Polish and Italian neighborhood. Did you have Polish friends?"

"Of course. I went to a Polish elementary school."

She should have thought of that. "Oh, yeah. You went to St. Casimir. Well, I'm trying to think of Polish last names, and maybe you can give me some."

"Yeah, I can give you some Polish last names." Her mother proceeded to reel them off, most of them ending in "ski."

She listened carefully, but none of them sounded familiar.

"Why do you want to know Polish last names?"

"I'm trying to find a guy who had a Polish first name. At least I think it's a Polish first name."

"What's the name?"

"Stanley."

"Yeah, that's a Polish first name. Along with Walter, it's one of the most common Polish first names. I learned from the nuns how to say it in Polish. Stanislaw."

"Was he a saint like Casimir?"

"Right." Her mother looked at her curiously. "So why are you looking for this guy named Stanley?"

She decided to tell her mother everything. "The detective who came to see me last month had news about Laura. They found her body on an estate near Peekskill, in a mausoleum, and now the detective believes that instead of getting on a train for Montreal, she was given a ride to Poughkeepsie by someone she knew in the East Village. He believes that after taking Laura to her home in Poughkeepsie the guy killed her and hid her body in the mausoleum. Whoever it was, he must have had a car, and musicians were the only people in our neighborhood who had cars. So I remembered a drummer named Stanley, who had a car, and he was one of the guys who hung out at the local coffee shop."

"Good Lord," her mother said softly.

"So that's why I want to remember his last name."

"I understand. Do you remember other people who had cars?"

"There were other musicians, and I'm still trying to remember their names."

After a silence her mother asked: "Weren't you renting the apartment from a musician?"

"Yeah, we were. But he was touring Europe at the time. He couldn't have done it."

"But didn't you have the use of his car?"

"We did. It was a van, which Kieran used for trips to New Jersey. He used it to pick us up at the jail when he got us released. What are you suggesting?"

"I'm not suggesting anything. I'm only saying you should expand your list of people in the neighborhood who had cars."

"I don't have a list to expand."

"Well, think of other people that Laura knew well enough to accept a ride from. People who had cars."

"Okay, I will. And thanks, mom."

Her mother put a hand on her shoulder, saying: "I hope you don't feel responsible for what happened to her."

"I don't, though I feel I might have done something to stop it from happening."

"You couldn't have stopped it from happening. You weren't there when she decided to accept a ride from someone."

She believed that her mother was right, and that made her feel better, not about what had happened to Laura but about her possible role in the matter. And that night, as she lay in bed awake, she kept remembering what her mother had said about the car that belonged to the musician they were renting the apartment from. Before going to sleep she even considered the bizarre possibility that the musician had stealthily returned from Europe and met Laura on her way to Penn Station.

The next morning, while she was seated at the kitchen table having coffee and checking her email, she saw a message from Kieran, which said he needed to see her urgently. This message was so unlike him that at first she wondered if it really came from him, but then after checking her schedule she responded, suggesting that they meet in her office at eleven-thirty. By then she should be done with her ten o'clock appointment, and her next appointment was at one, which would give her an hour and a half with him. Within a few minutes he replied to her message saying he would see her at eleven-thirty.

When he arrived, on time, he looked as if he had been up all night. In his eyes was a look of agony that made her wince. It was a look she had seen in the eyes of her patients many times over the years, so she knew he was in serious trouble.

She led him into her office and closed the door and invited him to sit down where her patients sat for counseling. She sat down in the chair opposite him.

"I'm sorry to bother you," he said humbly. "But I have three confessions to make today. The first was to a priest, and this is the second."

She waited for him to continue, giving him the time she would have given to a patient.

"You may have noticed that I was shocked by what you told me yesterday. I mean, about their finding Laura's body. And I'm going to tell you what happened to her."

She should have been surprised that Kieran knew what had happened to Laura but she felt as if she had known all along that Kieran was hiding something from her. It had only been an

211

intimation, which she had dismissed whenever it arose in her consciousness, and even now as she listened to him she couldn't believe what he was saying. She wondered if he was making it up, as she had occasionally made up sins when she was a child in need of something to confess to a priest.

As usual he had gotten up early on the day when Laura was going to leave for Canada. He said goodbye to her in the kitchen where she was having breakfast, and he left the apartment. He was walking to where he had parked the van, which he planned to use for a trip to New Jersey to reconnoiter the records center, when he ran into the assistant pastor of Most Holy Redeemer Church. The man was a Jesuit who had been assigned to that parish with a mission of reaching out to the poor, so they had a lot of things in common. They ended up talking for almost an hour, and as Kieran was driving the van around the block in order to head crosstown to the tunnel he saw Laura carrying her suitcase. Of course he stopped and offered her a ride to Penn Station, which she accepted. While they were waiting for a traffic light to change she wondered aloud if she should stop at Poughkeepsie and get some winter clothes from her home, and seeing an opportunity to convince her that his plan to bomb the records center would not have any risk of hurting people, he offered to drive her to Poughkeepsie. At first she declined, but then she accepted his offer, maybe because she saw an opportunity to convince him not to bomb the center.

On the way to Poughkeepsie everything went well until they got into the subject of his plan. Laura was adamantly against it, arguing that it was wrong to take a chance on the life of someone who might be in the building. He insisted that he could be sure that there was no one in the building, and she maintained that there was no way he could be absolutely sure, and they were still arguing by the time they arrived at her home in Poughkeepsie. She said it wouldn't take her long so he offered to wait and drive her to the Poughkeepsie train station. While she took her suitcase upstairs he sat at the kitchen table and decided he wouldn't have time to go to New Jersey that day.

Returning with her suitcase, Laura said she still had plenty of time to catch her train, so she made coffee. They sat at the table drinking coffee and recalling their experiences of that summer. It looked as if they would part on good terms, but then the argument flared up again, and Laura told him that if he didn't promise not to bomb the records center she would call the police and tell them about it. He didn't believe she would do such a thing, but then she got up and went to the phone that was on the counter. Holding the phone, she told him he had one last chance to promise not to bomb the records center. Angered, he got up and tried to take the phone away from her. While they struggled for the phone she lost her balance and fell backward, hitting her head against the counter. It snapped her neck, and she went down. He rushed to her, already knowing that something terrible had happened to her. Desperately, he looked for signs of life in her, but she wasn't breathing and her heart wasn't beating. She was definitely dead.

He got the phone and was about to call the police when he thought about the consequences. He hadn't killed Laura, but there would be questions. They would want to know exactly what had happened to her. They would want to know what a Jesuit seminarian was doing alone with her in the house. They would probably conclude that to some extent he was responsible for her death. And they would report the incident to his superiors, which could get him expelled from the Jesuit program and prevent him from carrying out his mission.

Still holding the phone, he sat down at the table and wondered what to do. He didn't consider simply leaving because if he did, her parents would come home from vacation and find their daughter's rotting corpse on the kitchen floor. He had to hide her, but where could he hide her? He wasn't physically capable of digging a hole big enough to bury her, so he had to find another way to give her a dignified resting place. And then out of nowhere he remembered the family mausoleum on the estate outside of Peekskill where he had gone in the summer with friends to drink and party beyond the purview of their parents. They had never gone inside the mausoleum because it had a padlock on the door, so if he wanted to hide Laura's body there he would have to break the lock and replace it, and that would mean going to a hardware store and getting what he needed. For a long time he sat at the table and finally, unwilling to accept the consequences of calling the police, he decided to hide Laura's body in the mausoleum.

The first thing he did was pick up her body and carry it out to the van. After laying it in the back of the van he returned to the kitchen, where he looked around. There was no blood or any sign of what had happened, but there were coffee mugs on the table and the coffee filter on the counter. He washed them, dried them, and put them away where he thought they should go. And finally, in an act that bordered on madness he used his handkerchief to wipe the places where he might have left his fingerprints. He got Laura's suitcase and her pocketbook and left the house, stopping outside the back door. He found the key in her pocketbook, and he locked the door. As an afterthought he wiped the doorknob and around it. He put the suitcase and the pocketbook in the back of the van, and then he got in and drove away.

At a hardware store that he found in Poughkeepsie he bought a crowbar and a new padlock like the one he remembered. He drove to Peekskill and killed time there, parked at a spot that overlooked the river, and after it was dark he drove to the estate. It had a driveway that had given his group of teenagers easy access, and he took the van as close as he could to the mausoleum. The padlock was rusted, so it was easy to break with the crowbar. He opened the door and confronted an old smell of death. He went and got Laura's body, which he laid carefully on a slab that covered someone's grave. He arranged her as if she was sleeping on her back. He went and got her suitcase and her pocketbook and brought them into the mausoleum. And then he knelt beside her and prayed for her soul.

It was after ten when he left the estate, and he got as far as Ossining before he decided not to return to the apartment. He called Brigid from a bar in Ossining to let her know he wouldn't be home that night, and he checked into a cheap motel.

"So that's what happened to Laura," he said, staring bleakly into space.

Brigid was speechless. In fact, she only managed to say: "So

214

you weren't in New Jersey when you called me that night. You were in Ossining."

"Otherwise known as Sing Sing, where I belong."

"I don't know where you belong, but you must have been in hell since then."

"I've thought about it every day. I've had nightmares about it."

She recognized this symptom from her patients who had PTSD. He suffered from the trauma of being involved in Laura's death and being in some way responsible for it, but she understood that the treatment she could offer wouldn't work for him. In his case he needed to pay for what he had done. "So where are you going to make your third confession?"

"I'm going to the police. Could you give me the name of that detective?"

"Sure," she said. "What do you think they'll charge you with?"

"I don't know. Concealing a death?"

"But that's not what you charge yourself with."

"No." He gave her a long tormented look. "I charge myself with putting my mission ahead of other human beings."

"You mean ahead of her parents."

"Yeah. I let them wonder all that time what happened to her. I should have called the police and told them, then and there."

She paused to think. "Is that why you decided not to bomb the records center?"

He nodded. "Yeah. I realized that she was right, and I felt I owed that much to her."

"Well, until I've processed what you just told me, I won't know how I feel about it." Though she had been professionally trained not to judge people, she still had to make an effort to say: "But I won't judge you."

"Thanks," he said. "God will judge me."

"God will have mercy on you."

There was nothing else to say for now, so they got up. As they stood here, for the first time since she had met him Kieran was accessible for a hug, and she gave it to him. She hugged him with all her heart and soul.

Her appointments with patients helped her get through the rest of the day. She left the office around six and walked home. On the way she processed what Kieran had told her. She still didn't want to believe it but she knew he wouldn't invent something that made him look so bad. It forced her to admit to herself that he wasn't the man she had thought he was. It toppled him from a level where she had revered him to a level where she pitied him. But she was also angry at him for hiding what had happened to Laura, she was angry at herself for being in love with him, and she was depressed, feeling that now she had nothing left from that summer of youthful hopes and dreams.

When she got home she found her mother in the kitchen preparing dinner. Her mother took one look at her and turned off the stove and made her sit at the kitchen table, where she sat next to her, gently asking: "What happened to you?"

"I found out something awful today."

"Tell me about it."

She told her mother what she had learned from Kieran, and she finally revealed that she had been in love with him since she was a sophomore in college.

"You were in love with a priest?"

"He wasn't a priest when I fell in love with him. He was a seminarian, and I was hoping he'd change his mind about being a priest."

"A lot of them did," her mother said, "and a lot of them left the priesthood."

"Yeah." She remembered how Philip Berrigan had left the priesthood and gotten married. "So it wasn't a crazy hope."

"No. But after he became a priest were you still hoping?"

"I guess I was. I wasn't always conscious of it."

Her mother nodded and then said. "Well, now you know what happened to Laura."

"Yeah, now I know. And it makes me angry."

"Angry at him?"

"Angry at him and angry at myself."

"But you understand why he hid what happened."

"I do understand, but I don't condone it. What he did to her parents was really horrible. Keeping them in the dark about it for all those years."

"It *was* horrible," her mother agreed. "But why are you angry at yourself?"

"I'm angry at myself for being in love with him."

With a look of compassion her mother said: "You couldn't help being in love with him."

"But all those years I looked up to him, and now I know he's no better than I am."

"I understand. He's fallen from grace."

"So maybe I'm angry at myself for being wrong about him."

"Maybe you are." Her mother paused. "Do you think he'll confess to the police?"

"I know he will. He needs to pay for what he did."

"They'll let him off lightly. It's not like he abused an altar boy."

"But he won't let himself off lightly. He told me that he thought about it every day and that he had nightmares about it. So he'll punish himself."

Her mother nodded as if she understood. "Well, I hope you don't punish *yourself* for being in love with him."

"No, I won't. I've already paid for it."

Two days later she got a phone call from Vijay who told her that Kieran had come to him and confessed. Vijay sounded happy that he had successfully concluded his investigation, and he thanked Brigid for helping him.

A week later he gave her an update. Kieran pleaded guilty to concealing a death and was given a suspended sentence of one year in prison. He resigned from his position at Fordham and was teaching at a Catholic high school in the South Bronx, filling a position that suddenly became open when the man who held it was killed on the street.

The big event of the year for Pax Christi, which she had joined while participating in their demonstrations against the current wars, was the Way of the Cross on Good Friday. Its purpose was to present issues of peace and justice by linking them to Stations of the Cross. At each station an issue was presented by members of local chapters of Pax Christi in the metropolitan area. Signs of protest were not allowed but participants were encouraged to wear visible crosses and were expected to maintain silence except when they were praying, singing, or chanting.

Brigid invited Nhu to join her, so they took an early train from Yonkers to Grand Central and walked to Dag Hammarskjold Plaza, which brought back memories of demonstrations against the war in Vietnam. About three hundred people were gathered on the plaza with leaders and helpers of Pax Christi in red tee shirts. A flatbed truck was parked at the edge of the plaza, with musicians and audio equipment on it. Promptly at eight-thirty a tall woman in a red tee shirt climbed up onto the flatbed and went to a microphone and welcomed them to the twenty-third annual Way of the Cross. A bishop gave the invocation, and the event began with the first station: *Jesus is condemned to death.* According to the programs that a helper had given Brigid and Nhu, the issue of this station was refugees, presented by members from a church in Queens. The station began with a prayer that they would say at each station: "We adore you, O Christ, and we praise you. By the power of your holy cross, change us and help us to change the world." The members who presented the issue did a reading from Luke about Pilate reluctantly letting the crowd condemn Jesus, and then they described the plight of refugees who were treated inhumanely by our government. This was followed by a responsive prayer and then by a song led by the musicians strumming guitars: "Be Not Afraid." They remained on the plaza for the second station: *Jesus is made to carry the cross,* which presented the issue of nuclear weapons proliferation, and then they began a slow march across the street and down Second Avenue, led by a strapping young man who held on high a large wooden cross. As they walked they chanted: "*Ubi caritas et amor, ubi caritas, Deus ibi est,*" which Brigid translated for Nhu as: "Where there is charity and love, God is there."

As their procession moved south and then headed west on 42nd Street she was impressed by the way their attentive police escort stopped traffic for them and cleared a parking spot for the truck at the next stations, where local chapters presented the issues of intolerance, health care, poverty, homelessness, hunger, denial of education, abuse of the earth, and human trafficking. At the eleventh station, *Jesus is nailed to the cross*, the issue was militarization, and the flatbed truck was parked near a U.S. Army recruitment center. The issue was presented by two students from a Catholic high school in the South Bronx, a black and a Latino, who effectively delivered their script, which ended with the lines: "Jesus refuses a dose of drugged wine to ease his torment. May we also refuse the drug the national security state offers us—the illusion that life is sustained by violence rather than compassion, reconciliation, and justice." The song that followed the responsive prayer was "Blowin' in the Wind," which everyone knew, and singing along with them Brigid consciously projected the words toward the army recruitment center.

When the students climbed down from the flatbed they were met by a man in clerical clothes whose face she didn't see at first, and then she saw that it was Kieran. She was still affected by the sight of him, but now it was a warm sisterly feeling.

She and Nhu were standing near the front of the crowd, so she easily got his attention. With his students he approached her, smiling as if he was glad to see her.

"You guys were great," she told the students.

"You really were," Nhu told them.

"They're great guys," Kieran said, looking happier than she remembered seeing him, ever.

By then they were beginning the next station, at the same location: *Jesus dies on the cross*. The issue was the death penalty. As she joined in the prayer asking for the power of the holy cross to change them and to change the world, she was thankful that Kieran had found a way to change the world in his position as a high school teacher.

The Lost Summer

Tom Milton

Introduction

After her sophomore year of college Brigid McBride spends the summer with her best friend Laura Hughes, living in New York City and demonstrating against the war in Vietnam. It's the summer of 1968, a summer of love and a summer of violence when the nation is divided on the issue of the war and a new generation is rebelling against the order imposed by the previous generation, engaging in actions against the war and for civil rights, women's rights, and protecting the environment. Brigid and Laura, who are students in the nursing program at St. Catherine College in Yonkers, are sharing an apartment in the East Village with Kieran O'Donnell, a Jesuit seminarian who is planning an action against the draft board to stop it from sending mostly poor young men to fight in a war that he believes is a crime against humanity. Brigid is in love with him, and Laura is in love with a conscientious objector who fled to Canada to escape the draft.

Brigid got to know Laura when they were assigned as lab partners for the required course in microbiology. Brigid is an excellent student, whereas Laura lacks confidence in herself, so Brigid helps her with the course and develops a relationship with her. Outside of their personal lives the major issue of their time is the war in Vietnam, and when Brigid learns that Laura's boyfriend is in Canada escaping the draft she understands why Laura wants to join the college's chapter of the Catholic Peace Fellowship, an organization committed to peace and justice whose main purpose now is to end the war in Vietnam. Since Brigid is against the war as a matter of principle she goes along with Laura in joining the CPF and volunteering to campaign for the antiwar candidate, Eugene McCarthy, whose first test against President Johnson will be the New Hampshire primary. With a group of fourteen other girls they spend the next six weekends in New Hampshire going door to door in its major cities and urging people to vote for McCarthy. When their candidate almost beats Johnson in the primary they have hopes for a change in government that will end the war.

Later that spring the CPF has a speaker, Kieran O'Donnell, a Jesuit seminarian who praises their work and suggests they take actions against the draft system like the one taken by Philip Berrigan, who with several companions destroyed records at a Baltimore draft board by soaking them in blood. Since the CPF is guided by the principle of nonviolence the members of their chapter debate whether violence against things as opposed to people can be justified as a tactic to achieve their goal of peace. The chaplain and the two nuns who mentor the students question the use of such a tactic on the grounds that it could inadvertently harm people, but Kieran argues that it's possible to commit violence against things without harming people, as proven by Philip Berrigan. At the sight of Kieran, with his wavy dark hair, his fine features, and his dazzling blue eyes, Brigid is immediately attracted to him, and her feeling for him becomes stronger when after his speech he joins Brigid and Laura in the college pub and shows an interest in them.

A month later Philip and Daniel Berrigan, with seven others, take an action against a draft board in Catonsville, Maryland, in which they destroy draft records with homemade napalm, making the argument that instead of burning women and children with napalm they are burning paper. Inspired by this action, Kieran plans to spend the summer preparing an action that will top the action at Catonsville, which he will do to fulfill the requirement of Jesuit formation to perform a ministry to help the poor. Since the boys being drafted are mainly poor he will help them by impairing the system that sends them to war. He has rented an apartment in the East Village from a musician friend who will be in Europe that summer on a tour. He meets with Brigid and Laura in the college pub and invites them to join him in the city for the summer, which will give them an opportunity to participate in demonstrations at prominent locations in the city. The girls like the idea, and they tell their parents they will be doing an internship with a priest as their mentor, embellishing his status and omitting the fact that they will be sharing the apartment with him. After checking the apartment, which is like the apartments where they grew up in the Bronx and Yonkers, Brigid's parents approve the project, and early in June the girls join Kieran in the apartment. They have only been there a few days when Robert Kennedy is assassinated, which makes it likely that Hubert Humphrey will get the nomination of his party to oppose Richard Nixon in the presidential election. So the purpose of the demonstrations is to get more people to oppose the war, which could help Humphrey defeat Nixon.

The apartment is a railroad flat in a tenement building with a living room in front and then a bedroom and then a narrow room, used as a walk-through closet, and then the other bedroom, beyond which there is a kitchen and a bathroom. The girls take the bedroom next to the kitchen, where there is a queen size bed. They have already shared a bed together in motel rooms during their campaign in New Hampshire, so they are comfortable sleeping with each other. In fact, it's like having the sister which neither of them had. And in bed they share secrets, the two most important of which are the fact that Laura has made love with her boyfriend and the fact that Brigid is in love with Kieran.

For the rest of June the girls go out every day except Sunday to join demonstrations at Dag Hammarskjold Plaza, the Isaiah Wall near the UN, the Empire State Building, Rockefeller Center, and Times Square, where they meet a lot of tourists from states across the country. They are spreading the message of love and peace, but Kieran tells them that they could achieve greater publicity by targeting the induction center at Whitehall Street. When they follow his advice they encounter protesters who are more aggressive than they are used to, and when they join in a group action to prevent inductees from entering the center they are arrested and put into jail. They give Kieran as a contact for the police, who don't call him until the next morning, evidently wanting to teach them a lesson by making them spend a night in jail. This experience convinces them that being martyrs for the cause is not for them, and they resume participating in peaceful demonstrations.

Meanwhile, Kieran is advancing his plans for a dramatic action. So far he has refused to tell them anything about it because he wants to protect them from the risk of being accessories to an action that will certainly be considered a felony. They finally get him to tell them about his basic plan, and when they hear that it's to bomb a regional record center for the draft they both oppose it, Laura even more strongly than Brigid. At that point Laura decides to leave and join her boyfriend in Canada. The next morning Brigid says goodbye to her and watches her go on her way to Penn Central Station, where she will catch a train to Montreal. Though Brigid feels lonely without her friend she stays with Kieran in the hope of getting him to abandon his plan and to love her the way she loves him. Laura has assured her that he only has to see what Brigid has to offer and he will come around, so Brigid tries to attract him at a level where she might at least be equal to him.

A conversation with Tom Milton

In this novel you return to the subject of your third novel, All the Flowers, *which was about the opposition to the war in Vietnam. What made you return to this subject?*

I wanted to look at other aspects of it. In particular, I wanted to explore the question of whether violence can ever be justified to achieve peace.

Your characters debate this question as members of an antiwar group at St. Catherine College in Yonkers, where All the Flowers *was set. You even have some characters from that novel play minor roles in this novel, which suggests that you are picking up where you left off.*

The questions raised in that novel have been ringing in my head ever since, so it was natural to use the same setting. But the points of view are different. In that novel the point of view was a man in his early twenties living the experience, whereas in this novel the point of view is a woman in her late fifties looking back at what happened many years ago.

I'm barely old enough to remember that summer, the summer of 1968, when it seemed like the whole world was up in arms. I was only ten at the time, but I watched the events on television with my parents.

It was an eventful year. In the spring I was in Paris when the students and workers tore up the streets and closed down the city. There was no public transportation into or out of the city, so I was trapped there. But I was able to watch what was going on.

When you got out, did you come back to New York?

I went back to Argentina, where I was living and seeing the events that led to the Dirty War. The mostly young people fighting the government at first used peaceful tactics, being members of a Catholic action group at the university, but finally they resorted to violence, which they came to believe was the only way to achieve social justice.

That was the setting of your first novel, No Way to Peace, *so with this novel you're going back to the beginning.*

A theme of that novel was that violence only leads to more violence, which you hear repeated in *The Lost Summer* at a meeting of the antiwar group. They're debating about the use of violence by the Berrigan brothers at Catonsville, where they destroyed draft records with homemade napalm. The proponents of this tactic argue that whereas violence against people cannot be justified, violence against things *can* be justified.

They also address the larger issue of whether war can be justified, applying the just war doctrine. A main character, a Jesuit seminarian, is moving toward the conclusion that no war can be justified, and that using the doctrine to condemn one war could lead to its being used to justify another war.

Which shows that you have to be careful in your choice of arguments. The basic argument against war is that killing is wrong, whatever the reason.

As in your other novels, the issues are framed within a story of characters who mean well but get into trouble. As usual there's a love story, but this one is different. Could we say that Brigid's love for Kieran, the seminarian, is almost hopeless?

It's almost hopeless. If it *was* hopeless, there wouldn't be a story. It's her hope that keeps her love alive.

Your story has other important relationships. I especially like the friendship between Brigid and Laura. At times I feel that Brigid loves Laura as much as she loves Kieran, though in a different way. You developed this relationship so naturally.

I didn't plan it, so maybe that's why it feels natural. It just happened.

Then there's her relationship with Dana, which is quite different from her relationship with Laura but becomes a life saver for Brigid.

At the time she needed a different kind of relationship. She had lost Laura, and Kieran went away to continue the process of becoming a priest, so she needed a friend who would take her into a different world.

And then there's her relationship with Parker, the doctor who hires her to work on a team doing hip and knee replacements. He asks Brigid to marry him, which forces her to make a decision.

It's a hard decision, and she could be wrong either way.

While all these things are happening she pursues her career, which evolves over time and gives her a mission. What's interesting is that both Brigid and Kieran are driven by their missions, which at times become more important than their relationships.

At times they do, but at other times Brigid's relationships are congruent with her mission.

Her mission to help veterans with mental disorders caused by war gives us the professional side of Invisible Wounds, *which is told from the point of view of the fiancée of a young man who returns from the war in Afghanistan with a mental disorder. It was interesting to see in* The Lost Summer *how this disorder could be treated.*

The methods of treatment are still evolving. As with other disorders, the goal isn't to cure people but to help them manage their fears and live productive lives.

This stage of Brigid's life involves her relationship with a psychiatrist who teaches her ways of treating such patients. So that relationship is congruent with her mission.

Right. And there's another relationship of that type.

You mean her relationship with Nhu, whom she adopts as an orphan of the war in Vietnam. After seeing her friend Dana's baby she realizes that something is missing from her life, and adopting Nhu completes her as a person.

As she says in a conversation early in the story, it compensates her for her losses, though at the time she doesn't know she's about to suffer another loss.

We should leave it there to avoid a spoiler. But while I was thinking about Nhu it occurred to me that you also dealt with issues of abandoned children in your novels Orphans of War *and* The Godmother.

My novels are all tied together. They're parts of one novel that deals with the triumphs and tribulations of unremarkable human beings trying to live meaningful lives.

Discussion questions

1. How would you describe the character of Brigid?

2. How would you describe Brigid's relationship with Laura?

3. Compare the motives of Brigid and Laura for joining the college's antiwar group.

4. Compare their motives for joining Kieran in the city for the summer.

5. Why is Laura more strongly opposed than Brigid to Kieran's plan to bomb a draft records center?

6. What do you think of Brigid's attempt to get Kieran to love her the way she loves him?

7. How does Brigid's relationship with Dana help her deal with the losses of that fateful summer?

8. Why was Brigid successful as a nurse on the team for hip and knee replacements?

9. What did her relationship with Parker offer her? What were the complications?

10. How did her career evolve in a way that helped her find a mission?

11. Why was her relationship with Wesley so important in her development?

12. How did her adoption of Nhu bring together all the strands of her mission?

13. Evaluate Brigid in her role as a mother.

14. How does the truth about what happened to Laura change Brigid's perspective on her life?

15. Did she ever put her mission ahead of other human beings?

16. Do you believe that violence can be justified to achieve peace?

17. Do you believe that war is justified under any circumstances?

CPSIA information can be obtained
at www.ICGtesting.com
Printed in the USA
BVHW081047291020
592123BV00001B/77